Other works by the author:

Catholic Boys (novel)
A History of Things Lost or Broken (stories)

Love in the Age of Dion (feature film)

JESUSVILLE

PHILIP CIOFFARI

LIVINGSTON PRESS
THE UNIVERSITY OF WEST ALABAMA

Typesetting and page layout: Joe Taylor
Cover design and layout: Jennifer Brown
Cover photo courtesy Library of Congress, "The Gran Quivera," photo by Charles
F. Loomis, 1890, reproduction number: LC-USZ62-48452, Library of Congress
Prints and Photographs Division Washington, D.C. 20540 USA
Proofreading: Connie James, Joe Taylor, DeWayne Crockett,
Shakendra Bowden, Jamarree Collins, Miakka Taylor,
and Sarah Cole

*The author wishes to thank Joe Taylor, the staff at Livingston Press,
and Beth Terrell-Hicks, for their help
in preparing this manuscript for publication.*

Livingston Press is part of The University of West Alabama,
and thereby has non-profit status.
Donations are tax-deductible:
brothers and sisters, we need 'em.

first edition
6 5 4 3 2 1

JESUSVILLE

This is a lonely stretch of desert: a wide basin of grey silt, sage and mesquite, forty miles of nothingness between the San Lorenzo Mountains on the west and Apache land to the east. An hour's drive to the nearest blacktop, *two* before you'll hit the Interstate.

No towns here. What you'll find is an occasional outpost like the one at Indian Point: a cluster of buildings, weathered, flat-roofed, a sagging gas pump out front of the general store, its plate-glass window obscured by beer signs, and next to the store—knocked sideways into permanent slant by the wind—a shed that sold, or had for sale, second-hand tires and automotive parts. Your car breaks down, might as well forget it. Start walking back to wherever it is you come from.

Takes its name not from the Catholic sanctuary at the Refuge of Good Hope nor from the remnants of the now-defunct Holy Land theme park—not even from the Apaches who have come for centuries, once openly and now secretly, to worship their ancestors—but from Joshua Farley, a retired teacher from New York, who came out to "commune with the Lord Jesus." He dedicated his life—till he vanished last year without a trace—to search for a rare species of the sage plant, rumored to grow wild in the hidden canyons of the San Lorenzo's. The leaves of the plant, according to legend, induce an ecstatic state, thrust you face to face with the living God.

Here the sun beats from skies of the purest blue.

In the radiance of day, under its glorious and constant stare, you might believe all things possible, that there is benevolence in the design of the universe.

Nights, though . . . nights you lose your faith.

Wind tears the surface from moonscapes of sand and rock. Time and space and self dissolve. Darkness unbroken. Darkness so long, so full of eternity, you'd swear morning's never going to come.

-- *PART ONE* --

—*1*—

The priest was still awake—another restless night—when he heard banging on the front door. The clock on his nightstand read 3:15.

He sat on the edge of the bed, thinking his disordered mind must have imagined the sound.

Then he heard it again: a slow knocking, the delayed cadence of a tolling bell, rising sharply above the rush of wind. Surely that was no human hand upon the door. Too slow, too unhurried. Not the hand of a traveler seeking refuge from a storm. He wrapped his robe around him and stepped into a hall that led to the common room with its high, beamed ceilings and Spanish oak furnishings. From here it was obvious the sound came not from the front door but from the hill behind the Refuge.

At the window he looked beyond the garden and the walled enclosure. The grotesque facades of Holy Land lifted above the cottonwood trees. He thought a shutter must be hanging loose. Then the banging ceased though the wind persisted, the shutter perhaps broken free, afloat somewhere in the desert air. He would be happy if the entire park blew away. How many times had he petitioned the governor's

5 *Jesusville*

office to dismantle it? It was an embarrassment, a nuisance, an *abomination.*

Inside his room he tried to calm himself, but nature's breath came vicious and snarling against the adobe walls of the building. It hissed in the leaves of the cottonwood trees. For a moment he thought he heard it *in* the house as well, moving with an intruder's stealth through the halls and empty spaces.

Or was it something else?

Don't tell me you believe in spirits now, a voice inside his head chided. *That's sacrilege, remember? You're a man of God.*

But surely he thought, as he had thought before in his weakest moments, there was every reason to believe this place he lived in *was* haunted—all those disturbed souls who had passed through here. Yes, they were gone now, the Refuge no longer a rehab center for troubled priests, but *they had been here,* lived in these rooms, walked these grounds. Surely they had left some of themselves behind: their tainted desires and unsettling urges, their nightmares. That was why he couldn't sleep. The very air was poisoned.

He had settled back in bed when the banging came again and this time he was sure it was the front door. Twenty-five past three. His new guests weren't scheduled to arrive for hours yet. He thought perhaps it might be a Farley disciple who'd lost his way. But that was unlikely. The encampment was miles from here, on the far side of the basin.

The knocking continued: four or five insistent blows in quick succession.

Pulling his robe tightly around him, he crossed the common room and stood at the heavy oak door. It wasn't fear that made him hesitate before throwing it open—he had long since lost any fear for his personal safety—but rather the anticipation of an obligation, what might be asked of him. He'd come to believe he had nothing left to give.

The night assaulted him, cold and raw.

The man who stood before him cowered against the wind. Even standing under the porch he had to raise his arm to protect his face and eyes from the biting sand.

"Hell of a night, Father," he said with a wry grin. He wore a thin leather jacket and jeans and a pair of square-toed riding boots. With his wind-blown hair, his unshaven face, he looked like someone fallen on hard times, a drifter maybe, or someone on the run.

"How can I help you?"

"Shelter, Father. Need a place to stay."

The priest folded his arms against the chill. He squinted into the mist of sand and darkness for a look at the car parked outside the gate. A dark coupe. Apparently unoccupied. At this distance he couldn't read the plates. "We don't normally—we like to have advance—"

"I know, Father, I know. Real sorry to come like this, middle of the night, waking you up. Real sorry, you know? But you see—" He shifted his feet, shoved his hands into his jeans as if to contain his energy, keep it under control. His eyes flared wide and bright in their sockets. "Circumstances, you see? This storm, you see? Things got a little crazy. Got my timing a little screwed up, knocked things off-kilter." He forced a smile. "See what I mean, Father?"

"What kind of trouble are you in, son?"

"No trouble, Father. Just need a place to stay." He moved directly under the porch light and offered his hand, his smile broad and white, a playful glimmer in the wild dark of his eyes. He was a good-looking man and he knew how to use that. "Name's Dillon. Joseph F.X. Dillon. That's for Francis Xavier. My mother was one of the Saint's biggest fans."

"You're not one of them, are you?"

"Who, Father?"

"The Farley people."

"Them nuts? Nah, not me."

The priest feigned a coughing spell to give himself more time. The Refuge had been officially closed for several months now. It was still open to guests, but on a limited basis: parish priests who needed a few days' rest, members of the laity in search of a spiritual retreat. Both the priests and the laity were typically from the western dioceses, referred by bishops or other church dignitaries.

"How did you hear about us?"

"Priest in Abilene. Can't recall his name. Thought it might do me good, clear my head. Been kinda hectic lately."

"Is that where you're from? Abilene?"

"Just passing through." Broad smile again—self-satisfied and self-congratulatory. It was charm the man was offering, not information.

The wind rose again. The man on the porch shivered, turning his body against it and pushing his dark hair from his face. He was at least twenty or twenty-five years younger than the priest, about the same height, 5'10 or 5'11, but built sturdier—someone who had spent time in the weight room.

Father Martin's instincts were to deny him entrance. If he was not *in* trouble, he was trouble itself. Maybe even dangerous. Maybe that, too. There was something—he couldn't quite identify it: his restlessness perhaps, the hard edge to the energy he gave off—something disturbing about him. But seeing him small and diminished in the wind's fury, hunched against the backdrop of the desert night, he ignored his reservations, his better judgment. This was a refuge, after all. And he had always been drawn to those in need.

"I'll have to charge you for the room," he said, in apology. Bishop's orders. The Refuge had to be self-supporting or it would be shut down completely.

"No problem," Joseph Dillon said. "No problem at all, Father."

The priest pulled the door closed behind him and led the man down a covered walkway that bordered the garden. A dirt path curled off in the direction of the hill. Along the path, and still within the walled enclosure of the Refuge, four flat-roofed adobe cottages stood fifty or so feet apart. Each had its own small yard and shade trees.

Out in the open here the wind's chill cut deeper. The leaves rattled like paper.

The priest stopped at the last of the cottages, the one closest to the hill and farthest from the main house, as if housing him out here made him less of a threat, offered some kind of barricade against his potential for violence. He pushed open the wooden door and stepped inside, flicking the light switch.

The man came in behind him, squinting against the sudden light and taking in the bare floor and walls, the two single beds. "A regular Hilton Deluxe."

"We live simply here."

"Fine by me. Could use a shower, though," he said, noticing there was only a washstand and a toilet in the bathroom.

"I'm afraid you'll have to go out back. We have showers there."

The man nodded thoughtfully, his eyes flat and without expression. "So, I've got neighbors out there or what?"

"At the moment, no. Later today we have two journalists arriving, a young couple. They'll be staying in the first cottage. You both should have all the privacy you need."

"Privacy's the name of the game out here, I guess."

The priest couldn't tell either from his tone or expression whether that pleased or displeased him. "If you've come to think something through, you've come to the right place."

"Sure thing, Father. You hit the nail on the head." He grinned and a playful light crept in behind the darkness of his eyes. This time the priest was sure the man was having fun with him. In the overhead light he could see that he was older than he'd first thought—mid-thirties maybe.

"How long will you be staying?"

"Not long. I get restless, you know?"

The priest wanted to ask if there was a destination involved, or was it simply motion for motion's sake. But he didn't think he'd get much of an answer, so he left it alone. "Meals are at seven, noon, and six-thirty. In the main dining room."

"Much obliged, Father. Much obliged."

"Our rules are few but necessary. No smoking in the room, no radios or TV, no alcohol or drugs. Guests are not permitted in the rooms. There's very poor cell phone service here, but in any case we discourage its use anywhere on the grounds."

"Whatever you say, Father."

"Is there anything else you need right now?"

The man stepped to the door and turned the handle. "How you lock this thing?"

"You don't. There are no keys in the Refuge."

"Honor system, huh?" He seemed amused at the concept.

"We've never had the need to lock our doors."

"That should make us all sleep warm and cozy then, right?"

The light in the man's eyes and the playful grin made it hard to take offense at the mockery. The priest thought of the ebb and flow of his own tortured thoughts night after night, so it was with more than a little irony that he replied, "Yes, I suppose."

"Oh, there is something else," Joseph Dillon said when the priest turned to leave. "When's that damn wind gonna let up?"

"By morning, the radio says. Things are always better in the morning."

Outside Father Martin stopped to search the sky for the first signs of dawn. Behind him the cottage door closed. He heard something scraping across the floor and then the sound of the door handle being jiggled. His instincts had been right. Joseph F.X. Dillon was barricading himself. The man *was* running from something.

Inside the cottage, Dillon stared at his makeshift defense system. The chair was a flimsy thing, spindly legs. Sure to break up under the slightest pressure. He'd have to use the dresser instead.

He lit a cigarette and looked around the room. The bare necessities. Who would've thought, he asked himself, that he'd end up in a monastery? Not him. Not Joey D, the man who always had the world at his feet.

He considered the weirdness of his present situation as he went to move his car. He drove it inside the gate and parked along the enclosure wall, under the trees. It was somewhat hidden there, at least to anyone outside the Refuge.

On the way back to his cottage he stopped at the garden, a small grassy square enclosed by colonnades. A tree grew in each corner of the courtyard, and a center fountain in the form of a winged angel spouted a stream of water. Real sweet, he thought. The damn monks must love it.

But what about *that*? he wondered, gazing at the dark specter of the hillside beyond the garden. Some kind of Christian Disneyland gone to seed. Through the hissing mists of sand he could barely make out the lopsided facades of the nearest buildings, shutters hanging from the glassless windows. Something moved between the trees and the facades, or he thought it did, pale headless figures. With his arm raised to shield his squinting eyes he saw that they were statues, or the decrepit remains of such. In the storm's ghoulish light, the hill's blasted look of chaos seemed to mock the civility and order of the walled Refuge.

Inside his room he set the dresser against the door. That's better, he thought. He leaned his weight against it to test its sturdiness.

Above the bed, a crucifix hung on the wall. He'd paid it scant attention before, but now he studied it with grim fascination. It was larger than the typical bedroom-wall variety and had been hand-carved out of dark wood. The features of Christ's face were over-sized and crude almost to the point of distortion. Vacant eye-sockets gave him a particularly tortured look.

"You got screwed, man," Dillon said aloud, speaking as much about himself as the figure on the crucifix. "You really got yourself into some bad shit."

Try as he might to laugh it off, the face disturbed him in a way he wasn't prepared for; it sent a shiver of fear through him and he finally forced himself to look away. He flicked off the light. At the front window he parted the curtain, felt the window pane tremble from the wind's pressure. His car's bumper glimmered in the shadow of the trees and beyond that, through the open gate, a section of road was visible. He didn't think he'd been followed. There'd been no lights in his mirror on the drive from the Interstate. There were no head lights out there now.

The way he figured it, he should have maybe forty-eight hours of breathing room. Right about now they'd be pretty sure he'd skipped town. They would have broken into his apartment in the Bronx, staked it out, while they asked around. Friends, neighbors, the bouncers and barkeeps of the clubs he'd frequented. Eventually they'd find their way to Phil, and Phil of course would spill the beans. Phil, the outlaw chemist, with his secret lab in the cellar of his house in Pelham Bay. Always trying to concoct chemical highs. Something *new*. Something more exciting than whatever the drug of choice was at the moment. Good old Phil. Fast-talking Phil. Dreams and schemes. A whirlwind of ideas, but scared shitless too. Look at him sideways and he'd swoon.

Dillon couldn't really blame him. The guy had his family to think about. Hell, he had his own ass to think about. He didn't cough up, they'd carve it up for him, scatter the parts on the streets of the Bronx like they did with Petrie. He'd known Phil since second grade, but in Dillon's line of work friendship only went so far. Law of the streets: sacrifice your mother if it meant saving your ass. Nothing personal.

Then they'd come for *him*. Fly to Vegas maybe, even though it was farther away than Santa Fe, because Vinnie liked to gamble. He'd drop a wad at Caesar's, his favorite, then drive down here. But more than likely they'd fly into Santa Fe, put them that much closer. Didn't matter, really. What mattered was one way or another they'd get here, and he'd better have something to give them.

On the bed he propped both pillows under his head and stretched out. He watched his smoke rings lift into the darkness and listened to the wind's hum against the windows. He could use a drink, he thought. Anything would do. Hell, right now he'd drink altar wine if he could get his hands on some.

He smoked the cigarette down, ground the stub into the floor.

A sudden wind gust rattled the door and his body tensed. He reached for the gun inside his jacket, a small Derringer, and kept his eyes fixed on the door.

Then the wind seemed to die away, absorbed by the night's deep silence and he leaned back into the pillows. He was too exhausted, too unnerved to sleep but God, was he tired.

He'd been driving day and night. Non-stop, it seemed. And now he was here. In search of a damn plant. On the wild-eyed notion that if he found enough of it, he might be able to buy his life back.

A marked man's last hope.

—*2*—

At dusk the journalist and his girlfriend reached the Refuge of Good Hope where Father Martin greeted them in the common room. "I thought perhaps you had gotten lost."

"No, no," the young man, Trace Burden, assured him. "The drive was longer than we expected, that's all."

"I'm afraid it's my fault, Father. I made him stop along the way," Vicki said. Her beauty startled the priest. Not quite a cover girl's face, but close. Brown, curious eyes that held his gaze as she offered her hand. His hand was cool and tentative in hers. He withdrew it quickly with a nervous laugh.

Trace watched her wander off, flinging her bag over her shoulder and swinging her hips as she moved to inspect the room's southwestern décor. This was something new, a flamboyance in her walk, that he first noticed three days ago at the outset of their trip. It coincided with a change in her dress to tight tops, short skirts—the way she was dressed now. At the university she'd been more sedate: turtleneck sweaters and baggy jeans. This new look seemed glaring to the point of excess, a threat to her safety.

At the reception desk Father Martin asked Trace to fill out the guest application. "I should tell you," the priest said, sitting across from him, "as a matter of policy we don't accept as guests the Farley people or anyone associated with them. We don't want to give their pilgrimage attention of any kind, so we're not usually hospitable to the media. But your work with *Catholicism Today*, your various efforts to expose false and idolatrous worship in your monthly columns has allowed me to make an exception in your case."

"Thank you, Father, I appreciate that."

"I especially liked your recent piece in which you exposed the fakery of that New Jersey couple." He rubbed his eyes, groping to recall the details. "The ones who claimed the Virgin Mary appeared to them on their front porch."

"The Meriwethers, yes. Ethel and Bob. They had nearly a thousand people showing up on Sunday nights, in hopes she'd reappear."

"That's exactly the kind of circus we'd like to prevent here." He shook his head in disgust. "You know what the locals call this place, don't you?"

"You mean the Refuge?"

"The Refuge, the rotting theme park next door, the section of the San Lorenzo's where the Farley people are searching for God in a plant, this whole godforsaken part of the world. You know what they call it?" His lips turned down in a sneer. "Jesusville. They call it Jesusville."

He looked closely at Trace, sizing him up. His guest was younger than he'd expected. Something almost fragile about him—his thin features, his neatly brushed light-brown hair—something unformed. He hoped he was strong enough to do what he had come to do. "It is our prayer that your expose' will discourage others, often well-meaning but misguided souls, from attending these annual excursions."

"How many are here this year?"

"Several hundred so far, from what I hear," the priest

said, taking the check Trace had written. "Since this is the first anniversary of Mr. Farley's disappearance, they're predicting a bumper crop. We're worried, of course, that his vanishing act will make him even more of a cult hero." He deposited the check inside a tin box that he kept, unlocked, in the desk drawer. "What have *you* heard?"

"Only that Farley's son, Ezekiel, is scheduled to arrive tomorrow. In my communications with him, he's been secretive about everything else. He assumes, given my track record, I'm out to disparage him."

"Aren't you?"

"Most likely. But I'm a journalist. I try not to let my biases keep me from the truth."

The priest raised his eyes. "But all truth is subjective, is it not? Except for the Divinity, of course."

"I try to keep to verifiable fact. In my writing, at least."

"You're a man of conviction, I see."

"I think a man has to know more than I do before he earns the right to have convictions."

"You're a man of humility as well." The priest's smile was vague, his eyes alight with curiosity. "I understand, from other things you've written, that you hold some intriguing ideas. About the clergy, for example. That we're of little use as a bridge between man and God."

Trace felt his face flush but he spoke evenly, without apology. "I've lost faith in the traditional ways of reaching the Creator. They just haven't worked for me."

"So drugs are the answer?"

"That's what I've come to disprove."

Father Martin shook his head sadly. "Yours seems like such a negative quest, for one so young. There seems no room for hope."

"I always have hope."

"For what, may I ask?"

"For whatever discoveries lie ahead."

The priest wanted to ask him if it wasn't lonely, on his own like this, without the matrix of the Church, without the counsel of those appointed as God's ushers. But he thought,

for the moment, he'd grilled the boy enough. As he got slowly to his feet he ran his hand back over his full head of greying hair. "I've enjoyed our little chat. These days stimulating conversation is hard to come by out here. I have to rely on guests, like yourselves. So I hope we can talk again, but right now we should get you two settled." He gave Vicki a nervous smile as she came across the room. "I'm afraid we've already served dinner, but Brother Brendan is still cleaning up in the kitchen. I can have him bring something to your room."

"Super," Vicki said. "I'm starved."

Night had fallen quickly, it seemed. On the way across the courtyard she noticed the walls and vacant windows of Holy Land rising dimly on the hill beyond. "What *is* that?"

"Our number one embarrassment after the Farley people," the priest explained.

"It's creepy looking."

"If you keep away from it, you'll have nothing to worry about."

She glanced back at it with a nervous shiver, then her attention shifted to the man at the end cottage. He was smoking, leaning back in his chair which was tipped on two legs against the porch rail. She thought he was looking directly at her but he gave no sign of acknowledgement.

Father Martin, as he pushed open the door to their cottage, said in a low voice, "That's our only other guest at the moment. I don't believe he'll be staying long." He flicked on the light and stepped aside for them. "Brother Brendan will help you with your luggage, should you need assistance."

"We're okay," Trace said. "I can handle it."

"Don't be alarmed by him. Brother Brendan, I mean. He

doesn't speak or hear. But he understands simple commands. He'll be able to comprehend what you say to him." He stood in the doorway, half in shadow, half in the light. "I hope you'll be comfortable here."

"Is this place weird or what?" Vicki said when the priest had gone. She sat on the bed and leaned forward to slip off her sandals. "Did you see that ghost town on the hill? And Father Martin. Man, is he nervous around women. I can't wait to see what this Brendan guy is like."

She balked about having to go outside for a shower but she had no choice. She was hot and sticky from the long day's drive and she desperately wanted to cool off, feel clean again. Trace came with her, the two of them sharing a stall on the women's side. It was called the Facilities Building according to the map of the Refuge they'd found in the room, but it was really only a collection of wood stalls several feet apart, two on the women's side, two on the men's.

In the stall they fooled around a little—wet kisses, touches—and she wanted to go on but Trace felt they were too exposed. The stalls were open at the top and bottom, the night air a constant reminder of that, brushing against their faces and necks, drifting around their feet. He splashed some water on himself and reached for his towel. "See you back in the room."

"Your loss," she said, feigning rejection and rubbing the bar of soap slowly between her legs in a mock rendition of the movies they'd watched for laughs in her dorm room.

His showers were always quick but she liked to dawdle, liked the feel of water on her skin, especially here with the added caress of the cool night air. She had her eyes closed, the water falling on her face and hair, when she first sensed she was not alone. She opened her eyes, blinked to clear them, to search the darkness above the top of the stall.

One side faced a narrow walkway that ran behind the row of cottages; the other side of the stall faced the back end of the Refuge, an open sandy area with the wind-shriveled branches of Joshua trees extending above the adobe wall. And beyond that the hill rose toward Holy Land.

She listened, heard nothing but the steady drip of water and the wind's distant whir.

The icy chill in her veins persisted. "Trace? Trace, is that you?"

She listened again, waited for a sound to break the stillness.

On the hill dark, glassless windows loomed like eyes brooding over her. The wind passing through them made a low, murmuring, plaintive sound. Like someone hurt, she thought. Like someone calling for help.

She dried herself quickly, pulled on her robe and crossed the narrow walkway to the cottage. The porch where the man had been sitting was empty. He hadn't seemed to her the peeping tom sort, more the kind of guy who would simply take what he wanted. Perhaps what she had sensed was all in her mind. She had an active imagination, she reminded herself, and night-time here was spooky.

In the room she saw, resting on the bed, the tray with its two plates of chicken and potatoes. "So what was he like?" she said.

Trace sat on the bed reading over his notes in preparation for his meeting with Ezekiel Farley tomorrow. "Who?"

"The food bearer. Brother Brendan."

"What you expected."

"Strange, right?"

"A little."

She picked at the chicken with her fingers. "Like how?"

"He's mute."

"Yeah—?"

"Just stands there and stares at you with these really flat

blue eyes."

"That's it?"

"Even after he gave me the tray and I thanked him, he kept standing there in the doorway, staring at me. I had to start closing the door on him before he backed away."

"Creepy."

"I felt kind of sorry for him."

She took another bite of chicken and sat on the bed drying her hair. "You think he was, like, into you?"

"I think he just stares a lot."

"Maybe *he* was the one—"

"The one what?"

"Oh, nothing."

Trace glanced at the dinner tray. Her plate had been barely touched. "You finished already?"

"I wasn't as hungry as I thought." She shook her hair loose and fluffed it out with her fingers. Her robe had fallen open revealing her breasts; her legs were exposed beneath the short hemline. She grinned at the way he was watching her. "I've been wondering what it would be like to do it in a monastery."

With the lights out she felt better, the darkness pushing away the haunting image of the ruins on the hillside, the disturbing sensation while she was showering. She wanted him to reach deep inside her. She wanted the force of him to keep at bay the uneasiness she felt, the longing that wouldn't leave her in peace. "Stay with me," she said, "Stay with me." And he did, an hour—maybe more, prodding and reaching, though nearly not long enough.

Too soon it seemed they were lying apart on the bed listening to the stillness and she thought she could feel it—the stillness—a palpable thing, not only in the dead air of the room but inside her as well, something liquid and sinister cramming itself beneath her skin, filling her up where she wanted Trace to be, filling her with an emptiness she couldn't bear.

"The museum today," she said.

"What about it?"

"That woman and her child."

They had stopped at a roadside Indian museum where she'd lingered before a display case that housed the complete skeletons of an Apache squaw and her child, the woman in a sitting position with her arms around the infant.

"They looked so desperate, dying that way. They looked so—I don't know." She was staring at the dull web of window light stretched across the foot of the bed. "It really
upset me." After a moment she said, "It's a sign."

"Of what?"

She flipped on the light and went into the bathroom, studying her face in the mirror. Trace rose, too, feeling the desire to get some distance, to walk alone in the night. He saw it as a failure on his part that he couldn't please her, that in their five months together he had yet to please her that way. At the window he gazed at the desert beyond the Refuge walls, a flat silvery expanse of hard-packed sand and salt flats.

"Trace?" she called from the bathroom.

He stood in the doorway, a thin uncertain figure with probing eyes, and watched her watching herself in the mirror. Before this trip she'd cut her hair. It was short and straight now, reaching just below her chin and raked to fall across her right eye. With her rigid gaze she seemed almost catatonic. She wanted him there, but it was as if nothing existed but herself and maybe not even that. Maybe simply her reflection in the glass.

Times like this he didn't know what to do or say. "You okay?"

"I feel different here. Don't you?" Only her lips moved.

"Kind of, yeah."

"Did you ever think when you look at yourself like this

that what you're seeing isn't really you?"

It was more, he thought, that what he saw in the mirror wasn't *enough*, that he was too insubstantial a being, too incomplete. Which was something his image in the glass couldn't conceal."No, not really."

"I do. I feel it a lot. I feel it right now."

"In the morning you'll feel different. Everything will seem normal again."

"Think so?"

"Yes."

"Why will it be different?"

"Night-time and its tricks."

"Is that all it is?"

In these moods she became like a child and, though she was two years older than he was, he responded to her the way he would with a child, speaking slowly, with patience, coaxing her back from her fears, telling her what he thought she needed to hear, things he himself did not necessarily believe. "That's all it is."

"I don't think I'm Vicki anymore," she said, turning to him. She stared hard at him, her hair falling across one eye, the set of her mouth firm and unyielding.

It had always astonished him how quickly she could change from playfulness to dead seriousness. He still hadn't gotten used to it and he was disturbed enough now to break his habit, to veer from the comfort he would normally offer. "You're scaring me, Vick."

"Vee," she said. "I'm not Vicki anymore. From now on I want you to call me *Vee*. Okay?"

—*3*—

The encampment was visible above a ravine: tents of various sizes and shapes, RVs and SUVs parked this way and that against rock walls that rose toward higher elevations. Backpack over one shoulder, Trace climbed toward it along a narrow, rutted road too much for his Chevy to handle.

In the early morning light a group of them were huddled around a campfire, middle-aged men and women drinking from coffee mugs. Beyond the fire a half dozen children chased each other across the dirt.

"Help you?" a grey-bearded man asked. He was the oldest of the group and his offer was without warmth. He'd been watching Trace's approach from the moment he parked the Chevy on the desert floor.

"I'm looking for Zeke Farley."

"What you want him for?"

"An interview. I contacted him about it." What he didn't say was that Farley had stonewalled him. Offered him nothing but a four-word reply via email: I don't give interviews. Trace had taken it to mean: *not to people like you.*

There was a long silence while the man sipped his coffee. "Zeke's not here."

"Know where I might find him?"

"Nope, can't say I do."

More people had gathered around the fire, emerging from their tents and forming a loose semi-circle around the bearded man. Twenty or twenty-five of them, Trace estimated, a few in their twenties or thirties but mostly forty and fifty year olds. They looked like left-over hippies, dressed as they were in jeans and T-shirts, some of them tie-dyed. A few of the women wore bandannas around their heads. He was clearly the stranger in his khaki pants and blue short-sleeved dress shirt.

One of the women stepped closer to the bearded man and took his arm. "He's up in the mountains," she said.

His first thought was that they were concealing Farley, protecting him from the tedium of the ordinary world. But it made perfect sense he would already be up in the mountains. Why wouldn't he be? Trace thought. Why wouldn't he get here ahead of schedule, especially when there might be reporters like himself snooping around trying to discredit him? Maybe Farley had also wanted to jump the gun on these disciples. If he was anything like his father, he'd consider even his followers as meddlesome. Trace admonished himself for being so naïve, for thinking the man would be easy to track down.

He stepped back from the fire to re-think the situation. The way they watched him with silent distrust made it clear they weren't willing to talk in any depth about their spiritual leader or his quest. He decided to try a different tack. "How long you folks been here?"

"Most of us got here last night," the bearded man said. "Not that it's any of your concern."

"No, no, of course not." Trace smiled graciously. Never push a hostile subject, not if you're soliciting information.

He lowered his gaze deferentially, kicked at the dirt with the toe of his sneaker. "Guess you'll have a sizable turnout. What do you figure? Couple thousand, maybe?"

"A goodly number," the man said smugly.

"Just one more thing, though, just so I have my facts straight, then I'll leave you folks alone. The actual anniversary of Joshua Farley's disappearance is Sunday, isn't it?"

"Yes," the woman said, "September 8th."

"You holding some kind of a ceremony that night?"

"Yes, sir. A prayer vigil." She lowered her head. "We'll be praying to the Lord to bring him back to us."

"Can you tell me why it is you don't go searching for the plant yourselves?"

"We're only disciples," she said. "Not our place. Though there's some that'd differ."

"Who would that be?"

Something had clamped shut in her eyes, the lines around her mouth had tightened. He understood she'd said as much as she was going to. "Thank you, ma'am. Thank you, sir. Forgive my intruding like this." He turned and walked back the way he had come.

When he reached the ravine, he took the trail leading up into the mountains. The bearded man called out behind him. "You won't find Zeke if he don't want to be found. He's even more of a loner than his father."

The trail hugged the base of a sheer rock wall. The encampment was somewhere below him, no longer visible, though he glanced around occasionally to see if anyone was tailing him. He'd have to watch his back. He was an outsider, and the Farleys had always been wary of outsiders.

Of course he could camp out here, simply wait for Zeke Farley to re-emerge and hope to get his story then. But his interest in the case had deepened since it was first assigned to him. It was the man's search that had come to fascinate him, the moment of discovery, should it come. He wanted to be there for that. He wanted to witness this allegedly magical plant in its natural habitat.

The sheer majesty of the rock face above him took his breath away, the upper reaches thrust like ramparts into the sky. Transfixed, he marveled at the grand and stately design. He could see why the Indians believed this to be the gateway to sanctified land.

This particular section, where Joshua Farley had last been seen, began with a series of interlocking canyons, many of them so remote as to still be pristine. In the university library Trace had pored over maps, examined satellite photos. It was in one of these hidden canyons—the *Canyon of the Gods*, the Anasazi and later the Apaches had called it—that Farley believed the plant he was seeking, a rare variant of the Salvia, thrived.

According to legend, when Cortez conquered Mexico, the Aztecs referred to the Salvia leaves as "God's flesh." They were using it in rituals as a primitive form of Holy Communion, a way of seeing and feeling God. Later, some followers of Cortez wandered north into the mountains of what would eventually become the United States and reportedly discovered a plant of similar appearance and taste that was nearly twice as powerful in terms of the visions it induced. After years of study, Joshua Farley determined *this* was where Cortez' men had ended up. He had written articles about the "secret canyon," a place he'd never seen but had visited in visions, though he was deliberately vague about the details.

Trace wondered if the old man had found the canyon before he vanished. Was he now holed up in it, hoarding his secret, engaging in ecstatic communion with the Divine?

The skeptic in him said *absolutely not*: there was no such thing as a Jesus plant; old man Farley was delusional, if well-intentioned. That was what he was here to write about. Delusion. Miscalculation. Faith gone awry.

But he was enraptured, too. By old man Farley, his son, the plant itself. By all those who, like his father before he was killed, devoted their lives to Godly pursuits. What did they know that he didn't? What had they found that he had not?

His nagging concerns about his own lost faith had driven him on this three day journey from the east coast. The old *what if*. What if old man Farley had really been onto something?

But the rising heat and the sheer magnitude of the landscape before him made him stop to reconsider. In the shadow of the canyon wall, he drank deeply from his canteen.

It was already past noon.

He couldn't go much farther and still make the return by nightfall. For sure, he had under-estimated what he was up against. And then he laughed at his staggering naiveté.

So much for his fantasy that he would interview Zeke Farley and that somehow, magically, he would accompany the man into the mountains. So much for his skills as a budding journalist. This was absurd, wasn't it? This effort of his?

But the old *what if* came back to nag him.

What if the old man had been onto something?

Trace stepped away from the wall's shade. A buzzard drifted above the canyon rim then veered sharply, its shadow crossing the ground ahead of him. In the quiet he could hear the beating of its wings.

What if, what if, what if. . . .

The loneliness of the landscape, the absolute stillness, unsettled him like a bad dream. Until he came around a bend in the trail and saw a figure ahead of him. A girl, it appeared, her bare legs dangling from the rock where she sat. Her arm was raised and she appeared to be waving to him.

A mirage, for sure.

He blinked to clear his eyes.

When he looked again, the girl was still there, still waving at him.

—4—

Trailside, above a gulley, the girl named Jessi Belle watched him approach. She wore short shorts, a bikini top and wraparound sunglasses. Her bare feet dangled off the rock, her ankle bracelet glinting in the sun.

He blinked again, to be sure he wasn't seeing things.

She smiled and leaned forward as he drew close. "You looking for Zeke Farley."

He squinted at her, still not sure she was real. "Who says I am?"

"Them." She jerked her thumb in the direction of the encampment.

"You one of them?"

"*They* don't think so."

He looked toward the camp which lay somewhere beyond the trail bend, then back at the girl. No more than fifteen or sixteen, he guessed. She had one leg cocked—hands around her ankle, chin on her knee—and she was rocking lightly. He thought maybe she wasn't right in the head. "I don't understand."

"They don't think I'm good enough."

"For what?"

"To be a disciple." She flashed him with her misty blue eyes, a look that was both mischievous and conspiratorial. "Which is pretty funny when you think about it. I know more about Joshua and Zeke than all them folks put together."

He stepped closer to see her out of the sun's glare. "How do you know so much?"

She smiled, more to herself than to him, and ran her hand slowly up and down her leg. "Got my ways."

"Meaning what?" he asked, though he had a pretty good idea.

"Been with them, like, three or four times."

"Yeah, right."

"I *have*." She rolled her leg side to side and smiled at him. "Joshua *liked* me."

He looked at her in disbelief. "How old are you?"

"Eighteen."

"Sure you are." He turned and began walking away. He'd been right; she was off in her head.

"I *am*," she called after him. "Got my driver's license to prove it. Here, look."

He stopped and looked back. She was fumbling in her beaded leather purse. Finally, she held out her license. "Says it right here. Jessi Belle Lynch. Born: June 18th, 1992. Which makes me eighteen and one-quarter years old."

He came back and took the license. Her small round face looked particularly cute and coy shining from under the laminated surface. The DOB was what she said it was: June 18, 1992. He handed back the license. "So what does that prove?"

"Proves I'm telling the truth. Proves you can believe what I say. I know where Zeke is. I know how to find him."

He stared hard into her eyes, which was like trying to see through a deep blue mist, to decide if she were telling a lie. "How do you know that?"

"Told you. I been with them, him and Joshua. Up in the mountains. *All* the way up."

"When?"

"Last year."

"Why aren't you up there with him now?"

She shifted her weight on the rock, her face drawn tight. "He don't like me. Not the way his daddy did. Says I'm a distraction." Her lips were half-pout, half-smile. In the sunlight her skin looked baby-smooth and copper-colored, glittering with tanning oil. She pushed her shoulders forward and he could smell the oil and it seemed to him between the bra-like top and her cut-off shorts she'd found a way to expose as much flesh as possible and still be considered clothed. "You think I'm a distraction?"

He pretended to be thinking it over while he sized her up: angel face and smile, teenage sexpot body. Most guys he knew would have a hard time saying no, jailbait or not. He glanced toward the barren slope of the gulley to clear his mind. "You tell your buddies back there about this?"

"They think I'm just sex-starved and delusional."

"How'd they get that impression, I wonder."

"They don't listen to a thing I say," she continued as if she hadn't been interrupted. "Fact, they kind of kicked me out. They think I give them a bad name. But I know what I know. The truth lifts one above the scorn of others. That's what Joshua used to say."

He was still trying to figure how wacky she was. "So in this regard, exactly what truth are we talking about?"

She shifted her position on the rock and sat cross-legged, watching him coolly, unaffected—it seemed—by the mid-afternoon heat. "In this regard we're talking about a certain hidden canyon where a certain highly desirable plant can be found to grow in profusion."

He stared back at her, unblinking.

"*What?*" she said, arching her back and lifting her nose. "You think because I look like the passionate person I am I can't sound smart like you?"

"I didn't say that."

"Sure you did." Then she tossed her head back and laughed at how uncomfortable he looked. "I ain't gettin' after you."

"Nothing to get after."

"Sure there is," she said, "but we'll save that for another time. Got to be going now." She hooked the strap of her purse over her shoulder, slid from the rock and started down the trail.

"Wait," he said, grabbing her arm. Her skin was as soft as it looked, softer even, if that were possible. He quickly released her as if she were contagious. "Wait." He said it softer this time.

"What's on your mind? 'Cause I got things to do."

"Your connection to Farley. I—I want to hear more about it."

"Oh, so now I got somethin' you want? Thought you thought I was delusional."

"I didn't say that."

"You ain't said a lot of things, have you?"

"I'm sorry if I—"

"Forget it," she said, "I'm only teasing you." She was all little girl again, showing her teeth, swaying her shoulders as she held the purse strap. "I was the second to last person to see him. That night. Before he disappeared."

"I thought he was alone up there."

"Not that night."

"The papers said—"

"They weren't up there. Nobody was. 'Cept me and Zeke."

"The police reports said—"

"Cops weren't up there, either."

"How do I know you're not making this up?"

"You don't." She held out her hand to show him the ring on her finger: a thin gold wedding band. "He gave me this. Joshua did. Belonged to his wife. He carried it around with him since she died. Gave it to me. A token of our love."

"You were jailbait."

"Some men got too much passion to be stopped by a technicality." She tilted her hand, held it out to the sun, admiring the way light struck the metal band. "Real pretty, ain't it?"

If she wasn't the craziest woman he'd ever met, she had the wildest imagination. For whatever reason, though—instinct, maybe, or because he was low on options—he couldn't simply dismiss her. "If you were the second to last person to see him, that means his son was the last."

"That's right."

"You really know where Zeke is?"

"Maybe I do, maybe I don't."

He stepped closer to her, shielding his eyes from the sun. "This isn't a game with me."

"Me, neither."

"Tell me serious then. Can you find Zeke Farley?"

She eyed him warily. "What you want with him?"

"I'm a writer. I'm doing a story—"

"Can't help you then. Sorry." She began to turn away again.

"Why not?"

"Zeke Farley's a serious man. Got no time for trifles. Me, neither."

"I'm *interested*—in his work, his research." There was something in his voice, a pleading quality, an urgency he hadn't heard before. He'd never thought of himself as a desperate man. A haunted one, yes, but not desperate. "This plant—I want to know if it can do what Joshua Farley claimed it could. Make us see Jesus. It's important to me, *personally*."

"Well then," she said, coming down the trail toward him. "Why didn't you say so in the first place?"

"You know how to find him then?"

"You a holy man?"

"No."

"But you want to be, right?"

"I want to know what's out there. I want to—I *have* to— know the possibilities."

"Course you do. It's written all over you. Why else would a body drag his sorry ass out in this heat?" She stared forlornly up the trail. "Why else would a guy like you want to climb up there into that hell hole?"

"You'll take me up there?"

She smiled sweetly. "We'll see." Her eyes were smiling at him now, too, and he could see by the way she stood there—head high, shoulders back, legs spread and planted solidly on the dirt—that she enjoyed her position of power. "Some things can't be rushed."

Again his suspicions fluttered to the surface. "What's in it for you?"

"Got my reasons." She sidled up to him, standing so close he could feel the heat trapped between them. She rolled her tongue, slowly, back and forth across her lip. "I like you, you know."

"Why's that?"

"You're a doubter like me."

—5—

In the early morning light, Joey Dillon had watched the guy in the far cottage take off across the desert in his Chevy. A reporter, the priest had said. Well, he'd be sure to stay the hell clear of *him*.

Now he lit a cigarette on the porch of his cottage and stared across the dirt yard at the Eldorado. Its black paint, which he'd waxed and polished to a high sheen every week since he'd bought it, wore a coating of dust and the damn bugs had made a mess of his windshield and grill; but he knew, beneath all that, the car's metal looked as good as it had in the showroom. A wash was all it needed. But it had to go.

Today, *now*.

Driving it was like leaving a trail. His clothes betrayed him, as well: too dark, too hip, too New York. They would be next to go.

Because by this time, Vinnie and his boys would have gotten to Phil. They'd know he'd come out here in search of the plant, but what they wouldn't know was exactly *where* in the San Lorenzo's he was staying. They'd have to catch a plane out, most likely today, then scout both the east and west sides of the range, with their tiny towns, their occasional motels. Then they'd have to drive this entire basin before they'd find the Refuge, tucked in as it was against the foothills. The lower his profile, he figured, the more time he bought for himself.

He drove the Eldorado into the hills behind the Refuge where he found an old mining road that snaked between the theme park and the higher ground of the San Lorenzo's. A mile or so in, the road dead-ended at an abandoned shaft and below the shaft a dry creek bed curled into the trees. It was onto the stony bottom of the creek bed that he guided his baby until he had tree cover, sparse though it was, on all sides.

Engine idling, the low understated throb of the powerful V-8 pulsing through the Caddy's frame, he sat a moment to savor the feel of his automobile one last time. When the engine began to overheat, he shut it down and lowered the windows. It was hot as hell, no matter what they said about dry heat. The weather, though, was the least of his worries. He tried not to think about what had brought him here. But his anger rose like an elevator inside him, unloading bitter memories at every floor.

Vinnie Fargo. Fat Vinnie. Brother of his boss, Nicky Fargo.

If it wasn't for Vinnie, he thought. If it wasn't for Vinnie. What galled him most was that it had been an easy job—one of the easiest he'd done for Nicky—a piece of cake, if there ever was one. One two three, really. As easy as one two three.

He stared through the windshield at the dry wash with its dead-looking bushes, its smattering of wispy trees, watching his undoing again on a screen clear as the desert sky:

Pick up Wilson and Petrie at 5 a.m.

Drive to the Hunts Point Market.

Park behind the Crown Fruit & Vegetable Distributors' stall.

Load six crates of zucchini into the Caddy's trunk.

Drive it to a house on a dead end street in City Island.

Unload the crates into the garage.

Lock the garage.

Finis.

Twelve kilos of uncut cocaine hidden in the false-bottomed crates delivered safe and sound. From there Nicky would have it transferred to his distributors in Jersey and the Island. But that wasn't Dillon's concern. He'd completed his leg of the operation. Except that before he got out of the garage two goons, two *goomba's* with assault rifles, pull into the driveway in a Mercedes.

Perfect timing, *too* perfect.

*Some*body tipped them off.

They want the crates loaded into the Mercedes. They stand around and smirk while he helps Wilson and Petrie hump the crates. So instead of a job well done, the three of them are standing in the driveway, the Eldorado slumped on its four flat tires, as they watch the taillights of the Mercedes fade down the street.

Nicky, of course, didn't want to hear about it. Nicky, who he worked for eight years, eight devoted years doing anything the man wanted him to do. Nicky turned a deaf ear. *You owe me*, he says. *You guys lost it, you find it. You owe me. Twenty-four hours. You get it back, you put it in the garage where it's supposed to be.*

Twenty-four hours? No way. All he could come up with was that it had to be Vinnie, Nicky's own brother, because no one else knew about the operation. Not even Sal, Nicky's brother-in-law at Crown Distributors. Sal thought Nicky had this thing for zucchini, that's all. For his restaurant on Zerega. So it couldn't have been Sal. Too dumb, anyway. He didn't travel in Nicky's circles. Sal was a family man, an ordinary guy, a member of the Knights of Columbus and the

St. Vincent DePaul society, for Christ's sake.

It's Vinnie, Nick, he tried to tell him.

My own brother? You're accusing my own brother?

No offense, no offense, Nicky, it's just—

Just what?

Nothing.

It's not nothin', Joey. It's 900G's is what it is. Is what you owe. How you gonna pay me back?

I'll figure something out.

Yeah, you do that, Joey. You figure it out. You got twenty-four hours.

Dillon stared into the dry wash and cringed at the memory, at how twisted everything became. The deafening stillness of the mountains seemed to mock him. Out here, in the desert, nothing changes in a thousand years; but back in the Bronx, your world splits apart in seconds.

Wilson got it first. They fished his body out of the Sound near Throggs Neck. In three dumpsters near Bronx Park, the cops found most of Petrie's body parts. Not the arms or the hands, though. Those they couldn't locate. Meanwhile I'm hightailing it west, Dillon thinks. Hiding out in this corner of desert hell, looking for a damn plant with magic leaves. *I'm* the lucky one.

And the ultimate kick in the nuts was this: Vinnie was Nicky's muscle man. It would be Vinnie coming after him. If he couldn't come up with the money, or at least with something of equal value, Vinnie's would be the last face he would see in this world.

Fat-faced, foul-mouthed Vinnie.

Dillon was enraged again and he thought if he didn't choke it back, swallow the whole damn thing, he wouldn't be able to think straight, get done what needed to be done. So he opened the door and stepped out of the car.

In the trunk he pushed aside the bag of rags and cleaning supplies, the tins of Raindance and Turtle wax, and removed the cover to the spare tire well which was filled to overflowing with packets of bills—twenties and fifties and hundreds. He stuffed them into a leather satchel that he'd found in a shop in the East Village, threw in his revolver as well, and fastened the bag with a rawhide tie. It had a western feel to it, the satchel, with its fringe and its shoulder strap. That's why he'd bought it. Little had he known he'd be playing cowboy with it one day.

It was one of two bags he'd brought with him when he fled. The other, a larger one, held most of his stash: the money he couldn't justify putting in his bank account, not on the salary he made as part-time maître-D, part-time bartender at Nicky Fargo's Bay of Naples Restaurant and Pizzeria. Before dawn, he'd hidden it under a pile of rubble at the theme park. He wasn't going to leave it in his room, not without a damn lock.

He flung this one over his shoulder and removed the ten-gallon gasoline can he'd kept in reserve—didn't want to run out in some god-forsaken place like this, not when you're being chased by someone who wants to cut your nuts off. He doused the black leather seats first then the engine, the interior of the trunk, and finally he splashed the remainder of the can over the hood, let it drip over the doors.

From the hill above the mine shaft he watched his baby burn, the flames bright yellow and red, the smoke gnarled and black, especially once the tank exploded, shooting flames and smoke even higher, above the tallest of the trees, the smoke drifting back over the hills in the direction of Holy Land.

The car that came for Dillon was an old pick-up, a '69 Ford gone completely to rust. Last night, on his way through town, he'd wandered the side streets until he found some half-wasted Indians lounging in the shadows of an alley, asked which one of them wanted to make some easy bucks.

The one he'd chosen—John Brown Bear, AKA "Brownie," the only one with a car, was a thin stalk of a man, a face so bronzed it looked petrified, the kind of face he remembered from the Indian head pennies he collected as a kid. Yesterday he was unsteady on his feet but today, behind the wheel of his truck, he looked cleaned-up and alert, almost dignified in the upright way he sat there, gripping the cracked and corroded wheel, grinning at Dillon with yellow teeth.

"You found someone who can help me?" Dillon asked as the geezer shifted gears and left the Refuge gate behind, the engine revving noisily as they picked up speed.

"Someone, yes. A holy man."

Dillon laughed. "How holy?"

"A man of great respect among the Mescaleros."

"You mean, like, a medicine man?"

"A man of many visions."

He looked at the old man to see if he were joking but his face, fixed on the road ahead, was composed and serious. "He's not loco, is he?"

"No loco. He knows many things. He speaks with the *hastshin*."

"The who?"

"The spirits who created the world."

No wonder they're a dying race, Dillon thought. They're either drunk or hallucinating. This heat can't help, either. Fries the brain. Even with the windows open the cab was beastly hot. Which made him miss the Eldorado, with its advanced climate control system, even more.

"He has been seen walking. According to the *hastshin*."

"Who has? What in hell you talking about?"

"Joshua Farley. He has been seen walking in the hills. The spirits have revealed this to George Rising Sun, the man I'm taking you to."

"You're scaring me, Brownie, you know that? You're giving me agita."

"We do not know if it was Joshua Farley himself or his spirit that was seen. The *hastshin* do not make such distinctions."

"Yeah, well, that doesn't make me feel a whole lot better." He studied the old man's face, but his expression hadn't changed. "Couldn't you find me a better connection? This guy sounds like he's still playing Cowboys and Indians."

"No one is better. He is a man—"

"Yeah, yeah, I know. A man of great respect among the Mescaleros."

John Brown Bear made a groaning sound deep in his throat. "You wanted information. No one among my people knows more about Joshua Farley." He squinted into the sun's glare on the roadbed, wrinkles so thick around his eyes his sockets seemed to disappear. "He heals many of my people. He protects our sacred ground from people like Joshua Farley. He can tell you many things. It is better that you do not try to disrespect him."

"Sure, sure, whatever. I only meant—"

He sat back in the seat and stared hopelessly at the flat blue hills they were heading toward. Whack job Apaches— perfect, he thought. This whole idea was a crazy long shot, so why not make it a little crazier? He cringed at what he was up against: finding enough leaves to send as a sample to Phil, back in the Bronx.

It was Phil, nearly a year ago, who'd first put the idea in his head:

I have this friend, guy named Tucker, works for J & J down in Jersey. Anyway he goes to these ethno-botany conferences, real highbrow stuff, professors and independent researchers— freaky alternative types, you know. Anyway, the point is, old man Farley was at the last one, right before he disappeared. He put a load on one night and he's sayin' how he's already found the plant and sayin' how it's gonna revolutionize the way we think about God and the whole religion thing, sayin' it's the biggest thing since the birth of JC himself.

All you have to do is bring me back a few leaves, Phil promised. *I'll do the rest.*

A crazy idea, Dillon had argued, time and again. Shit-ass crazy. Off the wall.

Salvia's the most potent natural substance for inducing visions known to man. It's not detectable via drug testing. Which, as you can see, is a major plus. And, plus of all pluses, it's not addictive. I mean, I'm telling you, this stuff's got it all, man. And if this business about seeing God has even a fraction of truth in it, we get the right-wing crowd as well. This could be the first drug sanctioned by the Church, for god's sake. We can't miss with this thing.

Dillon had to laugh now at their endless debates. A moot point. A sure-as-hell moot point. Because once he'd lost the cocaine shipment, he had to do something fast. Phil had insisted it was fate knocking on the door, the opportunity of a lifetime.

Until that point, fate had frequently been knocking at his door, dumping riches at his feet. *You lead a charmed life,* his resentful father liked to say whenever he wanted to knock Dillon down a peg. *But charms are fickle. They can turn on you like a snake.*

Dillon had scoffed at that. *Got it made, Dad. Don't you worry 'bout me.* Luck was on his side. It would always be on his side—or so he'd thought until now.

The truck rocked and jounced on the uneven road that led to the reservation. He watched the blue hills growing larger, thinking one man's dream is another man's necessity; necessity was all he owned right now. He had to admit, though, it was the kind of get-rich scheme Nicky might go for. High potential, low risk. And as far as Dillon was concerned, whether Phil could pull it off in the lab mattered little at the moment. If he could at least find some of the damn leaves, and Nicky bought into it, he got the most important thing he needed right now: time.

—6—

From the hill's crest John Brown Bear pointed out the man leading the line of dancers. "That's George Rising Sun."

On a small patch of cleared ground, a half-dozen masked figures gyrated to the beat of drums, their tanned and oiled skin shimmering in the sunlight. Each wore some kind of bird mask and each was dressed identically in loin cloths and moccasins.

"It is a war dance. To invoke the power of the eagle. They are declaring war."

"Against who?"

"Joshua Farley and his descendants. Those who trespass on sacred ground."

Great, Dillon thought. That's gonna make him real eager to help me find the plant. "I thought you guys lost the San Lorenzo's. One of the treaties you signed."

His eyes, hard and unblinking, watched the dancers. "It was *stolen* from us. In one of the treaties we were *forced* to sign."

Yesterday when he was drunk he didn't seem to care

about anything except making a few bucks to buy more whiskey. Dillon was surprised to see him now, controlled but deep passion quivering in his lower lip, in the steely glint of his eyes.

"In our hearts it has always been ours. It is ours, still."

The chanting and swirling dancers and the relentless beat of the tom-toms were nothing more than mumbo-jumbo to Dillon and he was glad when the dance and the drumming stopped abruptly. At the clearing's edge a water sack made out of animal skin hung from a tree limb. The Indians lined up for a turn under the spout.

George Rising Sun, breathing heavily, leaned against a rock. His eyes delivered a harsh judgment on the two men approaching him. Even unmasked, his face—with its tomahawk nose and glaring eyes—bore more than a passing resemblance to an eagle's. "What is it, Brownie?" he said in a tone that suggested he'd been the object of many such entreaties and that his patience had worn thin.

"My friend here needed some information," the old man began, clearing his throat several times over, his face abject, eyes lowered, as if in the presence of the tribal healer he'd been exposed once again for the shameless, pitiable drunk he'd become. "I thought you might help—"

"I thought we might help *each other*," Dillon broke in, figuring to seize the initiative before the old man groveled it away. Never come to a man of power on your knees. One of the first lessons he'd learned on the streets of the Bronx.

The healer stared at Dillon a long time without speaking. "How would that be possible?" he said finally in a flat voice.

"I'm glad you asked." Dillon smiled to show he was making light of the moment but neither Indian found him amusing. He cut the smile and cleared his throat. To stop his hands from fidgeting, he shoved them into his jeans. "George, ah, Mr. Rising Sun I mean, I understand you have a problem with a certain intruder on your sacred lands. And, you see, it so happens I'm trying to get a hold of this man myself for, ah, personal reasons. So I thought if you could put me in touch with him I'd be real grateful and to return the favor, show how truly grateful I am, I could fix it so he'd never have the desire to go back up there again. . .if you get my meaning."

George Rising Sun's face registered nothing but its own solemn composure. "You are a man of great persuasion, then?"

"You might say that." Dillon grinned shamelessly. "Back in New York, we have our ways."

"Yes, I have seen your ways. On television and in the movies. There are many, many stories about your ways."

"Yeah, kind of the thing now, I guess you could say. Everybody's getting in on the act." He was about to tell a joke about these two hit men who go into a bar, but the Indian's cold smile stopped him.

"Your ways are not our ways, Mr—"

"Joey. You can call me Joey."

"We prefer, Mr. Joey, to seek the help of our ancestors, those spirits who have gone before us. They have passed down to us the stories we live by, and they are different stories from yours. I will tell you one of them now." He leaned back against the rock, closed his eyes and tilted his head toward the heavens.

It seemed to Dillon a long time, though in fact it was a matter of moments, before he spoke. "A man who had a pretty wife and two sons went off alone on a hunting trip with Coyote. They made camp the first night and, because he was exhausted by the long day's hike, he slept late into the next morning. But restless Coyote was awake at dawn and set out by himself. He came upon an eagle's nest high up on a cliff wall and saw that there were young eagles in the nest. Upon returning to camp he related what he had seen and asked the man to help him reach the eaglets, explaining that he needed the feathers to attach to his arrows. The man, thinking there was no harm in helping, agreed. He accompanied Coyote to the top of the cliff where Coyote lowered him slowly and carefully, by rope, over the edge. Coyote held the end of the rope, which he had looped around a nearby tree for support. He peered over the edge and kept asking the man if he had reached the nest yet.

'Not yet, not yet,' the man replied.

'I will lower you some more,' Coyote said. And when finally the man said, 'Yes, I have found the nest and I see the eaglets, I can reach them now,' Coyote let go of the rope laughing and saying, as the man clung to the opening of the nest, 'Cousin, she who was your wife will now be mine.'

"Abandoned, the man crawled into the nest with the young eagles and vowed to protect them. When the father returned he brought, in thanks, a cup so that the man would have water; and when the mother returned she brought a dish of corn that never emptied no matter how much he ate. And soon many eagles assembled there and they carried the man into the sky world where they invited him into one of their houses. Still, he was steadfast about protecting them and he went out into the night and killed all predators of the eagle—bees and wasps and yellow jackets that had stung eagles to death, and deadly tumbleweeds that had killed eagles by rolling on top of them.

"When he had made them safe from all harm, the eagles gave thanks and flew him back down to earth where he found Coyote living with his wife and mistreating his children. In revenge he forced Coyote to swallow hot stones that his wife had baked in fire. This caused Coyote great pain and suffering. He fled the man's home in agony, forever homeless and on the run."

The Indian lowered his head and opened his eyes. They seemed unfocused, still lost in whatever trance had taken him. Then, as though a cloud had passed over the sun, the landscape of his face darkened, his eyes narrowed sharply and focused on Dillon—a long, penetrating stare weighted with judgment. Dillon shifted his feet, glanced away, but when he looked again at the man before him, the eyes had not wavered. Cool and hard and relentless they registered their dislike, *disgust*, at what they saw. Then the man said something to John Brown Bear in a language Dillon didn't understand, and went to join the other dancers in the shade of a desert willow.

"He will say no more to you," John Brown Bear said. "It is better that we go now."

The old man walked quickly toward the truck and Dillon hurried to keep pace with him. "What did he say? What did he say about me?"

The Indian waved away the question, his mouth tight, eyes fixed on the truck at the bottom of the rise. Inside the cab he seemed agitated, his composure slipping away. He reached under the seat, pushing bottles around, glass scraping across metal until he found what he was searching for: a half-filled pint of whiskey. One-handedly he uncapped it, bringing it to his lips as he cranked the engine.

"What the hell, man?" Dillon said.

They raced along the reservation road as if being chased. The Indian's silence added to Dillon's fury. "What was that? Who the hell's *Coyote*? Why's he telling me that story? I mean, what's the point? What's the damn point?"

"It's only a story."

"Yeah? Well it's a dumb-ass, stupid damn story, you ask me. Stupidest story I ever heard." He glared across the seat at the Indian as if *he* had told the story, as if he were to blame. "I didn't ask for any story. A simple proposition. A simple business deal. That's all I wanted. I would have paid him, too. He would have been damn well compensated for his troubles."

"George Rising Sun has no interest in the white man's money."

"Yeah, well, it sure looked like he could use some of it. Get rid of that cave man get-up, for one thing." He stared hard at his driver, waiting for a response, but the old man tipped the bottle to his lips and drank deeply. "Why don't you lay off that stuff, man?" He reached for the bottle but the Indian guzzled the last of the whiskey and flung the bottle out the window.

They were outside the reservation now, John Brown Bear's foot holding the pedal to the floor, the engine straining under the pressure.

"Where we going?"

"The Refuge," the Indian said. "I take you back."

"Hey, man, we had a deal. You're supposed to get me up in those hills."

"I'm thirsty."

"We had a deal."

The Indian wiped the sleeve of his plaid shirt across his lips. "Find Farley on your own. I did what I could."

"The hell with Farley. It's the plant I need. Just get me to the plant."

The old man sighed. "Me, I'm too old to go up in them hills. I'm too hot. Too thirsty."

"Someone else, then," Dillon pleaded. "I know you guys been tokin' up on all kinds a desert weed for centuries. Find me someone else."

"Don't know nobody else."

"*Think*, man. Think hard." He reached into his jeans and pulled out a handful of bills, held them up so they fluttered in the hot wind blowing off the desert. "There's more of this. Enough to keep you in hooch the rest of your days."

It wasn't until they reached the Refuge that the Indian spoke again. The truck was stopped in front of the gate. "I think I have someone," John Brown Bear said.

"Who?"

"Someone." The Indian was even more tight-lipped than usual. "I would not choose him for myself, but if you are desperate—"

He studied the old man's face to see what he was holding

back. "This guy, he knows the San Lorenzo's?"

"He takes rich white men up there for what he calls 'hunting excursions.' They drink too much and, without mercy, slaughter their prey. They are interested only in bringing back trophies for their living room walls. They leave rotting carcasses behind. He allows this to happen. He encourages it, I am told. He has no respect for our sacred land."

"He's an Apache?"

"He *was* an Apache. He has been disowned."

Dillon twisted in his seat to get a better look at the old man's eyes. "What in hell does that mean?"

The old man shrugged, as if all this should be obvious. "We do not have prisons on the reservation. If a member breaks our laws, he is cast off from the tribe, he is forced to leave the community and live as an outcast."

"Yeah, so what laws did this guy break?"

"He stole things. Another man's wife or his chickens or his cows. He took whatever pleased him."

Dillon laughed. "Sounds like my neighborhood. So, how do I meet this guy? What's his name, anyway?"

"Harry Smith."

Dillon laughed again. "What kind of weirded-out Apache name is Harry Smith?"

"When you are cast off from the tribe, you must leave your birth name behind. It is part of the punishment."

"Harry Smith." Dillon laughed again.

"Tomorrow, when you are buying your car in town, I will find him and bring him there."

"Today, man. I can't wait till tomorrow." He'd already figured out a likely scenario. The only direct flight from New York into Santa Fe left at 6 a.m., way too early for the likes of Vinnie. So that left a 10 a.m. flight via Chicago, or a 1 p.m. via Denver. The 10 a.m. got in shortly past noon today, which meant by the time they picked up a rental car and spent four hours on the Interstate the earliest they would get anywhere near this section of the San Lorenzo's would be about 6 o'clock. He checked his watch. It was 3:30 now. "We have to do it today."

The old man shook his head. "He is leading a hunting party today. He does not return until nightfall."

"Then find me someone else."

"I have already told you. I can think of no one else."

"Jesus," Dillon said in disgust.

"Do you want me to bring him tomorrow, or not?"

"Yeah, yeah. If that's the best you can do, bring him tomorrow. But early, man. Let's do it early."

"You will have to pay for this service." He turned his face to Dillon, his small eyes staring from wrinkled sockets. "I, too, am desperate."

"A hundred bucks," Dillon said.

The old man stared back at him, unblinking. "Two hundred."

"One-fifty."

"Two hundred."

The old coot's not so dumb after all, Dillon thought. "I'll pay you when you bring him."

"Half now, half then."

Dillon gave him a sideward glance. "You're a tough man, Brownie."

"I'm a man with a thirst, that is all. I, too, am a disgrace to my tribe."

Dillon counted off five twenties and handed them across the seat. He held another twenty out, but withdrew it when the old man reached for it. "Tell me something first. What did that Rising Sun dude say before we left?"

Blank-eyed and tight-lipped the old man watched him. Then he shifted his gaze to his lap, his gnarled hands curled on the worn denim.

"*Forty* bucks," Dillon said, holding up two twenties.

The old man hoisted his shoulders wearily and stared at the desert hardpan. It was a few moments before he spoke.

"He said, 'My brother, what kind of trash are you bringing me?'"

—7—

After Trace had left that morning, Vee lay on the bed in a T-shirt and shorts staring at the ceiling. He had said she should come with him, she could take photos of the desert, but the thought of walking around in the hot sun, in the mood she was in, had no appeal.

When she fell into states like this, she questioned all things big and small, but especially the grandest of issues: what was she doing with her life? At 26 she was out of school, out of a job, no real plans for her future. She was too old, she thought, to be so unsettled. Her mother had already had three children at her age, her parents had already owned the home they would occupy for the rest of their lives.

Her mind drifted like this, to no purpose or resolution, until fear invaded her inertia, made her finally get off the bed, made her too anxious to remain alone in the room, because when she was adrift like this anything could happen, she might *let* anything happen. And that's what frightened her most: that the danger awaiting her would be of her own making.

From the porch she saw their fellow-guest's black Eldorado was gone, nor was there any sign of the man himself. She felt grateful for that. There had been something disturbing last night, she thought, in the way he had looked at them, at *her*, and if she was going to have to run into him she wanted Trace to be around.

She walked along the path to the courtyard garden where the vivid green of the lawn and the red and yellow flowers seemed shockingly bright in the afternoon sun. It seemed such a peaceful haven, especially in contrast to the turbulence of her feelings, and she thought it might calm her if she lay awhile on the soft grass. When she closed her eyes there was nothing but the high-pitched, frantic chittering of birds and the fountain water dripping on stone.

A shadow crossed her eyelids and she opened her eyes to see a man leaning over her, staring blankly. Drawing her breath sharply, she pulled herself into a sitting position and inched backward on the grass. The man hadn't changed position; he didn't react to her reaction, but stood there looming above her, leaning in her direction and watching her with unblinking blue eyes. It took her a moment to realize— because he was dressed unceremoniously in a white jersey and grey pants, his work clothes—that this must be Brother Brendan.

"You frightened me," she said, rising to her feet and tugging down the hem of her shorts.

His gaze didn't waver and she couldn't tell if he was leering at her or simply staring with the unintentional rudeness of a child. He made a motion with his hands, pointing to the hose coiled at the garden's edge and she understood that he wanted to water the grass.

"Why didn't you just say so?" she said before remembering the man was mute. She stammered an apology though the expression in his eyes didn't change. She backed away and he continued to stare at her so she turned abruptly and slipped through the side gate. When she glanced back again the garden wall hid him from view and she felt relieved.

She wandered into the rear of the property past adobe storage sheds, the ground weedy and untended, and she was about to turn back when she spotted, to her surprise, a mini health spa: a cabana, a hot tub and a sauna. It seemed odd for it to be tucked away like this against the enclosure wall with nothing but the desert and the hill behind it but she thought maybe that was the point. The Refuge was a place of spiritual retreat and, from her Catholic school days, she knew the body must always take second position to the mind and spirit. Or maybe the priests simply wanted a private place for their orgies. She giggled at the thought.

At the tub she knelt on the stone rim and let her hand trail through the water. Under the hot sun she felt the urge to take off her clothes and soak in the pool but the thought of Brother Brendan, or anyone else who might be lurking around, suddenly popping up and gawking discouraged her.

From the enclosure wall she looked out on the desert.

Nowhere else to go.

Except on the hill.

Her eyes wandered upward over the uneven rows of buildings clinging to the hillside, and towering above them a gigantic cross, the figure of Christ hanging in the blazing sun.

The place repelled her but still she found herself climbing toward the entrance, a cut-stone arch buttressed by two large pillars, the words HOLY LAND chiseled across the keystone. Beyond the arch the air seemed different— denser, harder to breathe, a sickly sweet smell rising from the vegetation. Hedges withered brown and grey bordered the main walkway. Designated "prayer arenas" were situated on either side of the path, each a crude and unlikely rendition of a Biblical scene: the garden of Gethsemane, Moses and the Burning Bush, the nativity crèche—a lopsided shed-like structure with rotting beams and a homemade sign that read, *Birthplace of Jesus*, nailed to the roof. In each of the exhibits the statues had all been maimed in some way. Body parts cluttered the ground: fractured hands and arms, severed heads. Some statues still standing, others pushed face forward into the dirt.

She found the blank, silent facades of the buildings equally disturbing with their gaping windows, their uneven shapes propped against the hillside. A few had arched roofs, but mostly they were flat slabs of concrete or wood painted a greyish-white, with rectangular cutouts for windows. Vaguely Middle-Eastern in design.

In the eerie stillness of the streets, with the facades staring down at her, she felt like a figure from one of her nightmares, alone, tormented, terrified at the prospect of what was to come.

At the end of the uppermost street a sign with the word, *Calvary,* in red letters, pointed toward the crest of the hill. Along the main walkway she climbed past trees and dry hedges. The heat was more intense now and as the path grew steeper she stopped to catch her breath, looking back the way she had come. From above, Holy Land looked even stranger. The thin facades were exposed for the shams that they were and the toppled statues and strewn plaster body parts added a look of cartoon-like devastation.

As she climbed, the trees became gnarled and brutish and the vegetation grew sparser. Soon she was on bare ground, nothing but rock and sand, the sun a brilliant white in the sky's unbroken blue reaches. Above her, at the crest, the crucifix appeared thrust upward at a staggering height.

The ascent grew even steeper and the heat forced her to slow her pace. Amid a ring of huge boulders, stone steps led to the summit.

It was only when she reached the top of the steps, when for the first time she had a complete view of the massive cross, that her breath caught in her throat and her heart pounded furiously. On the crossbeam two black vultures roosted, one on either side of the vertical post. Against the stark blue depths of the sky and the wide vista of the mountains the figure of Christ seemed both small and humbled. He, too, had been vandalized. His left arm was missing so that he hung one-handedly from the beam. His eyes had been painted a bright neon red, the paint dripping in zigzag streams from his sockets.

It was then that she noticed him.

The man who had watched them arrive last night sat partially hidden, his back against the post, as he stared at the mountains. He must have heard her then or sensed her, because he turned his head and, seeing her, got slowly to his feet. For a moment she stood frozen, staring back at him, at the growing smirk on his face. She knew she should leave, there was something frightening about him; but she lingered, waiting for—*what*? When he moved toward her she turned and fled down the steps.

When she reached the trees she glanced to see if he were following but he stood at the top of the steps, a tall figure in clothes that seemed unusually dark against the desert sky, raising his hand to draw on a cigarette as he watched her descend.

—8—

Vee paced in front of the Refuge gate, walking the length of the wall then back again. Three, four, five times—she'd lost count. Every other moment or so she glanced at the road, following it with her eyes until it vanished in white haze.

She'd been calling Trace's cell phone; the NO SERVICE message kept flashing on her display. There were no cell towers in the San Lorenzo's, Father Martin had informed her. But she was more than welcome to make herself at home in the common room and use the library. It's small, he'd told her, but we carry some very good titles.

Truth was, she didn't feel comfortable inside the main house. It had a weird vibe, all those white walls and polished terracotta tiles—too monastic, too lonely—and he was an unsettling host. There was something haunted about him.

Finally, in her desperation and impatience, she'd ended up here like a streetwalker, enduring the sun's heat and glare, and grumbling to herself. From this distance Holy Land looked like a jumble of nonsensical structures slapped with no apparent design onto the hillside. Despite the sunshine, the dark green profusion of cedars and twisted-limbed Joshua trees deepened the gloom that hung like mist above the blighted exhibits. She turned so that she wouldn't have to face it. She'd had enough of it for one day.

For a few minutes she studied the Refuge itself, her attention drawn to the stone bell tower attached to the chapel. On each of its four walls, below the bell, the over-sized numerals of a gigantic clock had been carved from the stone. Such an ostentatious and unnecessary display, she mused, considering the seeming irrelevance of time in a landscape like this. Did it really matter that another minute, or five or ten, had evaporated in the desert air? At the moment, she was ready to find fault with everything.

She couldn't tell how much of her dissatisfaction was because of Trace—his age, his lack of experience. Two years, she reminded herself, what was the big deal? That wasn't much of a difference, was it? And in all fairness she couldn't really blame *him*. None of the guys she'd gone out with had ever made her feel complete and God knows, she had to admit, at least Trace tried. He would hang in there like a trooper until she called it off, pushing him gently away, feeling as bad for him as she did for herself, though she didn't know how to tell him that. She loved him, or thought she did. She knew at least that she loved the effort he made. It was endearing. It sometimes made her cry.

But she wished—what? She wished sometimes he wasn't so tentative, that he would simply take control of things, of *her*, their life together, that he would be strong enough, *confident* enough, so that she had no choice but to submit to his will.

A dust cloud took form in the distance. She stopped pacing to watch it grow. Out of its center emerged a red smudge which assumed the shape of the Chevy.

"What are you doing?" Trace wanted to know when he pulled alongside her.

She came around and got in, sinking back in the seat and sighing as if she'd found sanctuary at last.

Trace stared at her uncertainly. "Vicki—?"

"Vee," she said. "Remember?"

"*Vee*." It felt strange on his tongue, even stranger to his ear. "You okay?"

"No. I am definitely not okay. This is one strange place you brought me to." She looked at him, his face red from the sun. "Take me somewhere."

"Where?"

"Anywhere but here."

They drove the desert roads without destination, Vee chattering on about the day she'd had, though she didn't mention her chance meeting with the mystery man on the hilltop. I felt like a little girl, she said, a lost little girl. She confessed she hadn't taken any pictures.

"What are you waiting for?"

"I thought I'd look around first, see what's here."

"You should have come with me."

"I wasn't in the mood." She glanced at him and wanted him to understand.

"It wasn't much fun," he conceded. "But I've got to spend more time there."

"How *much* time?"

"Couple of days maybe."

She turned in the seat to see if he was kidding. "You said this would be an easy story, quick."

"I was fooling myself. My original idea, you know, doing a psychological portrait of Farley's son to discredit him? I thought I'd interview him, a few of the disciples, and that would be it. But there's a lot more to this. I see that now." He took his eyes away from the road, gave her an apologetic look. "I don't know, maybe it's this place, but like you I've been feeling different since I got here. I want to go into those canyons, see what's up there."

"Old man Farley," he continued, with an enthusiasm that surprised her, "was a fascinating guy. He's written up in all the journals of ethno-pharmacology. How he spent his summers with the curanderas and curanderos in Mexico partaking in their healing ceremonies. They're the ones who introduced him to rare and exotic species of hallucinogenic mushrooms and, eventually, to Salvia Divinorum, the "Sage of the Diviners.""

"Sounds like hogwash to me."

"That's why I didn't tell you any of this while I was doing my library research. I knew you'd think it was too weird. But keep an open mind." He tried to judge her level of receptivity but she'd turned away to stare at the desert hardpan.

"There's all kind of intriguing stories," he went on. "How first time he ate the leaves in a midnight ceremony the experience was so profound and spiritual he converted to Catholicism immediately. How he brought samples back to the U. S. for clinical testing but the leaves were mysteriously stolen from the laboratory and never recovered. How he returned to Mexico in search of repeating his mystical experience but was nearly assassinated by the very Indians he had befriended, supposedly because he'd betrayed the private, sacred nature of the experience by revealing it to the world. Then he retired from teaching and devoted his life to finding the plant here in the southwest. If the man was a self-deluded fool, he was a knowledgeable and determined one."

He glanced at her again but couldn't tell if she'd been listening. "So what do you think?"

"Libraries are dangerous," she said. "Imaginations go wild."

"Very funny."

"Next you'll be telling me you want to try the plant, see if it works?"

"I think I do."

She was speechless a moment. "A Jesus plant? Come on, Trace, I mean really."

"I know it sounds crazy."

"But that won't stop you, right?"

"I want to see if it can do what Joshua Farley claimed it did for him."

"You don't even believe in God."

"I never said that. I said I didn't believe mortal man has the means to determine whether or not he exists."

"Which, for all practical purposes, comes to the same thing, doesn't it?" She stared forlornly at the empty land ahead, the purple rim of hills barely visible on the horizon to the east. "I guess I shouldn't be surprised. Every project you undertake, everything you set out to debunk, you're really hoping you'll be wrong, aren't you? You're secretly hoping it will be the real thing."

He shrugged. "Yeah, I guess. I'm beginning to understand that now."

"This is really about your father, isn't it?"

"I have to know if he was a wise man or—"

"Or what?"

"Or a deluded one—if he threw away his life in vain."

"And why you're not like him."

"Yes. And why I'm not like him."

She thought a while before she said, "Sometimes I feel you're a stranger to me. There's so much you keep to yourself."

"You, too."

"I guess." Then she rolled her eyes and sat there quietly brooding. "This is supposed to be a vacation. We're supposed to be in Vegas on Monday."

"We will be," he promised. He felt he was letting her down again, but he couldn't help himself. "Unless—"

"Unless what?"

"Unless there are complications."

"You promised, Trace. You promised when we left the university. We both agreed we needed some time together, *alone*."

"Things changed a little, that's all."

She stared at the miles of road ahead and thought she might cry. "O Jesus," she said.

—9—

Dinner was served in the common room. Father Martin welcomed them, then took his place at the head of the table. "I believe we'll be dining alone this evening. Mr. Dillon seems to be keeping his own counsel. I don't believe I've seen him or his car all day. Have either of you?"

Trace said that he hadn't.

The priest smiled at Vee. "And you, my dear?"

"Only briefly. This afternoon."

Father Martin continued to smile at her, waiting—it seemed—for her to continue. She wondered if somehow he had witnessed the encounter, that he was waiting now for her to confirm what he already knew. But that wasn't possible, was it? There had been no one else on the hilltop at the time. "I was taking a walk through the religious park. I saw him there."

The priest seemed to be mulling something over. "You might want to stay away from the park. It has a somewhat unsavory history."

"Really? In what way?"

"In many ways, I'm afraid."

Brother Brendan emerged from the kitchen bearing a dinner tray and the conversation ceased. Slowly, deftly, he set a dish down in front of each of them. He stood to the right of Father Martin until the priest said, "That's fine, Brendan. We've got everything, I believe." Brother Brendan lowered his head and returned to the kitchen.

"Shall we?" Father Martin said. He blessed himself, clasped his hands and lowered his head. "Bless us, O Lord, and these thy gifts. . . ."

His dinner guests stared at their plates. When the priest finished, he raised his eyes to them. "Bon appetit."

They ate quietly for several moments before Vee broke the silence. "About the park, Father. You've sparked my curiosity."

The priest lay his fork down, daubed at his mouth with the linen napkin. "I shouldn't have brought it up. It most likely can be explained by coincidence."

"What can?"

He cleared his throat. A weak, apologetic smile crossed his lips. "Ezra Holmes, the man who built it, who *conceived* of it and then went on to build it, was a well-meaning but troubled individual."

His gaze turned inward as if he might be calculating what more, if anything, he wanted to add. "He was a frustrated man, a lonely man, with an almost messianic desire to leave behind a monument to his faith, and to himself perhaps as well. Apparently, he came up with the notion for the park because of this Refuge. He thought a theme park, in conjunction with the Refuge, would help attract visitors to the area. He thought it would make this a Mecca, of sorts. Of course that was precisely what we *didn't* want here. His notion flew in the face of everything the Refuge stood for: a place of solitude and retreat, free from the world's distractions."

He looked at his guests in a way that said, surely you understand. Again he appeared to be choosing his words carefully. "As you can imagine, the Archdiocese fought long and hard against him but he went ahead and bought the hillside from the mining company that owned it, hired a crew, and began construction. Within a month, first one and then a second of his crew fell to death from the scaffolding. And six months later, while erecting the crucifix, he himself fell from a ladder while adjusting the position of Christ's body on the cross. Apparently, it had been nailed on crookedly and it wasn't noticed until the cross had been mounted. Rather than take the whole thing down he tried to fix it himself."

"He died, too?" Trace asked.

"Broken neck. Like the two crewmen before him." The priest looked at them sheepishly. "Some believe the project was cursed. Certainly, the Mexican and Apache laborers he'd hired did."

"Do *you*?" Vee asked.

"As a Christian, of course, that would be sacrilege. But then some would say that the project itself was a sacrilege, a gaudy desecration of our sacred beliefs, and that it deserved to be destroyed. Whether some force of faith or destiny opposed its existence, is a matter of speculation. It never opened, you see. It was never completed." He smiled grimly at the irony. "One could argue that it is even more of an eyesore in its unfinished, deteriorating state, a mockery of man's lofty intentions. And it is repeatedly vandalized, several times a year, though there has never been any sign of the vandals. "

"Yes," Vee said. "The statues and buildings look as if someone took an axe to them."

"A hammer, an axe, in some cases a blow-torch. Whoever it is they do their damage under cover of darkness, and they leave no clues behind. The Sheriff's office is as perplexed as we are." He caught himself then and stopped. "I'm sorry. I don't mean to burden you with the many little mysteries we live with, out here in Jesusville."

Brother Brendan re-emerged from the kitchen, bearing a tray of dessert this time: over-sized bowls of butterscotch pudding. He set the tray on a stand beside the door, then joined them at the table. He ate slowly and steadily, a blank half-smile on his lips when he wasn't chewing.

"Perhaps I'll return another time and write the story of Holy Land," Trace suggested.

Father Martin dismissed the idea with a laugh. "I'm sure you have more important topics to concern yourself with, topics of significance, such as your present assignment."

"I did want to ask you, Father, about this plant that Joshua Farley has been searching for."

"The Salvia?"

"Yes. Or a close relative. He simply called it 'the voice of the Divine.'"

"Remember," Father Martin cautioned, "what the Bible tells us: I am the Lord, thy God. Thou shalt not bear false gods against me. Long before salvia, the Bible was deemed the voice of God."

"Yes, Father. I was brought up in the faith. I'm clear about the Church's position. But I'm reminded of the wisdom of the early Christian Mystics. There is only one God but many paths to Him."

"But some paths are sanctioned, others are not." The priest chortled, clearly enjoying himself. "It's been some time since I've had the pleasure of this kind of intellectual sparring. These past months it's been mostly with myself, and that's not nearly as much fun." He seemed to catch himself then, embarrassed by his display of unabashed enthusiasm. "But I'm afraid I'm not addressing your question." He nodded across the table. "Brother Brendan is the botanist. He takes care of our garden, and what a wonderful job he does. "Brendan, do you know anything about this plant we're talking about? The Salvia Divinorum?" He mouthed the words carefully, looking directly at his colleague who stared back with his unchanging half-smile.

"Alas," Father Martin said. "I'm afraid he doesn't understand what we're asking him."

"What have *you* heard?" Trace wanted to know. "What do the locals say about it?"

Father Martin laughed at that. "As you can see our association with the locals, what few there are, is limited."

"But you must have heard some stories."

"Stories, yes. That's all they are. Wild and fantastical. Like the stories that abound out here about extra-terrestrial visitations. The product of our lonely nights and howling winds. I've often thought the Creator gave us the night-time to remind us how much we need Him. Anyway, before all this Farley business these stories were simply part of the local folklore, handed down by one generation of Apaches to the next."

He pushed his plate away and settled back in his chair. "Supposedly the ancient ones, the early ancestors of the modern day Mescaleros, sent their tribal chiefs and elders—this was a male only thing—into the San Lorenzo's each month to celebrate the full moon. It was their way of communicating with the Great Spirit. Supposedly this plant you're talking about was the facilitator of such communication."

"Yes, yes," Trace said, "I've heard all that. I thought there might be more."

"Oh," Father Martin said dismissively, "there are all kinds of stories that spin off from that. How there were wild orgies of dancing and chanting, how the souls of deceased ancestors would assume human form once more and partake in the ceremonies, how some of the elders would die in the throes of the ecstasy and delirium that the plant supposedly induced. I've been told that the Mexican laborers would talk about the plant, how it grew in their homeland and how they'd heard stories about the trances and hallucinations it caused. There was even one story—apocryphal I'm sure, like all the others—that those who died during the construction had ingested the plant the night before. And there was talk of an ancient curse against anyone or anything that came too close to where the plant grew. Superstition, I'm sure. Man's feeble efforts to apply a rational formula to the vagaries of fate, or God's will, depending upon your beliefs."

"Would any of those workers still be living in the area?"

"I wouldn't know. Until recently, the Refuge has been a busy place. We've had more practical concerns to deal with, like the healing of tortured souls. No time for myth and superstition. I daresay we paid scant attention to Farley himself until he began to attract wider attention." He smiled kindly at Trace. "But that's why you've come. To lay this silly speculation to rest, once and for all, I hope."

Trace felt his face redden. "That was the plan, yes."

"Has it changed?"

"No, not really—"

"You look doubtful."

Trace thought a moment, limiting himself to what he could safely say. "I'm as committed as ever to finding out the truth."

In his chair, the priest settled back and studied him curiously. "It must be difficult, for your generation, to focus on the higher truths, given the distractions of technology which has become a god of sorts in its own way."

"That's precisely the point, Father. We've been astounded and distracted by it for so long, we've become anaesthetized, even bored by it. When we stop to think about it, those of us who do, we see—beneath the dazzle— how pedestrian the whole tech thing has become. It's only another version of the corporate world shoving its products down our throats."

"All that glitters. . . ."

"Exactly. So we've got nothing to fall back upon *but* the higher truths. Searching is our only option: Vee, for instance, through her art; and me, well, in my writing. "

"Well put," Father Martin said. "It seems the case, doesn't it, that no matter where mankind is in time and space, no matter what our accomplishments—scientific, technological, whatever— the question always comes down to the Divinity at the heart of the universe, and our relation to it."

Only the ways we search for the Divinity have changed, Trace was thinking. In the developed world, at least, the Church had lost its relevancy. But he said none of this to the priest. Vee was fidgeting in her seat and he turned to her.

She leaned close and asked if they could leave. During the priest's discourse, Brother Brendan had stopped eating and turned his attention on her, his eyes blank and strikingly blue, his lips parted in a cryptic smile. The man's stare had unnerved her. She'd done everything possible, short of leaving the table, to avoid eye contact. What was he thinking? What did he want?

She whispered again to Trace, "Can't we go? I'm awfully tired."

"Oh, but surely you don't want to leave without trying Brother Brendan's pudding," Father Martin interjected, his hearing more acute than she'd suspected. "Over the years it's won raves from our guests." Without waiting for a response, he motioned to his assistant to serve the dessert.

"It's been a long day, for both of us," Trace explained.

"Just a taste and then we'll release you," the priest joked. "But I hope we'll get a chance very soon to continue our conversation from last night about the relationship of contemporary journalism to truth."

"I'm sure we will." Trace tasted the pudding and had to admit it was quite good. But he could feel Vee's discomfort and impatience. "Thank you both for a delicious meal," he said finally, getting to his feet. Vee was already standing, waiting to leave. Though he didn't think it necessary, it occurred to him to ask, for her benefit: "She'll be safe here on her own for a day or two, won't she?"

Father Martin gave them both a broad, reassuring smile. "We'll take sterling care of her, Mr. Burden. You have nothing to worry about."

"That *man*," she said when they were outside on the dark path.

"What man?"

"The cook, the gardener, whoever he is. He totally creeps me out."

"He's afflicted. Show some compassion."

"Easy for you to say. He wasn't staring at you the entire meal with that psycho smile."

"He's not a psycho."

"How do you know that? This place used to be where they sent their child molesters, their sexual predators."

They had reached their cottage. Trace looked at her under the porch light. "Yeah, so what are you saying? This Brendan guy's a left-over. They've kept him on for old times' sake?"

She knew she sounded paranoid, silly, but she couldn't help herself. "It's creepy, don't you think, living here? With that kind of history?"

"You knew about this place. When we first talked about coming out here, I told you what it used to be."

"But it's different *being* here. Especially at night." She looked around helplessly. "It's so dark, so. . .endless. It's like I can feel things. I don't know. . . ." She shuddered in the cool air and her voice trailed off. Ahead of them the dark row of cottages were lit only by their porch lights. "Maybe I'm going crazy."

"You're not going crazy. You're a sensitive person, and sensitive people, well, you know, feel things deeply."

"Is that all it is?" She looked at him with dark, imploring eyes.

He slipped his arm around her shoulders and hugged her. "It's only a few more days."

Inside the room he flipped the light switch, the room reborn in brightness, the ghosts she imagined fleeing with the darkness. She stood in the doorway so hesitantly that he felt compelled to add to what he'd said. He could think of nothing but the obvious. "There wasn't any other place to stay, Vee. You know that. This was the closest. Besides, bishops and monsignors and all kinds of ordinary people come here now. It's not what it used to be."

"What *is*?" she said. It seemed her sense of herself was shifting again, she was standing on unsteady ground, and it was not so much fear that she felt as a kind of resignation. She was moving toward something or away from it, she couldn't be certain: an inevitability as large and looming as the cross on the hillside.

He was stuffing things into his backpack, preparing for tomorrow, and she wandered into the bathroom where she gazed at herself in the mirror, as if she might watch her future unfold before her eyes.

Then she was standing in the doorway watching him. He looked up and stopped what he was doing. He touched her face; her eyes looked down at his hand rather than into his eyes.

"Why don't you come with me tomorrow?"

She shook her head no. "I'm being a baby. I'll be fine here, whatever happens."

"Nothing's going to happen."

"Something always does."

He laughed because he thought she was being clever, but her eyes didn't share his amusement. "What is it?"

"Make love to me," she said. "Make me feel safe."

With the lights out and the wind knifing at the windows she lay on the bed and guided him inside her. His movements were slow and deliberate and she tried to ride them like waves, feeling their rhythm, the ebb and flow, urging herself forward. She wanted the ride to be continuous, a rising that would not falter, that would take her surely and steadily to that place where loneliness died, if only briefly, where she would be delivered to a comfort she'd never known.

She felt the shape of the waves in his shoulders, his back, the smooth skin of his neck: wherever her hands could reach him. She felt the sweat building between them, heat choking the space where they joined. In his face she read the strain, the determination, and she knew this must be a reflection of her own, this must be what he saw in her; and she wondered if he hated her for that, for making him as desperate as she was, a contagion he hadn't counted on when he first longed to touch her.

The waves, the waves, she reminded herself, *think only of the waves* and she imagined herself at sea being carried in the immensity of its arms—her thin pitiable self and this immense thing she could not comprehend—rocking with the motion of the tides, adrift at the whims of the moon. She felt herself edging shoreward, *please, please*, with an urgency that was itself a form of ecstasy, *the waves, the waves*, taking her closer, so much closer than she'd been, the strain in his face almost unbearable to look at, his breath rasping against her own, her breath rushing through lips that had turned dry as dust.

The waves, the waves, please, please. It was nearly a prayer and she was rising with the tide's upheaval, rising and rising, grabbing to hold on: to something, *anything.* But his flesh slipped through her fingers, she was losing him, she was sliding backward. Though he continued to move inside her, his thrusting as deep and determined as before, the rhythm unraveled, there were no more waves. Only a dead place that was flat and hard. A sweat-damp mattress in a dark room in the desert.

"I can't," she said. "I can't.

She wanted her words to release him, to ease the strain in his face, the tautness in his limbs. She wanted to give him permission to salvage whatever pleasure was left in the wreckage. But he said, "I can't, either," and he rolled away from her, his sex swollen and hard and glistening with her juices. She wrapped her hand around it but he said, "That's all right, you don't have to."

"You sure?"

"No, of course not." He laughed at himself. "Yeah, I'm sure." He pulled her hand away and held it against the sheet in the space between them.

She leaned close to kiss him but when she saw the defeat in his eyes she hesitated, touched her lips only briefly to his then settled back beside him.

She listened: to his breathing—steadier now, not as deep; to the low swirl of wind in the spaces between the cottages; to the indefinable sound silence makes in a dark room. She listened to her heart beating much too loud. Louder than it really must be, she thought. Thump-thumping in its cage.

And sometime later—with Trace still awake and restless beside her, their hands still clasped, though loosely now—after the silence of the room had become inseparable from the silence inside her and she felt herself slipping away, no longer a person but a space empty as air, she thought she heard the sound of a car motor approaching. Or maybe it was only the wind.

She imagined the black Eldorado slipping into its shadowy berth beneath the trees.

Outside, the air had cooled and the wind could be heard, even at this distance, gusting through the empty streets of Holy Land, though Father Martin knew there would be no storm tonight. The forecast was for milder weather. Before bedtime, he always checked the report, as if knowing what the night would bring might calm him.

It had no such effect. Warm or cold, hissing wind or

silence, his nights had developed a pattern of nearly constant restlessness. So that before he retired to his room he would step out into the colonnade like this, take a deep breath—the air was clean here, he could say that at least—and begin his nightly walk. An objective observer would call it *pacing*, traversing as he did the length of the colonnade, some fifty or sixty yards, between the main building and the chapel, then back again in relentless repetitions, the object of which was to tire himself, drive out night's jitters. A hopeless task, he had come to believe, but he made the effort nonetheless.

He checked his watch. Tonight it was his turn for the bells, so he had nearly twenty-five minutes. Enough for, he estimated, twelve or thirteen round trips.

He walked at a brisk pace, the brisker the better for his purposes, his heels clicking against the tiled floor. The sound was quickly absorbed by the darkness of the garden and the deep shadows between the dim, occasional lights of the colonnade. It often seemed to him that the night with its overpowering silence was mocking his efforts, erasing them before they could take effect. *Walk all you want*, it seemed to say. *Walk from here to kingdom come. For the next six hours I own you. I'll do with you what I will.*

Usually he read late into the night—spiritual tracts mostly—searching for answers to the questions that came at him harsh as the desert winds. Then, blear-eyed and unsatisfied, he would lie in the dark, the hiss of sand against the window glass like a failed lullaby. Or he would pace the corridor between his room and the common room. Or go to the kitchen to make tea, secretly hoping Brendan might awaken and join him. Even silent company was better than no company at all. But of course the man slept deeply as a child. Nothing seemed to trouble his dreams.

Restless nights hadn't always been his curse, he reminded himself. They had developed slowly, several years into his tenure as prefect of the Refuge. Before that his life in the priesthood had been well-organized, focused and rewarding. In fact, he was quick to admit, his entire youth had been focused because he was one of those fortunate few who knew early on what he would become. His earliest memory was of his mother reading the lives of the saints to him at bedtime: his favorite, of course, Martin De Porres, after whom she had named him, a man who lived nearly his entire life in a friary in Lima where day after day he ministered to the sick and impoverished beggars who came to the friary gate.

From that early age he held his sixteenth century hero in the highest esteem, an exemplar of the ideals to which he aspired.

As he hurried along the colonnade, Father Martin took some comfort in his childhood memories. In the El Paso grade school he attended, he would collect nickels and dimes and pennies from his fellow students then take the money in a cigar box to the homeless men who lived on the neighboring streets. His classmates would chide him, calling him Martin De Porridge or Marty Oatmeal, but that never stopped him from the mission he'd chosen for himself. When he was of age, he joined the Augustinian monastery at the edge of the city, continuing his work as an almsgiver, running the soup kitchen and the homeless shelter there. His days were full and exhausting, and he slept soundly, dreamlessly, at night.

It was ironic, he thought now as he reached the chapel at the end of the colonnade and turned to re-trace his steps, that it was his concern for the dispossessed that prompted his superiors to recommend him as prefect of the Refuge when that position became available. If they only could have seen how it would turn out.

"It's perfect for you, Martin," his spiritual adviser had told him at the time. "With your generosity of spirit, your deep and unwavering commitment to those in need—who better than you to lead our wayward brethren back to the flock?"

And for a while, for the first three years or so as chief

administrator and counselor at the Refuge, he thought that yes, it was true, this was the challenge the good Lord had been preparing him for all his life, this was the ultimate service he could offer.

Why did it all go wrong? Why did he lose his way? he asked himself again. It was the interrogation he'd endured every night since the Refuge closed.

What could he say in his defense? Other than to suggest that he had simply been worn down: by the isolation of the place, the interminable nights, the hopelessness of the task he'd been given. Typically, there would be ten or fifteen "re-habbers" residing at the Refuge at one time. There was a psychiatrist on premises and a staff of assistant counselors, but as chief spiritual counselor he felt ultimately responsible for the troubled souls who'd been sent here, or who had come voluntarily, to heal. When he'd see them return— and all of them did return, often time and again—or worse, when he would hear through channels that Father So and So had been "transferred" from parish to parish, he took it as a personal failure. One more soul who had slipped though the safety net of his love, his concern. One more servant of Christ lost to untamable lust, or unquenchable thirst.

So that somewhere between his third and fourth year at the Refuge, self-doubt invaded the fortress that housed his faith. With it came the sleepless nights, the agonizing self-recrimination. And less than a year later the diocese decided to close the Refuge as a rehab center—a decision he took as yet one more personal failure.

"The closing has nothing to do with you, Martin," the archbishop had assured him. "We're consolidating our operation, that's all. We'll do all of our re-hab work out of Phoenix now. It makes more sense for a number of reasons. . . ."

But Father Martin paid scant attention to the reasons. He was too involved with blaming himself, too busy apologizing to his namesake for failing to live up to the ideals he had set.

Not only had he failed his charges, he'd turned his back on them as well. He'd come to believe that their maladies were impervious to faith, to redemption.

And worse even than that was the terrible thing he had learned about *himself*, what lay at the heart of his despair—but he pushed that memory away.

It would haunt him through this night, as it did every night. He would be forced to live with it again. But right now he needed to prepare himself for what he liked to call "the ecstasy of the bells"—one of the few pleasures left to him here at the Refuge.

He was moving along the section of the colonnade that abutted the garden. He stopped to check his watch. There was still enough time for one lap around so he struck out across the grass that was, as always, manicured as neatly as a putting green. He passed the fountain with its poised stone angel and bubbling water, then the row of cottonwoods along the west wall.

Whenever the wind shifted the shadows, he thought it might be Brother Brendan lurking about. Often he would encounter his sole companion suddenly like this, at the unlikeliest moments, in the oddest places. What else was left to them now but prowling the grounds at all hours—in search of what? It was a testament to the magnitude of his own self-doubt that he hadn't even petitioned to have himself reassigned to the mission in El Paso, as if his experience here had scarred him for life, rendered him forever ineffective.

When he reached the corner of the garden that overlooked the cottages, he stopped. In each, the windows were dark. Only two vehicles were parked near the gate—his own and the journalist's. No sign of Joseph Dillon or his Eldorado.

It was a disquieting moment. Had the man left? *Why* had he come here? If the fellow was still here, should he demand that he leave in the morning? All his misgivings about the stranger rose once more to the surface.

He found himself shivering in the chilly breeze. He

stood there staring into the darkness for several moments before checking his watch again. Time for the bells.

At the rear of the chapel, he climbed the stairs, eighty-two in all, to the top of the tower. This was the tallest man-made structure in the basin and from the small, square room open on four sides to the elements, one stood witness to forty miles of night's darkness—a microcosm, he liked to think, of the infinity of the heavens. Directly above him, in the room's black upper reaches, hung the bell with its coil of rope reaching the floor. The bell was struck four times each day: for morning mass at six a.m., for meals at noon and six p.m., and to signal the end of day at midnight. Brendan and he took turns, on alternate days.

It was a simple act he looked forward to. He liked the feel of the rope in his hands, the strain of drawing down on the heavy metal, the imperious sound that rang out into the desert night heralding the significance of this particular day, of time itself, in all this emptiness. He could no longer say with any certainty what that significance was, but that only marginally diminished his pleasure. The act of ringing the bells connected him to a time when he *was* sure of himself, his life's mission, just as it connected him to all those who had come before him in the monasteries of the world, men who— like himself, once— dedicated their lives in the service of Christ's all encompassing love.

Now he took the rope in his hand and checked his watch. At the stroke of midnight he drew it downward, the clanging metal breaking the night's stillness, each chime it seemed more heartfelt and thunderous than the one before, the sound building to all-consuming proportions, his spirit for these few moments at least—before night's gravity took hold— rising above the limitations of his flesh, rising as high as the constellations beyond the windows, where the sky dazzled with a wondrous light that seemed nearly close enough to touch.

-- PART TWO --

—10—

In the headlights' glare Jessi Belle leaned against a beat-up Jeep with its canvas top in tatters. She seemed impatient, jiggling her leg and squinting in the brightness to be certain it was him. She wore cut-off denims even shorter than yesterday's and a bikini top—this one a neon yellow, a sweatshirt thrown over her shoulders.

She'd climbed into the jeep and fired the engine by the time Trace parked the Chevy and slid into the passenger seat. In the pre-dawn darkness the jeep lurched forward, taking on the rutted path that climbed toward the encampment. The engine coughed and heaved. Shreds of canvas clinging to the roof bars snapped like flags.

"This going to make it?"

She gave him an indignant look. "This old thing's taken on worse hills than this." To prove it she downshifted and gunned the engine. The jeep jumped ahead, tires grabbing for traction on the hard ground, shooting back sand and stones in a hissing spray. When it crested the rise she glanced at him and smirked. "JB2's never let me down yet."

"JB2?"

"Jessi Belle the Second. My shadow self."

"Kind of like an alter ego."

"Sure. Whatever."

The encampment lay above them, no lights, no movement, the tents hulked like silver shrouds in the moonlight. She took a short-cut through the ravine so they wouldn't have to pass directly by them. "Let sleeping dogs lie," she said.

"That what they are? Dogs?"

"Some of them, yeah."

"Thought they were visionaries."

"Don't mean they been absolved of meanness." Her hands clenched the wheel, her eyes fixed on the cracked and creviced incline ahead.

Off to the left, he saw the rock where she'd been sitting yesterday. *Yesterday.* The notion of days, the taxonomy of time, seemed irrelevant here. Yes, there was a point when he had met this woman, this *girl,* and now he was riding beside her in the ghost-blue light of the moon on a narrow strip of sand that could hardly be called a road and soon they would be toiling on foot under a blazing sun and maybe there was some sense to that, this collision of strangers in the strangest of lands; but at this moment as he was rocked and jounced without mercy, as the engine wailed in pain against the rugged ascent, even the notion of sense made no sense.

One thing he did know, though, was that he had violated nearly every rule of journalistic technique he'd been taught. He'd arrived here without a pre-determined list of contacts, he'd vastly under-estimated the enormity of the task, he'd changed his focus mid-stream and for personal rather than professional reasons, he'd teamed up with the most unlikely of guides, a girl, a *kid,* about whom he knew nothing, and for no other reason than that he was desperate and short of options.

"You remind me of my boyfriend." She had a vague smile on her lips, her face catching the silvery light of the moon.

"Oh, yeah? Why's that?"

"Always asking questions."

"My nature, I guess."

"That's what he would say."

It was colder than he'd expected so he zipped the windbreaker tight around his neck. She, however, seemed unfazed by the chill, her shoulders bare except for the draped sweatshirt as she strained forward at the wheel.

The road had gotten rougher and he let himself be rocked this way and that, concerned at times at how close they were to plunging into the gulley but impressed, too, by the skill she used to maneuver the old jeep, forcing it to do her will, sure-footed in its way as a donkey. He found himself watching her leg, sleek and tanned, as it guided her foot deftly and without hesitation from clutch to pedal. She noticed him watching her and smiled. He shifted his eyes away.

"Your boyfriend—"

"Where's he at? That what you're asking?"

"Yes."

"California. La Jolla."

"He's not a Farley disciple?"

She laughed. "Wouldn't be caught dead out here. Ocean's his thing. Can't stand the desert."

"He doesn't mind your running around like this?"

She gave him a stern look. "Like what?"

"I don't know—" He wanted to say flashing your tits and your legs like this, meeting a guy you don't know and driving in the dead of night onto some lonely and god-forsaken mountain. But he didn't want to provoke her. Not on this road. What he said was, "Alone like this. Out here."

"Don't matter if he minds. He does what *he* does, I do what *I* do." The road flattened out and she glanced at him to see how he took that. "He's real rich. Forty years older than me."

Trace whistled. "Wow."

"You think that's weird?" She said it aggressively, challenging him.

"I don't know. A little, maybe." He studied her cute baby-doll face, the soft curve of her shoulders.

"I know what you're thinking. I look so young and he probably looks like my grandfather." She shook her head. "No way. He works out. He's in real good shape."

Trace, still in placating mode, nodded in agreement. "I'm sure he is."

"He is, too."

"I believe you. Really, I do."

"Besides. We got a lot in common." She said it suggestively and rolled her leg side to side.

"I'm sure you do."

She glanced at him to see if he was covering up a deception and in that moment the back wheel slipped off the road bed. She shifted, the gears shrieked and for a moment they hung suspended above the abyss, before she pulled the jeep back onto solid ground. "Everything's cool," she said looking at him again and smiling. Her face glowed as if she were ruminating over some secret pleasure. "You like looking at me, huh?"

It took him a moment to catch his breath and settle back in the seat. At times he found her attractive in a nearly irresistible way, but he forced himself to keep things on a professional level. "I'm curious about you, that's all."

"That's good. I like to make men curious."

He sat in silence, keeping his body still, eyes fixed on the windshield. As they climbed the final steep stretch of navigable road, he wasn't going to distract her in the least way. When the road quit and she stopped the jeep, he rested his head against the seat back and sighed in relief.

She turned off the engine but it wouldn't go quietly. It shook and shuddered and made clanking noises.

"Your boyfriend—"

"What about him?" she said defensively. He figured she

must take a lot of flack about the age difference.

"If he's so rich why doesn't he buy you a new car?"

She looked at him in disbelief. "You got a complaint with this vehicle? You got some negative thing you're dying to spit out?" She stared as though she was ashamed of him. "Got you here, didn't it? Saved you a mile and half of walking in the black of night, didn't it?" She shook her head like she couldn't believe such lack of gratitude. "Besides, I pay my own way. I don't take handouts."

The rising sun grazed the top of the cliff walls with pink light as they climbed toward the first of the canyons. She estimated it would take them at least twelve hours to get where they were going. Which meant, if all went well, they should encounter Ezekiel Farley sometime that night.

He didn't know much about the man they were seeking, other than that he'd recently turned twenty-one, had accompanied his father—partway at least—on these quests for the past several years and, according to Jessi, was the last one to see him alive. After his old man's disappearance he dropped out of Michigan State where he'd been studying Botany, purportedly for the sole purpose of carrying on his father's work. He was quiet, introspective, a serious student who kept mostly to himself. This, the consensus of the profs at Michigan State Trace had contacted.

Now, as he hurried to keep pace with her on the trail, questions ran amok in his mind. "What's he like? Zeke Farley."

Her smile was bittersweet, not directed at him but at the path ahead where her eyes were fixed. "Don't know anybody can answer that. Keeps to himself."

"That's what I heard."

She looked at him askance. "Why'd you ask me then?"

"Thought you might—" He tried a more indirect approach. "Guess he's not going to be thrilled to see me."

"Guess you're right."

"You, either. From what you've said."

"He pretends he doesn't want a thing to do with me." She smirked, her eyes glimmering. "But deep down I know he wants me. I can tell."

"So you figure, what? He'll shoot at me and let you live?"

"Can't say what he'll do. Now if it was Joshua, that's a different story. He'd be real happy to see me. And *you*? Would depend on what you were after."

"If I wanted to experience what he'd experienced. If I wanted to see Jesus—"

She shook her head. "He wasn't ready to share that with anyone."

"Not even you?"

"Not me. Not even Zeke."

"You said you were with them—that last night. Did he show you the plant, where it grows?

"Un-unh."

"Did he at least say he'd found it? That he knew where it was?"

"Not exactly."

"What does that mean?"

"It means, not exactly."

"So you don't actually know if he located it or not?"

"I didn't say that, did I?"

"Maybe it's a hoax. Maybe he was fooling himself and everyone else.

"It's no hoax."

"You can't be sure of that, though, can you?'

She shot him a fierce look. "I can be sure of any damn thing I please."

He pushed on, walking faster to keep pace with her, grasping for something, the tiniest shred of certainty. "You think Zeke knows where to find it? I mean, if he's got his father's journals. Maybe the old man left behind a map—"

"You're gonna kill me with these questions."

"Sorry, I—I guess what I wanted to know is—"

"I don't talk with strangers about that night." She stopped on the path and fixed him with a hard look, her blonde hair pulled back in a ponytail, her face pink in the early light. "And far as I'm concerned you're still a stranger to me."

"I just want to know if he *saw* the plant, if it grows anywhere near that canyon we're going to." But she had already turned from him, striding quickly up the path, her ponytail swinging across the delicate ridge of her shoulders, her sneakers kicking up dirt behind her.

He ran to catch up, his breath coming fast and quick in the thin air. "Wait up," he called after her.

"We got to keep moving," she said when he came alongside her. "These canyons wait for no man. That's what Joshua used to say."

"Can I ask how you came to know him? I mean, I wouldn't think you guys traveled in the same circles."

"Depends on what circles you mean," she said with a slow smile. She shifted the straps of her backpack. Red lines appeared where the vinyl had rubbed her skin. "San Sebastian. He was giving a talk in a church there." She ran her fingers over her sore shoulders. "Love at first sight."

"So, what, he invited you to join him on his next trek up here?"

"I wouldn't say he exactly 'invited' me. I'd just be waiting for him when he came down the mountain. He'd be real discouraged on account of not finding what he was looking for." She gave him the slow smile again. "I kinda helped him unwind."

"You did that every year?"

Her eyes shone triumphantly. "Three years running. Fourth time—that was last year—he didn't want me waiting for him down below. Wanted me right by his side."

"I bet your boyfriend was thrilled about that."

She looked at him sharply. "You got a narrow view of the world, don't you?" She had begun walking again, a more moderate pace this time. "Like I said, he lives his life, I live mine."

Sometimes it seemed she was miles ahead of him, experience-wise, and he felt ashamed. He wanted to pull her back to his level: the literal, rational world he thought he understood. So he asked, "Where you from?"

"Told you. California."

"Before that. Where you got your accent."

"Mississippi, Florida, Georgia. I been from all those places."

He felt ashamed again. He'd been from one place—an unremarkable city in New Jersey—and then, of course, he'd been to the university, not so much a place as a state of mind, where he'd learned about the world from the books he read.

He'd never encountered anyone like Jessi Belle in those books. No one like Vee, either. The nation of pussy ain't like no place else on earth, his first year roommate from Tennessee had remarked one night, late, after hours of drinking. Trace had laughed when he said it. He thought it was a joke and he was supposed to laugh.

One thing he was sure of: he'd definitely under-estimated Jessi Belle. Crazy or not, she fascinated him and he felt himself being drawn into the labyrinth of her mysteries. He found himself envying her closeness with old man Farley, unproven though it was, and regretted his own bad timing, that he'd never gotten a chance to talk to him directly, that he would most likely never know what the man experienced during his transformative, "profound and spiritual" vision.

But climbing the mountain now behind this girl who claimed to know where Farley was last seen alive, the day brightening with golden light around them, he was filled with a strange and exceptional hope.

—11—

Outside a car lot in Cactus Springs, Dillon leaned against a grey '99 Toyota Camry and checked his watch. John Brown Bear had been gone nearly an hour. More than once the thought had crossed his mind that he'd been stiffed.

Five minutes. Five more minutes and he'd—what? He didn't even know what he'd do, he was that low on options.

Hot and disgusted he stared at the empty street, then at the Toyota. Back in the Bronx he wouldn't have been caught dead driving a car like this—it was an affront to his sense of style, his sense of driving pleasure—but he'd told the salesman he wanted the most dependable car on the lot and, without hesitation, the man had gone directly to this one. It was with great pain that Dillon had counted out the money for such a boxy, middle-of-the-road set of wheels.

He checked his watch again, entertaining once more the possibility the geezer had skipped out when he heard the clatter and jangle of the old pick-up on the next street over. In a matter of moments the '69 Ford came around the corner and chugged its way toward him.

Harry Smith had his arm dangling out the window and when the truck stopped he was out before the old man turned off the engine. He was a gaunt man with eyes that darted around like they were being chased. He held out a thin, sun-spotted arm at the end of which dangled a withered hand. "Yer lookin' for a guide, Brownie tells me."

"That's right." Dillon took the hand tentatively, the small shriveled thing fitting easily into his own.

"I'm your man. Been over them mountains a thousand times. Know 'em like I know my own hand. The good one *or* the bad one." He winked at Dillon.

"I'm lookin' for a certain plant—"

"Don't know anybody who can say for sure, or *will* say, where that plant's at."

"What about Farley, the old man or the kid?"

"Seen the boy two days ago when I was up with a huntin' party."

He sounded to Dillon more like a redneck cowboy than the Indians he'd met here, and he figured that came from rubbing elbows with the hayseed types he took on his hunting expeditions. The shifty eyes, though—maybe that came from his outcast status. Dillon thought he'd better check himself in the mirror next chance he got, make sure it hadn't happened to *him* yet. "If you can get me to Farley, I'll make it worth your while."

"And what would that be, I wonder," Harry Smith said with a slow smile, "to make it worth my while?"

"A thousand bucks minimum. The faster you get me there, the higher that goes."

Harry Smith was nodding slowly. "Yep, that'd be worth my while."

Dillon went to the street side of the truck to settle up with John Brown Bear. "This guy, you're sure he can get me to Farley?"

"I can only say he knows the mountains well. I can say

nothing for his character." The old man turned a weary gaze at Dillon. "I will tell you one more story."

"Please, no more stories."

"You may want to hear this one."

There was something in the way the old man spoke that forced Dillon to choke back his impatience and lean against the truck's cab.

"At one point in our history," the old man began, speaking slowly, leaning close, "the legends say there was a separation of the sexes. In order to prove that women were not capable of living on their own, the men abandoned them and traveled some distance to live apart. During this time of isolation the women used all types of objects—fruit, sticks, cacti, whatever they could find—to satisfy their desire. Their offspring from this period were monsters, deformed in body or spirit. Much like those who, in present times, we cast out."

Dillon looked across the truck's roof at Harry Smith who raised a cigarette to his lips with his good hand and watched them. He had stepped toward the curb, leaning forward as if to listen in.

A grave sadness descended upon Dillon. He saw how alone he was in this world. "There's no one else, right?"

"I'm sorry," the old man said and Dillon came around the truck to a grinning Harry Smith.

"You drive," Dillon said. "I'll follow you."

"No car. We'll have to ride together."

For a moment Dillon thought about calling it off, but he knew that was out of the question. He'd been dealt a hand, he'd play it out. In the Bronx he'd handled slimier looking guys than this weasel.

When they were in the car the man said he needed to stop at home, pick up some supplies. Dillon scowled and Harry Smith said, "Got to, man. Can't go up into them hills with nothing. 'Sides, got to get me some smokes." He pulled a nearly empty pack from his shirt pocket as proof.

It occurred to Dillon the guy might simply want to pick up a piece but he stopped the car where the man directed him, across from the Hoot Owl Saloon. "It's a bar, for Pete's sake," he said.

"Live upstairs there." He motioned toward a curtain-less window on the second floor. "Back in fifteen minutes."

He needed clothes, anyway, Dillon reminded himself so he picked up a few T-shirts, a pair of khakis and a pair of sneakers in a hardware store. When he returned to the car Harry Smith was already there, waiting for him, a backpack tossed into the rear seat.

"What you got in there?" He indicated the backpack.

Harry Smith gave him a lazy smile. "Supplies, is all. You want to check?"

Dillon felt the bag, felt the soft give of two cigarette packs, the pencil-like sticks of what might have been beef jerky, then something long and tube-like and hard. "What's this?"

"Flashlight." Harry Smith said matter of factly. " 'Case we ain't back before dark."

Dillon handed him the keys. "You drive. You know the way." He figured with his bad hand the man would have to keep both paws on the wheel.

No way was he going to let this guy get the drop on him.

"How long this gonna take?" Dillon wanted to know when they'd been driving for some time.

" 'Nother fifteen minutes driving. Three, four hours maybe up in them mountains. You got real lucky finding me. I know the shortcuts. Otherwise, you'd be least a day and half finding Farley." He drove mostly with his left hand but he kept the withered hand pressed to the wheel as a ballast. "Yessirree, I'd say you got real lucky."

Dillon stared out at the forlorn stretch of desert ahead. "I'll feel a hell of a lot luckier when we find Farley."

"You in a hurry, ain't cha?"

"Let's just say I'm on a schedule. I don't have time to waste."

"Must be nice havin' a schedule. Must make a man feel he got a purpose in life, an importance. Most folks I know just waitin' around for something to happen." He glanced sideways at Dillon. "What you want with that plant, anyway? You a holy man in disguise?"

Dillon kept his eyes straight ahead. "I'm not in the mood for chit-chat."

"Just passing the time, is all." He lifted his foot from the accelerator and the car slowed.

"What now?"

"Got to relieve myself."

"You just did. Not ten minutes ago."

The man shrugged. "Bad bladder. Like I tole you."

"How do your hunting parties put up with it, you having to goddamn pee every five minutes?"

"They ain't got no choice." Harry Smith grinned across the seat at him. "Just like you."

He stepped off a few paces from the car and stood with his back to it. Dillon figured it was a stall, maybe give his buddies back in the bar time to get out there in advance. But like the man said: he didn't have much choice, did he? He slipped his hand into his boot, let the cool metal of his Derringer reassure him.

"Trust," the Indian said when he got back into the car.

"What about it?"

"Makes life a whole lot sweeter. Lets a man breathe easier. Take me, for example." He put the car in gear and started off again for the mountains. "Used to be like you, always worrying, always calculating, the tension twisting me into knots inside. Then I learned to trust. Made me easy within myself. Like now, for example. I'm trusting you to give me that grand like you promised. I didn't ask for it up front. Didn't ask but for a small deposit. I put my trust in you, took you at your word. Some might say I'm a fool, but I'm doing what my heart tells me, and it makes me feel more kindly toward my fellow man."

"Thanks for the advice."

Dillon kept his eyes on the mountains ahead, watched them grow larger in the windshield, and when the car finally reached the foothills the Indian parked it against a slope of hard-packed dirt.

"Got to hoof it from here."

Dillon stepped from the car and looked around skeptically. There was no sign of life anywhere. "Where are those Farley people? Thought there was a campground or something."

"This is that shortcut I was telling you about. Them followers of his'd just get in the way anyhow." He pointed above the dirt hill to what appeared to be a steep rocky ascent. "We got a straight shot up the mountain here."

"How we gonna climb that?"

"I'm gonna show you. If you can find it in your heart to trust me." He spoke over his shoulder as he stood peeing into the base of the hill.

Dillon looked back at the car. He didn't like leaving it here, but what choice did he have?

The Indian zipped himself up. "You got a backpack in that trunk?"

"No."

"No matter," the Indian said with a faint smile. "I have everything we need here." He used his left hand to sling the backpack over his shoulder. "This way."

Dillon clicked the remote again to make sure the Toyota was locked. He glanced up at the rock outcroppings for any sign of movement then followed his guide up the hill.

The higher they climbed, the stronger the heat rising around them, the worse Dillon felt about the situation. The path was narrow and anything but straight. Flat rock surfaces acted like mirrors glinting in the sun, hurling back knife-blades of light. Shielding his eyes against the assault, he wiped the nearly constant bloom of sweat from his forehead. His feet hurt; he had cramps in his legs. In the city he would have raised his arm to hail a cab. Here he was a mule, plodding behind the lead mule. A dumb animal following a dumb animal. One foot forward, then the next.

Time and again he stumbled because, mistrustful as he was, he kept his eyes on the back of the man ahead instead of on the stony ground.

How had it come to this? A week ago his life had never been better. He had a boss who loved him, he was making more money than ever before, had more women than he had time for, had friends up and down his block. He was the crowned prince of his neighborhood. A prince, *period*. No ifs, ands, or buts. Riding the rising tide of his life.

And what was he now?

A slab of meat for the buzzards making lazy circles in the sky above.

One week and his universe had turned on its side. He laughed at the person he'd been, his foolishness, his belief that the bad times were all behind him.

And there *had* been bad times, early on, with his zealously upright father who beat him mercilessly, and sometimes beat his mother too, for the slightest disobedience—failure to do his homework, smoking in his room, talking back to a teacher—which had driven him to even deeper levels of rebellion, which nearly got him kicked out of school, which made him hate school as much as he hated his old man. So he rejected all those things his old man pushed him toward: career, marriage, family.

Instead he fell in with the neighborhood toughs who liked his attitude, liked his style. He was tough, too, like them. Tougher, maybe, with sharp good looks. A smart dresser with an easy, innate sense of cool. Petty crimes at first, nicking tires and hubcaps, which led to stealing the whole vehicle, which led to catching the eye of Nicky Fargo, the slickest operator in that corner of the east Bronx. Nicky, too, liked his attitude, liked his style.

It was around that time, the year he turned twenty and dropped out of college, that he learned how to use his looks, his charm, to his advantage. Make 'em smile, make 'em laugh, show them your razzle-dazzle, and while they're under the spell, take what you want. Take *whatever* you want, whether you need it or not. It was a game he excelled at, especially with the babes, *especially* with the married ones, his specialty—no hassle, no long-term commitment, just the fun; and he liked taking something secretively from other men. Served them right, didn't it, for not treating their women decent enough to keep them faithful? When it wasn't fun anymore, he moved on to the next one. Seemed there was an endless supply. He met them in the bars, on the street, in playgrounds and parks.

And he was a games-man with the guys too, with guys like Nicky who was using him as much as he was using Nicky. What difference did it make, if everybody was getting what he wanted?

Maybe that was what disturbed him most: that he'd clawed his way out of hell, that he'd proven he was better than that miserable little kid cringing at his father's feet, that he'd lived high and mighty all these years, only to have it all ripped away from him, and the hell he was now in was hotter and more desperate than anything he'd known before.

With every twist of the trail, with every arduous step up the mountainside, he thought he might scream out in protest. Damn Vinnie. The gutless low-life who had brought him to this. Why? *Why?* What had he ever done to Vinnie? He stared at the blank rock faces around him. *It's me. Cool*

Joey D. I'm better than this. I am. I am.

But the rock walls rising on each side of the trail, the stoic unforgiving landscape around him, seemed to mock his distress. Under the sun's glare, the dry treeless surface of the ridge, the unyielding faces of the rock, offered no comfort to any living thing—least of all man, who seemed to Dillon to count as nothing more on this earth than a trifling intruder.

He stared at the sky until his eyes hurt, until he felt tears forming. There was nothing, *no one*, here to charm. No one to hear a complaint, no one to blame.

This was no game.

Live or die, thrive or perish, he would have to find some other way out this time. His wavy hair, flashing eyes, wide smile? Useless to him now.

It was a realization that knocked him senseless, that went far beyond the extreme physical discomfort of the climb or the feeling of injustice seething within because fate had turned upon him its blind eye.

Up ahead Harry Smith turned and offered a crooked grin. "Pretty country, ain't it?"

Dillon scowled a response.

"Each to each, I guess," the Indian conceded. "You're a city boy. Me, all this rock and sand and such, it's in my blood. Ancestor to ancestor. Passed down so long it's who I am. Makes me love this here dirt. Love it to death."

"Not what I hear."

"How's that?"

"Nothin'."

Harry Smith stood sideways on the trail, a heavy sadness in his eyes as he gazed across the jagged terrain. "Funny what some folks'll say, just to hear themselves talk. Like they was appointed judge or somethin', settin' down the rules, layin' it all out. Who gave them the right, I wonder. Who said, this man speaks the truth, this one don't, this one's right, that one's wrong? Who, I wonder?" He was shaking his head slowly at the mystery of it. "Who, you figure?"

Dillon waved his hand in dismissal. He was in no mood for philosophy. Not, at least, from the likes of the broke-down creature before him.

"A man's got a right to eat, don't he? Got a right to find his way in this hard-luck world, don't he? Who's to say he don't? Who's to say he done this wrong, or done this right?" He stared angrily at Dillon, as if he was the source of the accusations against him. "Let him say it to my face," he said, but Dillon waved his hand again in dismissal.

"Plenty of folks like me woulda give up, feel sorry for themselves." He raised his shriveled hand as evidence. "Not me. I took what God give me and made the best of it. Done the best I could." He directed his pointed stare again at Dillon. "Dare any man to say I didn't."

Dillon checked his watch. "Ain't got time for this, man."

"I know, I know. You got a schedule to keep. You got the world waitin' on you. You're just dropping by, then you're gone. Wham, bam, thank you ma'am. Ain't that right?" He started to climb again, dragging his withered hand along the craggy face of the wall. "Me, I'm right at home here. Got all the time I need. Got my history right here in this rock." He was quiet a moment before asking in a friendlier voice, "How 'bout you?"

Dillon had only been half-listening. It was *time* he was thinking about, a commodity he would soon be without. "What *about* me?"

"How far you go back? Family tree-wise."

"My old man. That was enough for me."

"Shame," Harry Smith said, shaking his head. "Damn shame."

Dillon, thinking about how much his feet hurt in the new sneakers he'd bought, thinking he wouldn't even be able to run good if Vinnie and the boys caught him by surprise, said nothing.

"A man who's got no past, don't have a future, either."

"That's no concern of yours now, is it?"

"Just sayin', that's all, just sayin'. All that money you got, and you still ain't happy."

"How you know whether I've got money or not?"

A snake-like grin coiled across the man's lips. "Figures, that's all. Man comes all the way out here from New York City. No regular job or nothing. Offerin' big bucks for taxi and guide service. Way I figure, must be a payoff waitin' somewhere."

"That's not your concern. Your concern's getting me to Farley."

"We're getting there."

Dillon checked his watch. It was already close to noon. If he was right in his calculations, that Vinnie and his boys had flown into Santa Fe yesterday, then they'd already be somewhere in this desert, going motel to motel in search of him. He wiped his sleeve across his forehead and squinted against the bright glare on the rocks. "How much farther?"

The man offered his crooked, serpentine grin once more. "Be there before you know it."

They hadn't been climbing ten more minutes before Harry Smith signaled—his third time in the not quite forty-five minutes they'd be on the mountain— that he had to pee again. They'd been moving between thick boulders, sometimes the passage so narrow there was barely enough space for a man to slide through. If there was a more perfect place for an ambush, Dillon couldn't imagine it. He stuffed the Derringer inside his belt for easier access.

Sunlight poured down heavy as rain. He watched as the exiled Apache stepped behind a rock several yards farther up the trail and held out his hand for Dillon to wait.

The space between the boulders was wider here, as much of a trail as they'd been on so far. Dillon leaned against a rock to catch his breath, keeping his eye on the Indian. For a moment the man's head dipped out of sight and Dillon tensed, reaching for his gun. He listened for the sound of water hitting rock, thought he heard it but wasn't certain. The Indian's head reappeared and Dillon relaxed.

"Let's go," Harry Smith said.

As Dillon took a step forward the Indian emerged in full from behind the rock, standing above him on the trail. He held his bag in his withered hand; in his left hand there was something long and dark. The bag came at Dillon first. The Indian let out a yell and leapt on him wielding the hard metal flashlight which glanced off Dillon's skull, sent him slamming back against the rock.

The flashlight, heavy as a night stick, came at Dillon again. He raised his arm to take the blow, the metal making a cracking sound as it struck bone, Dillon crying out and grabbing for the man's good hand, twisting it backward until the Indian screamed and fell against him, dropping the flashlight. Dillon kicked him from behind to send him spinning hard against the rocks farther down the trail.

A shadow dropped from the ledge above, knocking Dillon sideways but he was able to grab the flashlight where it had fallen and swing it at the dark, pony-tailed figure before him. The man's mouth bloomed suddenly with blood, spitting teeth in an aerosol-like spray of red mist, and the face was gone as quickly as it had appeared, pressed hard against the stony surface of the ground.

Then he saw the others, two more of them, crouched above him on the ledge.

He had the Derringer out and he held it on them, saying, "I wouldn't even *think* about jumping. Not unless you want to end up like your buddies here."

They were gone then, out of sight somewhere farther back on the ledge, and he looked at the two bodies on the trail. The jumper lay out cold, blood pooling beneath his head, branching into rivulets that added a bright red sheen to the drab earth. At the base of the rock he'd collided with, Harry Smith lay in a twisted heap. He was moving, if one could call it that—more a twitching of his limbs as he moaned in agony. Blood seeped from his scalp. His left arm, his good one, was turned under him in such a way that the bone of his elbow had pushed through the skin.

Didn't look like he'd be leading an expedition into the mountains any time soon.

—12—

Father Martin drove the Good Hope van through the desert east of the Refuge, feeling giddy as a teenager. It wasn't often he was in the presence of the female sex and it had been years since he was this close to one so attractive. Her outfit, of course, did nothing to hide her charms: form-fitting jeans, skimpy top, bare midriff. Even when he kept his eyes on the road, when he was successful at conquering his impulse to turn and face her, the wild orchid scent of her bath soap taunted him. An exquisite torment.

She seemed as lost, now staring out the window as she had earlier in the day wandering with her camera around the garden. When he asked if she might want to get away for a while, she'd surprised him by saying yes, she'd been reading in a guide book about a museum she'd like to visit called Miss Bonnie Tauber's Lost World of Exotic Dance, if he wouldn't be too scandalized to drop her off there.

He would have liked to think now, sitting beside her like this with the air-conditioned van pitching and heaving even over relatively smooth ground, that his offer had been made out of kindness, but it was *his* need more than hers that had motivated him. He wanted company, especially today on this lonely drive to visit his dying friend. And he liked the way he felt in this woman's presence: part shepherd, guardian of the emotionally orphaned, and part man of desire. Life had awakened within him, as thin and solitary and beautiful as a flower's bloom from the dry bedrock of the desert.

They were ten miles from the museum when he broke a long silence. "You're a professional photographer, I take it."

"I wish." She shifted in the seat and stretched her legs. He caught the motion out of the corner of his eyes and resisted the impulse to look at her directly, though he would have preferred nothing more. "I just finished Grad school," she said. "We both did."

"Your husband—"

"Boyfriend."

"Your boyfriend. He seems like a fine young man."

"Yes, yes, he is. Too fine for me, I sometimes think."

"Why do you say that?" He wanted to know more about what troubled her, assuming of course he was correct in his assessment that she was in fact troubled, that he hadn't simply invented that to make himself feel purposeful: a new soul to save. That was the lie that had prompted his entry into the priesthood—to minister to the souls of the lost. It was only in the past months, since the official "closing" of the Refuge that he had exposed the lie. It was his own soul that needed ministering to. It was himself he was trying to save.

"He knows exactly what he wants," she was saying. "Like right now, for instance, he's focused on two things: becoming a professional journalist and regaining his faith. And he's figured out a way to pursue both at the same time. The way I see it, he's *totally* directed, even though he doesn't think so."

"Oh?"

"He's got this father thing." She stopped to consider if she was betraying a trust. The vast, empty space around them convinced her she wasn't. Things had to be expressed, she decided, or you couldn't survive here. You'd die of loneliness. Besides, it was a priest she was confiding in. No one who would do Trace any harm.

"His father was a religious man, totally devoted to his family, to his parish church. I never met him, he died when Trace was a boy, but he told me all about him. How strong his faith was. How happy he was. How sure of his life he was. When he wasn't at his job or with the family, he helped out at their church. Every Sunday at masses. Weeknights, too. Fixing things—he was kind of handy, I guess. Helping out at social functions, running the annual bazaar, serving as president of the Knights of Columbus, conducting clothes and food drives for the Vincent de Paul Society." She thought a moment. Did she leave anything out? "Anyway, Trace adored him, wanted to be like him. Still does."

"That seems an admirable goal."

"He doesn't have the faith his father had. What faith he *did* have—he worries about this all the time— he says he lost after his father was killed."

Father Martin glanced away from the road, turning to her. "How was he killed?"

"In the church."

It was a brutal murder, from what Trace had told her. He cried in the telling. There had been a series of break-ins, robberies. The neighborhood was turning bad. The police couldn't, or wouldn't, catch whoever it was. So his father took matters into his own hands. He'd let himself secretly into the church after it was locked at night, and wait. When the thief came the next time, he tried to stop him.

She told all this to the priest.

"How awful."

"Trace took it hard. He still does."

"Of course. Anyone would."

"It was more than the death itself, the horror of it. It left him with something he had to prove."

"His skepticism?"

"Just the opposite. He wants to justify his father's death. He really wants what his father had, an all-consuming faith."

"Don't we all." Father Martin laughed at himself, then quickly sobered. He was moved by the story. Why were there so many things to weaken our faith, so few to strengthen it? She was looking at him sharply. "I only meant that would give us *all* purpose," he explained. "If there were no doubt."

"It's one thing I can't help him with. I'm not a believer myself."

He searched her eyes. What was she thinking? "I'm honored that you—that you would share—" He was embarrassed at the strength of his need, so he stopped himself. She had turned again to the window, as if she'd said too much. "And you?"

"What *about* me?"

"How do *you* live your life?"

She stared at the parched land around them. "I drift."

"You're such a lovely young woman—" He stopped himself again. He didn't want to appear foolish, a lovesick boy in a man's body, a *priest's* body. "You have your photography—"

"I like to take pictures, that's all. It's not a job or anything. Nobody's paying me to do it. I don't have any *plan*." She looked at him to see if he understood. It was obvious, she thought, she was nothing like Trace. "That's what drew me to him, I think. No matter how unfulfilled he thinks he is, he has more sense of direction than I can even imagine. I guess I was hoping it would rub off."

"Purpose is an elusive thing. It comes and goes." I should know, he thought. He resisted the urge to speak of his own despair.

"I love him, I'm pretty sure of that." She spoke so softly he could barely hear her over the road noise. "I've never felt that for anyone before."

He found himself nodding, as if agreeing with her.

"I guess I expected things to be different, being in love."

"Different how?" He leaned closer to be sure he would hear.

"I don't know. . .different. From what I thought it would be."

Most things are, he thought. Being a priest had taught him that. He'd assumed living a religious life would bring him closer to God but, if anything, he felt more removed than ever from his Creator.

The wind made a thin hissing noise against the windows. He adjusted his glasses to fend off the glare of the road ahead. Once—briefly, it seemed—he'd had both purpose *and* love. But they were not always one and the same. He said that to her now, aloud.

"I wish they were," she said. "I wish they were one and the same."

He hoped he hadn't sounded foolish or pretentious. Or worse, simply irrelevant. She *seemed* to have taken what he said to heart, as if she were pondering it in her silence. Now, as he drove alone toward the Church of the Transfiguration, he thought again about her.

When he had dropped her at the museum she'd lingered before leaving the van, the silence between them like an intimacy exchanged. Or so he thought, until a quirky light flared in her eyes and she asked if he wanted to join her inside. Wasn't he the least bit curious?

Obligations, he said. Priestly duties. And she shrugged, said "Whatever."

"I hear Miss Tauber's got quite a collection of memorabilia. You'll have to give me the highlights on the ride back."

"Vicarious experience."

"That's what's left to me these days, I'm afraid."

She walked toward the bright purple cinderblock building, her shoulders swinging, legs thin and graceful as any ballerina's, her body moving in a lilting rhythm that called to him like a wisp of song so melancholic and from so long ago that he could not recall the memory attached to it.

—13—

"Are you an Exotic?" a voice from behind Vee asked.

She'd been listening to the piped-in music and staring at a sequence of blown-up, black and white photos on the wall, six of them in all, depicting stages of a striptease—from fully clothed to the bare essentials: pasties and a g-string—performed by a one-time burlesque queen known as Trixie DeLuxe. She turned to the owner of the voice, an older woman in her sixties, with flowing blonde hair.

The woman stood tall and statuesque and when she crossed the room she did so, despite the weight she'd put on, with the elegance of a runway model, a woman with a sense of herself, of what her body was capable of. "Are you an Exotic?"

Vee didn't understand. "Excuse me?"

"An exotic dancer. We get many young dancers stopping by. I thought you might be one."

Vee blushed at the thought. "Oh, no. I can't dance like that."

"That's what *I* thought when I was your age. But times were hard. A woman didn't have many choices. A woman on her own had even fewer." Her face showed all the expected signs of age but her eyes were bright and her smile beguiling. She appraised Vee thoughtfully. "You're a good height. You've got the right proportions. You wear clothes well. That's important, you know. Most folks think it's all about taking *off* your clothes. But you've got to look good in them first. That's what draws your audience in. That's what makes them want to see you *without* them."

"I wouldn't want to do that. I couldn't—" She'd been raised conservatively, to say the least. Catholic girls' schools, through college. Not until Grad school had she been introduced to co-ed classes, dorm parties, the free-wheeling social life of a secular university.

"Could have fooled me, honey," Miss Tauber was saying. "The way you were studying the photos of Trixie there. I could feel the connection. Like a buzz in the air. I can usually tell when a girl's got a yen for the life." She stepped back and smiled. "Walk around me, honey. Let me see you move."

Vee blushed again, embarrassed by Miss Tauber's insistence, the woman prodding her with her eyes. She had a kindly, almost motherly face, and Vee found herself doing what was asked, strolling across the room, exaggerating the thrust of her hips as she had been doing lately. Halfway across the room she stopped, too embarrassed to continue. Miss Tauber nodded and smiled as if something had been confirmed. "Yes sir, honey, you sure have it. You sure you're not fooling with me?"

"I dance at parties, that's all. Always with a guy. Mostly, the guy I'm with."

"That's a whole different thing. This here—" She nodded at the photos of Trixie DeLuxe. "This here's an art." She stood beside Vee and admired the pictures, as if seeing them for the first time. "Trixie was one of the best. Maybe *the* best." She exhaled softly. "She was a real good friend."

"*Was?*"

"Gone, honey. Five months now. Those are her ashes

up there." She indicated a brass urn on a shelf above the photos. "She wanted them kept here. Donated all this stuff you see. This room's kind of a shrine to her."

Vee was impressed by the dazzle of it all: sequined gowns, glittering shoes, brightly colored boas.

"The rest of us are in the next room."

Vee followed her into the second room, a larger one, past exhibits devoted to women with names like Alaska Heat Wave, Tempest Storm, Gail Winds, Jennie Lee, past posters and costumes and bras and all manner of artfully detailed pasties, mostly bejeweled with rhinestones, but the one at the end was the real thing, Miss Tauber explained. She lifted it from the wall hook and held it out so it caught the rose-blue light of the room. "This belonged to Suzie Suzie who made the fan dance famous. You might remember her from your history classes in school." Her laugh was deep and throaty. The diamond-studded nipple-shield shook and glittered in her hands. "Suzie had half a dozen a these, one for every day of the week. She was the only one could afford them." She stopped herself then, took a deep breath. "Listen to me going on. An old goat chewing your ear off. And you know, funny part is, when I was your age I swore I'd never get like this." She smiled in apology. "I'm gonna let you be now. You have any questions, I'll be in the back."

Vee had been mesmerized by the woman and she watched with a reverential awe as she slipped behind a curtain. Despite the gaudy displays, the shifting rose and blue light and the gritty bump and grind rhythm of the piped-in music, the room felt empty without her.

She stood there, slowly turning in a circle, until she found the section of the room devoted to Miss Bonnie Tauber, the Torrid Flame of the Tropics, as the posters proclaimed. The woman was a stunning beauty in her youth, wild blonde hair even longer than it now was and shapely curves—and her smile. The smile had not changed with the years. No trace of false gaiety, nothing forced at all, only a straightforward and obvious enthusiasm.

Yes, Vee thought, she had known it as soon as the woman had appeared: there were things she could learn from her, questions to ask. So she pushed aside the curtain and stood in the open doorway.

The room was a living room of sorts, with a plush couch, an armchair and a TV. Miss Tauber sat at a desk near the window, making entries in a ledger.

"Would you mind—?" The sun had slipped free of the clouds, bright light filling the window, touching the woman in a way that made her hair glimmer, her face partly in shadow. "Would you mind if I took some photographs?"

"Sure, honey, you go right ahead. Take all you want."

"No, I meant of *you*."

"My picture taking days are over."

"I'd really like to. It would mean a lot to me."

She laughed her deep, throaty laugh. "Hell, it's your lens that's gonna break. Where you want me to stand?"

"Right there. You don't have to move." Vee slipped the camera from her bag, an old 35 millimeter single lens reflex that she preferred to the newer digital ones.

Standing, kneeling, moving quickly around the small room, she shot from various angles, hoping the light wouldn't change because she wanted that interplay of sun and shadow on the woman's face, her body. The act of shooting, as it always did, freed her from her inhibitions, gave her permission to ask questions of her subject that under other circumstances she wouldn't. "I notice you still call yourself *Miss* Tauber. I'm curious—I hope you don't mind my asking—but does that mean you never married?"

"Show business, honey." She sat there poised but natural, undaunted by the presence of the camera. "Back then you wanted your audience to *think* you were available, even if you weren't. But no, to answer your question, I never did marry."

"You obviously made the choice, with all the men who

must have been in love with you—"

"I liked men, don't get me wrong. Maybe a little too much. Couldn't settle for just one. Always wanted to see what the next night would bring. And I didn't want anyone getting in the way of my work. It wasn't just a job for me. It was my life. Hell, I'm the only dancer I know used my real name. Made up my mind I was never gonna apologize for who I was, what I did."

"When you retired from dancing, though." Vee stopped shooting for a moment, thinking about this woman who was so unlike her own mother who had lived a sheltered, conventional life, who had such limited experience about the world outside their home, their town. "When you weren't onstage anymore, didn't you feel—I don't know—empty?"

"Hell, yeah. Empty as sin. But I wasn't going to latch onto some bloke just because I was feeling down." She sighed then, her eyes gone inward. "I'm no feministic hero, honey. Don't want you thinking that. A woman gives in sooner or later. Got me a man now, living with me. Old codger who came through here, remembered me from the days. Why, he remembered things about my act that even *I'd* forgotten. Kept coming back day after day, begging me to marry him. Well, no way in hell was I gonna make it legal, but I got to feeling sorry for him, told him he could move in if he wanted."

She sighed again, more deeply than before. "Funny thing, though. Didn't take me long to see it was me I was feeling sorry for. I *needed* the old geezer. Needed to know I meant something to someone. I'd look at him and see it in his eyes."

She came out of herself then, regarded Vee curiously. "What about *you*, honey? Why you in here listening to an old lady like me when you could be out there having fun? Now's your time, you know."

How many times had Vee heard that? A woman's time is short, so make the best of it. What you don't do now, you'll regret later. She *wanted* to make the most of her life. She was trying. She really was. She thought of her mother again: how uneasy she had seemed in her skin, always covered up, long sleeves, turtleneck sweaters or high-collared blouses, always cold. "You seem so. . .*comfortable*. . .with yourself, your body."

"Do I?" She considered that a moment. "Used to *think* I was. Onstage, you know, that's all you had, your bod, your only friend, so you'd damn well better be on speaking terms. But we were talkin' about *you*, honey. You got someone who needs you?"

"Yes, I think so."

"Someone *you* need?"

"I think so, yes."

Miss Tauber looked at her sharply. "*Thinking's* got nothing to do with it. You got to be sure, honey. You got to feel it deep down. That's one thing I learned."

Miss Tauber showed her the adobe-walled garden out back, a square of desert sand that she'd converted into cultivated rows—more than half the plot in tomato plants, the rest in squash, cucumbers and corn. "Wasn't easy," she said, "making this dry earth do what don't come natural. Sure worth it, though." She held up a ripe tomato and turned it slowly in her palm. "Know why I planted so many of these?"

Vee shook her head no. Her eyes were still adjusting to the sudden light. She hadn't yet gotten used to how bright the days were here in the West, the sky a boundless blue, the air quivering with sparkle.

"They remind me of my girls," Miss Tauber was saying. "Round and plump and so, so sweet and juicy." She caught herself then and laughed. " 'Course on stage we couldn't let ourselves get *too* plump, but the sweet and juicy part, that we were."

"You were all so daring. Getting up like that, I mean. In a room full of strangers. In a room of men."

Miss Tauber laughed again. "You could say that, I guess. But we didn't think of it that way. 'Least, I didn't. Matter of simple economics, that's what it was. I needed a job bad and I had no skills, to speak of. I had a good bod, that I knew. Men seemed to go for me, that I knew too. So it just made sense. Take advantage of what the good Lord gave me. 'Cause it was just a loan anyways, right? Temporary thing. Till we get to where we all get to"—she pinched the flab on her neck—"the point of negative interest. Where the last thing anyone wants is to gape at your titties."

She set the tomato on a bench along the wall and stood with her hands on her hips, taking in the garden. "Don't seem fair, does it? Have something one day, have it gone the next. Like you was just being teased. Somebody up there yanking back the toy and saying, 'It wasn't really yours, you know,' after you got used to playing with it. I was sore a long time. Did my share of cussin' and complainin'. But what the hell. You get used to it, the *in-dis-pu-ta-bil-ity* of it."

She laughed at the word, the length and fanciness of it, the trouble she had rolling it off her tongue. "Just the way things are. So you deal with it. Open a museum, grow a garden, find some old geezer to hold your hand nights."

"You seem really happy now."

"Don't know whether happiness has much to do with it, honey. Like this plot of sand here. You work it and work it till the earth gives you at least some of what you asked for."

A Joshua tree grew in one corner of the garden, its long horizontal branches waving over the rim of the wall. Vee took pictures of her standing beneath the gnarled limbs, her face again partly in shadow, partly in light. She was thinking of what the woman had said inside, about being sure, about feeling things deep down. "How do you know? About a guy. Whether he's the one."

The woman sighed, as if this was one more thing she'd

learned the hard way. "If you're lucky, your body tells you. And your heart. All the questions get erased."

"But what if they're not all erased? What if sometimes you think they are, and sometimes you think they're not?"

Miss Tauber had been there, too. Her throaty, knowing laugh testified to that. "Then you're like most of us, honey. In the Zombie Zone. And the only way out of there's step by lonely step." She settled on a bench in the tree's shade and tapped the seat beside her.

Vee sat down, holding the camera on her lap, her mind racing with a thousand questions. "I don't understand."

"For most of us gals, I think—I know it was true of me—there's no one-plan-fits-all. You make one move at a time and hope it's the right one. Then one day you stop and look and see there's a whole life trailing behind you, like the plot of a book, and if you're lucky maybe it even makes some sense."

"What if it doesn't make sense?"

"You're young yet, honey. Give it time."

How much time? Vee wondered. It seemed she'd lived a lifetime already without any discernible pattern, with nothing that was hers to keep.

"For a while there I wasn't sure myself," Miss Tauber was saying. "Had me a heap of doubts. But now, now I think it all does make sense—my life, that is. See, I was the kind of girl who wouldn't take advice. Had to do things my own way. Ornery, I guess. Nobody could tell me a thing. So I made a helluva lot of mistakes along the way."

The bell rang inside the museum which meant another visitor had arrived. She pushed herself up from the bench and stood framed against the rows of tomato plants, grinning at Vee. "But here I am. Got my own piece of ground. Got my memories. The Torrid Flame ain't so torrid anymore, but I'm still standing, still smiling. What more could a gal like me want?"

It was the moment before Father Martin entered the priest's room that was the most difficult. Once he had pushed open the door, crossed the threshold and stood before his old friend he had a better time of it. Death was easier to handle face to face than in the imagination.

He raised his hand and knocked gently. No response. Not the usual dry-voiced, "My door is always open."

He pushed the door, took in at a glance the empty room, then turned to cross the dirt yard, scattering the three chickens and a rooster in his path.

The Church of the Transfiguration, a peaked-roof building made of stone, served a community of Indians who stubbornly clung to their ancestral life-style, living high above the desert on the mesa's flat surface, without benefit of electricity or running water. There were no cars here. You had to climb by foot from the valley below.

At the moment the church was empty. He came down the narrow aisle past rough-hewn wooden pews and brightly colored murals to a door that opened into the cemetery. Father Avila sat on a wall beyond the rows of stones.

"You insist on wearing your cassock, Paul, in your condition. In this heat, too, and in your off-duty hours."

"A priest is never off-duty. Not in a community like this." His voice was thick and dry, nearly a rasp.

They shook hands, a formality they'd established years back in their seminary days.Father Martin found it difficult to believe his friend's hand had once been larger and more powerful than his. Now, thin-fingered and bony, it fit easily into his own. There was no pressure in the grip. "I envy you, you know. Your devotion to your work. Your faith."

"*Habit's* a better word. It's habit that keeps me going."

After so many years his skin had taken on the bronzed look of those he served. His hair remained dark but his eyes seemed to have grown greyer with time, sinking deeper above the leathery folds of his cheeks. He smiled thinly at the irony. "Faith initiates, but habit sustains."

"Then I envy you that. Having *some*thing to sustain you."

"There'll be a vacancy here before long, Martin. It would console me to know you were the one to fill it."

"No one can fill your shoes." Father Martin sat on the wall and looked down nervously. It always made him uncomfortable to sit like this at the mesa's edge, several hundred feet above the valley floor, but it was cooler here than down below, thanks to the near constant breeze and he felt grateful for that. "*No* one, Paul. And in my present condition, I'd make a mockery of the attempt."

A playful light crept into Father Avila's eyes. "Remind me again, would you? Just what your present condition is?"

"Ineffectuality."

Father Avila laughed, a dry laugh like his voice. "There's a difference, you know, between *feeling* ineffectual and *being* ineffectual."

"How could I *not* know that? You remind me every week."

"You're a slow learner, then."

"One of my many failings."

"You underestimate yourself. You always have."

"How is it I come with the intention of giving *you* comfort and I leave with you having comforted *me*?"

"There you go again," Father Avila chided. "You've *always* been a comfort to me. Even when we don't see each other. Simply knowing you're out there, only sixty miles away."

He had felt that, too, the comfort of knowing his friend was in the region. He would miss him terribly when he was gone. "How have you been this week?"

"Good. I've been good."

It was what the ailing priest said every week. And

Father Martin wished it were true. In a year's time, though, he'd watched him become a shadow of his former self, thin, stooped, having more and more difficulty walking. This, a man who had played in the backfield at Notre Dame, who had weighed in at 220 pounds in his prime. "You're eating okay?"

"I'm eating fine."

"I still wish you'd come to the Refuge where I could care for you properly."

"Not while I have my flock. Dwindling though it may be. We lost another one this week." He looked toward the cluster of squat adobe dwellings beyond the churchyard where women washed clothes in the community basin or baked bread in the clay ovens. "We're down to less than a third of those who were here when I arrived. They don't want to live without TV."

The wind gusted and his grey eyes watered. Father Avila blinked against it, looking out toward the red and brown hulks of distant mesas. "It's curious, when you think about it. They came up here to preserve their way of life and escape their enemies—the white man, other hostile tribes— and they survived here. It took such a Herculean effort to build this village, to carve steps out of the rock face, to haul water and supplies from below. But they made that effort, for a hundred and fifty years they continued to make that effort. And now all it takes is a little box with pictures for them to give it up."

"What will you do if they all leave you?"

Father Avila nodded at the neat rows of gravestones, each one washed clean of dust and decorated with a tidy arrangement of desert plants. "I'll tend to their dead. It's a good occupation for an old man."

"Your spirit is as alive as it was when we were at seminary." Father Martin was thinking that death was not the human tragedy. Dying before we've exhausted our usefulness was.

"What's troubling you, Martin?"

"Nothing, why?"

"I've known you long enough. This is different than one of your usual moods."

"It's nothing, really." What he meant was: *it's nothing compared to what you're going through.* Under the circumstances, he felt guilty talking about his own problems.

"Tell me, Martin." The priest's pale, watery eyes were insistent.

Martin took a breath and exhaled slowly. "It's a kind of dread. I'm *afraid,* especially at night. Something's happening, *about* to happen. I can feel it. It's inside me and it's outside me. Two forces about to collide."

He hesitated, fearing he wasn't making sense. "And I've been having these dreams. Nightmares, really. In most of them I'm carrying the baby Jesus somewhere, across water or sand or mountains. I'm carrying Him on my back and there's always some threat to His safety, something shadowy and undefined. I know we're going to die, the both of us, and it will be my fault, and I feel so helpless to do anything about it. I wake up with this terrible feeling. Like my entire life has been wasted. Like it means nothing at all."

Father Avila stared at the church with its thin wooden cross framed against the enormous sky. He leaned forward then and with his emaciated hand patted his friend's knee. "You're so convinced you're the bad guy, Martin. But, remember, we're *all* the characters in our dreams. You're the baby Jesus, too."

—14—

They climbed higher on the mountain, passing through canyon after canyon, moving toward the sun then away from it, so that Trace was constantly checking his satellite map to see where they were. "My map's in here," Jessi Belle had said early on, tapping her heart. "No need for paper."

Maybe it was the heat, the arduous ascent, or simply the long silence—they hadn't spoken in what seemed like hours—but by mid-afternoon she was talking to herself, or to the mountains. She walked ahead of him on the path which had leveled out at this point, juniper shrubs and thorny bushes on either side. Every inch of her exposed skin ran slick with sweat.

"Got to find out," she was muttering. "Got to."

He lengthened his stride to keep pace with her. "Find out what?"

"Got to know. Got to." Her face was red from sun and exertion, eyes fixed on the trail ahead, her lips a tight line around her mouth.

He thought maybe she was suffering from sun-stroke. What would he do then, if she lost it? Got delirious on him? "What do you have to find out?"

"*Got to.*"

Her shoulders tilted forward as if pulling her. Some time ago she'd taken off her sunglasses. She held them now in her hand as if they were useless to her, but how could that be, Trace wondered, given the brightness of the sun, its reflection off rock walls and sand?

"Last year? The night Farley disappeared. Is that what you mean?"

"He *knows.*"

"Who knows? Zeke?"

"He knows what happened."

He wasn't going to remind her she'd vowed not to talk about that night. Her delirium, or whatever it was, might be working in his favor. As long as she didn't flip out completely. "He knows what happened to his father?"

"He's got to. He was there." She said it as if confirming what she already knew.

"You were, too, though. You said you were there, too."

"Of course I was there. But they tricked me. They went off alone—"

"Where? How did they trick you?"

She stumbled then and pitched forward, face down on the dirt, her sunglasses flying out from her hand. He helped her up and she stood unsteadily, a stunned look on her face as though she'd awakened from a trance.

"Are you all right?"

"Why wouldn't I be?" She squinted in the light. "I lost my shades."

He reached for them on the path and held them out to her. "So this is what this is all about."

"What what's about?"

"This trek. You think Zeke knows what happened to his father but he's keeping his mouth shut."

She'd told him earlier on the climb that the guy had wanted nothing to do with her this past year. She'd phoned, written, emailed, even showed up once at his door. He'd refused to talk. "Yeah," she said softly, "that's what I think."

She seemed steadier on her feet now. Her eyes, before she slipped on her glasses, looked sharper, the haze gone; but he suggested they rest a minute anyway. In the shadow of a rock wall, their only refuge from the sun, he offered her his canteen. "Got my own water," she said, pulling out a bottle from her pack.

"You suspect foul play?"

She laughed at that. "Foul play. How quaint."

"Do you?"

"I'm tired of questions. It's answers I'm looking for." She tipped back her head and drank from the bottle, then gave him a shrewd look. "They're some kinda defense, you know. The more you ask the less you haveta say 'bout yourself. Questions keep you high and dry."

Trace grimaced, as if he'd been slapped. "What is it I'm not saying?"

"You tell *me*, Mr. Soul Searcher." She smirked. "Mr. Little boy blue who's lost his faith."

She was right, of course, Trace thought. *That* was not something he told her about. In fact, he'd told no one about it, save Vee.

He guessed it made him ashamed, the way things had changed on him, taking him by surprise. Beginning with his father's death, the shock of it. No one even knew he'd been slipping into the church, nights. He said he was picking up extra shifts—night-time security duty— at the Transit Authority where he worked. The killing itself? No witnesses except the thief. So the police had to reconstruct what happened from the position of the body, the blood spatter, what little the killer confessed to when he was finally caught.

His imagination filled in the details. Even now, ten years later, it was like a movie always playing somewhere in his head. *His father asleep in the choir loft. He hears something downstairs: the vestibule door opening, a footstep. Below him, he sees a man's shadow moving down the center aisle. By the time his father descends the stairs, the man is at the altar. He has a gold candelabra in hand, yanking the burning candles free one by one, dropping them on the marble floor.*

His father, in his indignation, says something direct and obvious: "You're taking something that doesn't belong to you," or "that's church property you're stealing."

Panic lights the thief's eyes. He doesn't know whether to drop the candelabra and run, or stay and fight. His father comes quickly down the aisle. When he reaches the altar, the thief has already made his decision. He comes at his father fast, wielding the candelabra like a hammer. His father falls backward, landing hard on the stone floor, face up, eyes staring into the high, dark shadows of the nave—the last thing he saw, Trace imagines, before leaving this world.

So in the space of a single night, in a matter of hours, he lost the man who had helped him with his science projects, taught him to hit a curveball, took him hiking Saturday afternoons, whose whistle he heard in the hallway outside their apartment every night when he came home from work, whose hand on his shoulder carried enough affection to get him through whatever obstacle lay ahead, who showed him by example what faith was.

For a while he tried to reach his father through prayer. He would conjure up his face—the sympathetic eyes and reassuring smile—and he would talk to him as though he were alive: what team should he try out for, baseball or basketball? What should he give his mother for Christmas? Sometimes he would address him in hurt and anger: why did he risk his life like he did? Why did he leave them? Did he love the church more than he loved his wife, his son? But even before he asked that, he knew the answer. He could hear his father saying, *God and the church and family, they're all the same love.*

In time his father's face grew dimmer, harder to recollect, until sometimes he couldn't see him at all, and even worse he couldn't *feel* him, couldn't feel his presence beside him. Just as he could no longer feel the presence of Jesus beside him. Jesus who had been as real to him as his friends, someone right there within calling distance, a bodyguard of sorts who watched his back on the mean streets of Jersey City.

In college when he started taking girls out, not *going* with them so much as *taking them out*, he found them mysterious for a date or two or three and then found them not so mysterious, so that he would have to search for a new woman, a new mystery, the mysteries of women replacing the mysteries of his faith. Jesus became a spotty presence flickering at the edges of his consciousness. They were like old friends who would cross paths occasionally, promise to call one another, then not do it.

In God's place was an absence that Trace tried to fill with books and writing and the evanescent wonders of whatever new woman had invaded his senses. When he met Vee, the mystery of her refused to vanish as it had with those who came before. The more he thought he knew about her, the more he saw that he didn't know. And among the things that most fascinated him was the seeming ease with which she had left her faith behind. It was simply gone one day, she said. Vanished without a trace. No remorse, no looking back. It was like she had never even been a Catholic, as if she'd never believed in God. It was one of the differences, he thought, that kept them together. If he could learn to leave *his* past behind, neither search to deny or affirm the existence of Divinity, he could move on with his life, couldn't he? Maybe find peace, after all.

He said much of this to Jessi Belle who thought a while before saying, "So, bottom line is, you blame your father for two things. One—taking himself out of your life and, two, taking Jesus with him."

"And for taking away the example of living such a satisfying life."

She gave him a disapproving look. "He already gave you that. It's up to *you* to find a way to duplicate it."

"Which is what I'm trying to do."

She was quiet again. In the shadow of the rock, she looked at the path ahead, her shoulders tipped forward as if she were already in climbing mode. Finally she said, "So you got a lot riding on finding this plant."

"Nothing else has worked, so far."

"You ever think, maybe it's not some outside thing?"

"What do you mean?"

"You ever hear the expression, one person's dream is somebody else's nightmare?"

"Yeah, so—?"

"Maybe one person's faith is somebody else's hogwash."

He wiped the sweat from his forehead and laughed. He didn't think he could explain away faith, or the lack of it, so easily. "Faith's got to be something more definite, more absolute."

"Yeah? Why's that?"

He tried to think what his father would say, but came up short. It seemed, looking back, questions like that never troubled him. *Because I need there to be*, he wanted to say. *For my father's sake, for my own.* What he said was, "What about *your* father?"

Her body stiffened. Her eyes grew tight. "What about him?"

"What was he like?"

"I don't talk about him," was all she said.

She turned away and tipped her head back against the rock. Eyes closed, she was thinking hard on something. Then she was looking at him sharply. "You believe in dreams?"

"In what way?"

"You think they're prescient?"

"I don't know. Maybe."

" 'Cause I've been having these dreams." Her brow furrowed at the recollection. "All year. Couple times a week." She was looking toward the opening of the next canyon several hundred yards ahead, preoccupied in a way that made her seem unreachable. "About Josh. Wandering lost in these mountains. It's worse than if I knew he died. The thought of him being lonely and afraid out here, it's awful. It tears my heart to pieces. It really does."

"Maybe he doesn't want to be found."

"But he'd want *me* to know he was all right. He made a promise to me." She was crouched, stuffing her canteen into her pack, a pained look on her face. "At first I thought maybe that was what he was trying to tell me in my dreams. But they're so sad and dark. I think he's calling out for help. I think he needs me."

"So you really think—?"

"I don't know what I think. Like *you*. Which is one more thing we got in common." She flung her knapsack over her shoulder and stepped away from the rock. "C'mon. We got to find Zeke before dark."

Behind the wheel of the Camry, Dillon drove stone-faced, tearing across the desert, a rooster tail of dust spinning in the air for a quarter mile behind. His left wrist ached badly where it had taken the blow from Harry Smith's flashlight; he massaged it and cursed himself for getting set up like that. But what choice had there been? *Desperation breeds bad luck*, Nicky Fargo used to say. The trick, according to Nicky, was to never let yourself get desperate.

Easy to say, hard to do, Dillon thought, under the circumstances. But truth was, desperation was new to him. For so long he'd been swinging free and easy, it had taken him off-guard, a stranger that slipped past his defenses.

He'd been caught. Pants down, butt to the wind, as they said in the neighborhood. Only this was no joke. He saw desperation as a debilitating disease which he was much too young to contract.

Anger built again inside him: at fate for casting him off, at Vinnie for sabotaging his career, his life, at the slack-handed Indian for wasting his precious time—hell, for trying to kill him. Because there was no doubt in his mind they would have left him for dead up there, if they didn't finish him off themselves. The guy was scum, a low-life, native American trash through and through. No wonder he'd been exiled.

You've been exiled, too, he reminded himself.

Yeah, yeah, but it's not the same thing. I've been set up. No way is it the same.

He tilted the rearview mirror toward him, studied his face. It was nothing like Harry Smith's. It was a strong, good-looking face. Women loved it. Hell, *he* loved it. No jitter in his eyes. No haunted shadows around his sockets.

He pushed the mirror back into position and stared at the wide, flat expanse of sand. Not even a tree for distraction. Everything here was revealed for what it was: empty and endless. Whatever had once existed had been erased. He pulled the mirror toward him again. It was the face he knew. He'd swear to that. The face that paid his bills, got him laid. Desperation hadn't yet taken root in his eyes.

Or had it?

The words of George Rising Sun came at him like a blow to the gut. *What kind of trash are you bringing me?*

No one had ever called him trash. Not even his old man.

He felt the pain of that word again—*trash*—sharp as a blade to his heart.

And that story the Indian told about that dude, Coyote, tricking some guy then shacking up with the guy's wife. Was that supposed to be him, Joey D? He remembered the way the medicine man or whatever the hell he was had stared at him, he remembered feeling as if he was standing trial. But George Rising Sun didn't know anything about him. How could he? They'd never met. They lived thousands of miles apart. Still, the Indian's stare had been relentless. It was a look others had turned upon him once or twice before. It was a look that seemed to say, *I know more about you than you know about yourself.*

Okay, so like the Coyote dude, he had taken what didn't belong to him—tires or cars or women. So, big deal. Everyone did that, one way or another, didn't they?

But he saw again the Indian's eyes: cool, judgmental, unforgiving.

In the mirror George Rising Sun's eyes had replaced his own.

He blinked to clear his vision. It had been a trick of the mind, that's all. His own eyes stared back at him. He pushed the glass away and gunned the engine as if he might outrun the judgment that had been levied upon him. But the open road, with its nightmare of endless space, offered no hope of that. For the first time in recognizable form, he felt shivers of guilt pushing up inside him like shoots through dry earth.

And he felt afraid.

The words from George Rising Sun's story came back to haunt him: *forever on the run and homeless.*

That would be his fate. Unless—

Unless *what*?

Unless he made amends.

He looked to the sky but in all the brilliance of its blue expanse he could find no sun. There was no center here, nothing holding this world together, just a man alone driving at incredible speed. In the loneliness of that moment he came as close to prayer as he had since childhood. He addressed the sky, the sand, whatever was or wasn't out there: *if I come through this, if I find the plant, I'll change my ways. I swear it. I'll be a different man.*

When he reached the Refuge he wasn't so much relieved as restless. He walked past the cottages, through the garden, into the main building. No one in sight. Not the chick with the great body, not the Head Honcho, not even the retard gardener, Brendan the Silent.

He was hungry so he helped himself to what was in the refrigerator—left over chicken legs, cornbread, refried beans which he ate cold—thinking again it had been a whacko idea to try to find Farley in the mountains. What he figured he'd do now, what he should have done to begin with, was wait for the guy to come down from the hills, point the Derringer in his face and follow him back to where the plants grew. All he'd have to worry about was getting the guy alone, without his lunatic followers gumming things up.

Yeah, he thought, that's what I should have tried first. Desperation. Impatience. It had nearly done him in. Nicky was right.

But in the next instant his mind was off in a contrary direction, undermining his logic and his Monday morning quarterback line of reasoning, calling him an asshole, a loser, a two-bit punk with mush for brains. *You don't have time, remember? That's why you did what you did. They're gonna extricate your balls from your body.*

That was the point at which he headed up into Holy Land, figuring there at least he'd be able to see them coming. They wouldn't be able to take him by surprise.

Once through the gate, he followed the second path on the right as it curled upward through a thicket of trees. Exhibits were built into the rock crags and every seventy-five feet or so another path split off from the one he traveled.

His guide-post was the crumbling Tower of Babel. But the tower was nowhere in sight. He thought he should have come to it by then and he stopped to get his bearings. It was a maze, all right. Exhibits collapsing all around him and paths running off in every which direction. The worst of it were the broken body parts strewn across the path. Sometimes he'd come upon one like a sudden apparition: a head fallen into the bushes, a leg or an arm lying at the bottom of a ditch. Made him think of his hapless buddy, poor Tommy Petrie.

He climbed the path to the next level and there he saw the top of the round tower, a grey stone turret—aslant and looking more like the Leaning Tower of Pisa—lifting above some yellow-leaved shrubs. The exhibit directly behind it was the Temple of Jerusalem where he had hidden his two satchels of cash. One half of the temple's wall had been intentionally demolished, the gold sign read, to show the extent of Christ's wrath when he chased out the money lenders.

On either side of the Temple, trees with gnarled, brutish limbs cast shadow-images of themselves on the tiled ground. Bending over the rubble he pried the stones apart to be sure the satchels were still there. This place was so freaky it made him more paranoid than he already was. In a gap between the stones he spotted the leather handles of the larger bag and sighed in relief.

Okay, okay, he could put his mind at ease.

Carefully he replaced the stone chunks, then let his eyes range over the entire exhibit which reminded him more of modern day Beirut than anything Biblical. He hadn't really paid close attention to the Bible lessons the nuns at St. Teresa's had taught him, but he was pretty sure JC had only *chased* them from the temple, not *destroyed* the damned place as well.

He was thinking this when he heard something move.

Far below, a figure had passed through the gate and was toiling its way up the main path.

Dillon crouched to conceal himself, his eyes hawking

after the man as he climbed the hill. It was Brother Retard. Despite the heat and the burlap sack he carried over his shoulder, the man moved with a steady, purposeful gait. From time to time he glanced behind him. At other times he shielded his eyes with his free hand and stared out at the Refuge and the desert beyond.

Dillon moved along the Temple wall to keep the man in view. *What's he up to?* He seemed to be heading for the cross but when he passed between the cluster of rocks beneath the summit he fell out of sight and did not re-emerge above the rock line.

What the hell? Dillon wondered. *What the holy hell?*

He half-slid, half-walked his way until he reached the main path then followed in the man's footsteps. When he reached the rocks he searched for some kind of cave or hole but found nothing. So he continued up the steps until he reached the cross at the summit. From there he saw the retard on the far side, several hundred feet below the shadow of the cross, moving into a thicket of trees and shrubs, a flat stretch of land nestled between the hills. If Dillon wasn't such a skeptic, he would have thought he'd witnessed a miracle. Somehow the man had passed through the hill without crossing the crest.

Hurrying after him, Dillon slipped several times, tearing his pants on the rocky soil, setting small landslides in motion. Stealth wasn't his strong point. In the Bronx it didn't make much difference how noisy you were. There was always some greater noise on the street to cover you.

Dillon made his way into the trees where he could view the proceedings safely. The Brendan dude was standing over a small garden, dribbling a few drops of water from a gardener's can over the rows of various-sized plantings. When he had doled out his sparse allotment to the pale, grey-green plants he stooped over a row of the tallest ones and picked off the largest of the leaves, the way Dillon had seen the Italian women in his neighborhood pluck their basil plants. He stuffed the leaves into a plastic zip-lock bag and, in turn, slipped the small bag into the burlap sack. He hoisted the sack over his shoulder and came toward the thicket.

Dillon had to scurry on hands and knees to conceal himself. The gardener, passing by within twenty feet, climbed to the ring of rocks below the cross, and disappeared between the boulders.

So there was some kind of cave or tunnel that bore through the summit.

Standing next to the cross Dillon had a view of both sides of the hill. He squinted through his shades, waiting for the man to emerge; and emerge he did some few minutes later from the ring of boulders. As he headed down the main path to the gate, he was whistling. Something by Sinatra, catchy and familiar. The one about strangers in the night.

Whistling.

Dillon thought that odd for a deaf man.

Give him time, give him some distance, Dillon told himself.

He waited before walking down to the ring of boulders. It took him several minutes searching among the craggy rocks before he found the opening of what he thought was a cave. He had to crouch to get through the entrance but once inside he found that it wasn't a natural cave at all but rather a man-made passageway with alcove niches, lit by candlelight, that housed shrines of the saints. In the cool shadows a faded Holy Land sign which once must have stood outside the entrance had been turned upside down and pushed against a wall. He flipped it right side up to read the inscription:

THE CATACOMBS OF ANCIENT ROME

The passage, no more than four or five feet across, moved in a fairly straight direction. The statues were in varying states of disrepair but the candles were new, and lit, and there were two or three spares in each alcove, which he figured meant that the Brendan dude, maybe not such a retard after all, had to be making frequent use of the place.

And then the passage opened into a larger shrine, a room of sorts, with at one end an over-sized statue—taller than Dillon—of the Sacred Heart, bleeding organ exposed; and at the other end a small table and above the table wooden shelves filled with plastic zip-lock bags.

For a moment he was too dumb-struck to move.

Then he was at the table where the newly picked leaves were spread out to dry. He picked one up and held it to his nose. It gave off a musty, earthy smell, vaguely reminiscent of sage. Enough like sage, at least, to set his heart beating hard. He reached for one of the bags on the shelf and brought it across the room, held it close to the wavering candles at the statue's base. Dried leaves. Papery and crisp.

Back at the shelves he made a rough tally of the bags. About fifty, maybe more. He brushed a lock of hair from his face and stood there with his mouth hanging open. If this was what he thought it was, his luck had finally changed. If this was what he thought it was, he'd found his ticket out of hell.

—15—

Holding a zip-lock bag in one hand and a few of the freshly picked leaves in the other, he stood on the hilltop and chewed on a leaf, his second of the afternoon. The first had yielded no measurable results.

It had taken him nearly an hour to get this far. Because if, as Phil claimed, the high was so powerful as to bring you *mano a mano* with the Almighty, well, the very thought of that made Dillon uneasy. Would it be the sweet, nurturing Jesus the nuns at St. Teresa's had described? Or the severe, reproachful eye-for-an-eye God of the Old Testament? He imagined a Divine version of his old man, fierce and unyielding. He didn't think he could withstand another withering assault on his worth as a human being. If his old man beat him senseless, if George Rising Sun called him trash, what would the Lord of the Universe do to him? He didn't care to dwell on that.

So he had hesitated. But the thought of Vinnie and the boys heading his way in a black limo had now forced him back into action. Tentatively, at first. A nibble here, a nibble there. He wanted to take on the Deity in small portions, sneak in the back door if he could, steal a glance at the Big Guy before the Big Guy got a look at him.

So far, nothing. No hallucinations. Not even a buzz.

This second leaf had a bitter taste and it was difficult to chew but he worked at it until he'd consumed it thoroughly. He hated the taste, the *feel* of it going down his throat; but then he had never liked lettuce either, anything remotely leafy or grassy. What kind of Italian are you, his mother had asked him more than once, you don't like a good salad? Half, he would say, I'm only half Italian. The only good half, she'd say, insisting on having the last word.

He waited now for the plant to take effect. He had no idea how many leaves were necessary for the damn thing to work, or whether they were more potent fresh or dried. If his damn cell phone worked out here, he could call Phil; but on his own like this he figured he'd better start off slow. Wrath of the Almighty aside, no way could he get blotto here; he had to be ready when Vinnie showed. He had to be lucid enough to explain the benefits of what he'd found. If, in fact, there were any.

He was at least pretty sure this was the real deal. Before he'd left, Phil had shown him pictures of the fabled plant, the Mexican version at least, and this leaf matched up damn near perfectly. Look for the little bumps along one edge of the leaf, had been Phil's advice. The little bumps are the giveaway.

He walked around the giant cross, hoping to hasten digestion. He swung his arms, breathed deeply into the wind.

Whoa, whoa, he thought he felt something.

A little dizziness maybe, a lack of balance. The feeling grew into nothing more substantial and he guessed it was some combination of the wind, his deep breathing, the heat and the dazzling vistas that made him light-headed.

Try again. Try again. He chewed another leaf, grimacing with each bite, grinding his teeth and straining his mouth muscles to get it down. *Get me high, goddammit. Get me high.*

Again he paced around the cross. Clockwise. Counter clockwise.

No dice.

Maybe dried they were more potent. He unzipped the bag and gingerly lifted a crisp leaf that looked like something from his ex- girlfriend's spice rack. In his mouth the leaf made a light crackling sound, turned quickly to dust on his tongue, resisting every effort he made to swallow it. What he needed was water to wash it down but he didn't want to wait. He wanted at least a glimmer of a high, something to tell him he'd hit pay dirt, that Phil wasn't just some dream-dopey, nutcase nerd playing with his chemistry set in the basement.

Finally he worked up enough saliva to get it down. Circling the cross again, he gazed at the thin strips of clouds, as if contemplating the vast reaches of the heavens might lift the chemicals within him to heights of their own.

But what did he know about pothead drugs? He was a beer and ale man, maybe a whiskey or two on a big night.

Come on, he urged the laggard hallucinogens within him. *Come onnnn.*

He stared at the nearest mountain peak rising beyond the garden, and a profound melancholy fell upon him. For the outcasts of the world. For himself. For the possibly not so deaf and dumb gardener. "Don't be a retard," he said aloud, as if it were a prayer. "Be a sly fox. Don't be a retard."

He leaned back against the base of the cross and closed his eyes. The sun pounded mercilessly on his head. He heard wind. Not really a whistle the way books described, more of a whir, the sound of bird wings beating the air. When he opened his eyes he expected to see huge buzzards flying overhead, but the sky was clean and clear and blue. The clouds had drifted off to the west.

He was still waiting to feel something. Maybe the leaves

had to be cooked or soaked. Or they had to be distilled to a powder or heated over a flame. Or they had to be smoked or injected. Maybe you had to eat bagfuls of the damn stuff.

When he lowered his gaze he saw the car, or was it a van, moving across the grey-white sand toward the Refuge. He relaxed when he saw it was the priest's van, and then he thought *he felt something*. It wasn't much, but it was something. A little haziness in his vision. A giddiness. A light-headed, airy sensation behind his temples. It wasn't much. Hardly a full-blown buzz. But it was *some*thing.

Enough to give him hope.

—16—

In the Refuge parking area, Father Martin turned off the van's engine and looked at her with eyes large and curious, expecting—what? Vee didn't know. On the ride back she'd told him about the museum, but especially about Bonnie Tauber, how fascinating a woman she was. Inspiring. A true pioneer. An independent woman's hero.

Father Martin nodded solemnly when she ran out of words to praise the woman. "Heroes often turn up in the unlikeliest places."

She thanked him for the ride, for having the opportunity to talk with him. He wasn't a weird man, she'd decided, so much as a sad one.

"I hope I'll be seeing more of you," he said. "Feel free to drop by the common room anytime. As I've said, we've got a nice little library and, of course, it's air-conditioned."

"Maybe I will. Later on." Then she was outside the van, walking toward the cottages.

It took a moment to realize that the black Eldorado was gone. In its place beneath the trees was a grey car, smaller, less stylish. She turned to the priest who was lifting his briefcase from the van.

"New guests?"

"I suspect it has something to do with Mr. Dillon in cottage #1. Shedding his skin, most likely." He winked and then his face turned serious. "I've been meaning to. . .I'm going to have to have a chat with him." He turned toward the main building, walking with a slow, determined step.

She stood there wondering what he meant, before shrugging it off. After all, it didn't concern her.

At the garden entrance stood Brother Brendan with his blank smile, leaning on a shovel and waving at her. Briefly she waved back and hurried on. She wanted to take pictures in Holy Land. Something had inspired her today. She had an idea for a photo collection: bleak images of the desert and the theme park's deteriorated exhibits set against the gaudy and decadent hedonism of Vegas. It was the first artistic urge she'd had since this trip began.

She began at the bottom of the hill, working her way upward exhibit by exhibit. She saw that, contrary to her first impression, the layout had been designed—however loosely—according to a plan. The Holy Mysteries, in ascending order: Joyful, Sorrowful and Glorious. With a sprinkling of Old Testament scenes for good measure.

What she wanted to capture were images of fragmentation: the broken statues and crumbling walls of these pseudo-Biblical structures. She zoomed in on faces cracked and fissured, noses hacked away or chipped, eyes that had been gouged out. Everywhere she turned, grotesquerie presented itself.

She was particularly fascinated with the Nativity scene where the carnage seemed even more extreme: the collapsing roof of the manger; donkeys, goats and pigs lying flat and bludgeoned on the ground. The figures of the holy family huddled in a heap on the flooring, like bodies tossed into a mass grave.

It was like a crime scene and she was an investigator gathering evidence. But for what purpose? she asked herself. What was she trying to prove?

An artist doesn't have to prove anything, her mentor at the University had constantly reminded her. *Your job is to show us what's there, what the world's made of. Your viewer will draw his own conclusions.*

Stop intellectualizing, she told herself. Get out of your head and into the shoot. Go with your gut.

She shot nearly a roll of film before she stopped to take a breath. So absorbed had she become, she hadn't thought once about the searing heat. Now standing back and surveying the scene, she felt both the heat and a stab of fear. Like that night in the outdoor stall. A tremor in the stillness, more felt than heard.

She was being watched.

She turned and gasped. A man stood behind her, at the edge of the trees, so still he might have been one of the park's stone inhabitants.

"Hey," he said, a quiver of a smile forming. "I know you."

It took her a moment to recognize him. His clothes were different: bright shirt, khaki pants. "*You.*" It sounded like an accusation. "You frightened me."

"You hang around here long enough, you hear the damn statues talking to you." He smiled then, a full-fledged smile that made his good looks even more obvious.

"How long were you watching me?"

"Ten minutes. Maybe fifteen." He laughed, ran his fingers through his thick dark hair and came toward her. "Only kidding. Saw you from up top. Thought I'd come down to say hello. Being as we're neighbors and all."

She was ready to bolt, if need be, but he came slowly in a low-key, friendly way with his hands hooked into his pants pockets. Like a boy, she thought. Except that he wasn't a boy. He was a good ten years older than she was. At least.

He cast a disdainful nod at the wreckage around them. "You like photographing this stuff?"

"Yes I do, as a matter of fact." She held the camera close as he made a slow half-circle around her, looking from the exhibit to her, figuring something out. There was something not quite right about him, she decided. He was drunk, or high, maybe both. The way he walked, too deliberate. And his eyes. Too wide open. Burning with an unnatural light.

"That why you came out here? To God's Country?"

"No. I—we—didn't know about this. A case of serendipity, you could say." She saw by his look that he didn't understand. "My boyfriend had to come on business. This happened to be here and caught my interest."

"Where's he at, your boyfriend?"

"Working."

He chewed on his lip, estimating something. "Working, huh?"

"He's a writer."

"Left you here by your lonesome?"

"Who said I was lonesome?"

He shrugged. "Just a feeling." He tapped his skull. "Instinct."

She didn't like his half-quiver smile. She didn't like his questions, or the tone behind them. "He'll be back shortly."

"Hey, I had a girl like you I wouldn't be leaving her alone, short or long."

"What he does is none of your business though, is it?"

"No offense." He held up his palms and took a step back. "Just passing the time. Slow, hot afternoon like this."

She decided she didn't like anything about him: not his cocky stance, not his insinuating grin or the way he kept his shoulders hiked like he was somebody she should be impressed by. She didn't like the way his presence seemed to fill the space around them, crowding her out. So when he asked, did she mind if he hung around and watched her take her pictures, she surprised herself when she said it didn't matter to her one way or the other, he could stay or he could go, it was all the same to her.

"That's kind of you," he said, his smile so ingratiating she had to look away.

She turned her back and focused on the scene. What had she missed? What in this carnage was left for her to capture? She began to shoot again, but his presence behind her was distracting. Why had she said he could stay?

"Somebody did a real number on this place."

She mumbled a *yes* without looking at him. Then she decided it was time to move on. She stooped for her camera bag, flung it over her shoulder and started up the hill.

"Where to, now?"

She hurried along, hoping he wouldn't follow, but she heard his footsteps slow and heavy on the gravel. Despite the heat she walked even faster, nearly breaking into a run, and either he had fallen far behind or had stopped altogether because she no longer heard his steps.

When she reached the Sorrowful Mysteries she was out of breath and sweating profusely. She leaned against a Styrofoam boulder in the Agony in the Garden exhibit, afraid to look behind her. Instead she concentrated on re-loading the camera. She heard him then, his breathing like a deep sigh in the stillness, and his footsteps slow but determined. For a moment she wasn't sure whether she was relieved or angry that he'd followed her.

When she turned around he stood there grinning, holding a plastic crown of thorns. "Found this."

He held it out to her. Almost innocently, trying to please her, she thought. As if offering her flowers.

She ignored him, turned to the garden in search of something to shoot. For some reason there were no statues here, vandalized or not. Nothing but Styrofoam boulders of varying size and shape. They had been arranged in a circular configuration with an entrance to an open area inside the circle. She looked around despairingly for a broken limb, a severed head. She didn't want to appear uncertain, indecisive. She didn't want to look like an amateur in front of this man.

"Why don't you shoot *me*?" he said. "I can wear this." He put the crown on his head, cocked at a rakish angle, and stood at the entrance to the garden.

It made her laugh. "Jesus with a Brooklyn accent."

"The *Bronx*. We beat the piss out of guys from Brooklyn." He extended his arm to brace himself against one of the boulders but it compressed like a sponge at his touch and he was bent sideward, staring at her from an awkward angle, offering his shining eyes and ingratiating smile. "Come on. It'll give you something to remember me by."

"One picture," she said, giving in. "That's all."

He turned down his mouth in an exaggerated pout. "That's all I'm worth to you? One picture?"

"I've got to get back to work. I'm developing a theme here."

But contrary to her declaration, she didn't stop at one shot. She had him take the crown off and she went in close on his face, from different angles. It was a strong face with hard, intense eyes that seemed to soften under the scrutiny of the lens. Without the dark clothes, with his charming smile, there seemed little trace of the mysterious, brooding man she had first seen watching her from his porch. He seemed less threatening. As if in some way the camera made her his equal. She held herself with more authority, felt the swagger in her walk as she moved around him. She asked him what he was doing out here at the Refuge. After all, she said, he didn't exactly look like a spiritual retreat type of guy.

"That's a good one," he said. "I like a woman with a sense of humor."

"You didn't answer my question."

He grinned back at her, playing dumb. "What question

was that?"

"What you're doing here."

"Business."

"Any particular *type* of business?"

"Nah. Just business. It's personal."

The phrase that Father Martin had used, *shedding his skin*, flashed through her mind. Something clicked. "*Shady business?*"

Blank face. A look both bland and innocent. A look, she thought, he had down pat. "Whaddayou mean by that?"

"Kidding you, that's all." She stopped shooting and glanced down the hill where afternoon shadows had begun to darken the displays. Higher on the hill the sun was still bright.

"What *kind* of business is that boyfriend of yours doing out here?"

"Just business. It's *personal*."

"Clever," he said, nodding begrudgingly. "Real clever."

"Not really. Just passing the time. Slow, hot afternoon like this."

He smiled, brief and knowing. "Like your style. Real hip and sassy. Like your irony. I been to college too, you know. Didn't finish, though."

"Why not?"

"Other opportunities presented themselves."

I can imagine, she thought. *I don't want* to imagine, she corrected herself. "Got to get back to work now," she said.

She picked up her bag and began walking toward the Calvary exhibits, a series of them along both sides of the main path as it climbed upward. Quickly he was beside her, matching her stride. "Got something to show you," he said.

She kept walking, eyes fixed on the next exhibit. "Yeah?"

"You're gonna like it."

"Why's that?"

"You're a curious lady, I can tell. You're looking for something special."

"Am I?"

"You're gonna like this place, trust me. It's real secret. You won't find it on your own."

"Maybe I will."

"You won't, I'm telling you. You'll never know it's there." He stopped and held out his hand. "I'm Joey, by the way. Joseph Francis Xavier Dillon."

The stuff was working, he thought. A long time coming and with a veneer of subtlety, but it *was* working.

A giddiness propelled him. He felt on top of the world. He wanted to climb to the hillcrest, raise his arms, and float high above the mountains: arms extended and bent upward in a V like the buzzards, only he'd be their king, the Buzzard King. Cool Joey D, the Buzzard King. Screw Vinnie Fargo. Screw Harry Smith and his ragtag band of renegades. Screw this ghoulish hellhole with its non-stop parade of mutilation and destruction. The Buzzard King rules. The Buzzard King flies above the world.

Well, he wanted to fly above the world *later*.

Right now he wanted to get laid.

And he would. Soon. He felt it coming, felt the tingle of his nerves in anticipation, though it had been touch and go there for awhile. This chick's cold front would have withered a weaker man. But he knew when a woman wanted him. He'd been blessed with a personal heat detector that rarely malfunctioned. He knew it before *they* knew it. And this one, this one gave it off like smoke from a brush fire. He'd seen it smoldering in her eyes the first time he saw her walking behind her boyfriend. It was in the *way* she moved, too, the way she held herself.

He took his time now, walking up the hill to the

catacombs. No need to rush, better to make her wait. They were all the same, women. Hold something back and they want it. They'll beg you for it. A man with secrets turns them on. Can't help themselves. Like dangling a big fat worm in front of a fish; that sucker's gonna open its mouth, wide. So he never gave away too much. Show a woman all you've got and she's not yours anymore. It was the rule he lived by. So even now he hadn't told her *where* they were going. Up the hill, that's all. Follow me, trust me, you're gonna love this, baby, I swear.

"How far is it?" she asked.

Impatience was a good sign. He liked that. "Not far." He smiled at her reassuringly. "You're gonna get the best pictures you got all day."

They walked in silence past a series of pillaged Christs, some beheaded, each with shoulders bent under the strain of a cross.

"Your boyfriend know you prowl around up here?"

"I'm not *prowling*. I'm working."

"Yeah, that's what I meant."

"What concern is that of yours?"

"None really. Trying to hold up my end of the conversation, is all." He had reached the ring of boulders, the real ones, and stood before the catacomb entrance with his chest puffed out. He grinned triumphantly. "This is it."

She stared at the hole without interest. "What? A cave?"

"Secret passage," he said. "Goes clear through the hill. Full of shrines and things." Her look had turned decidedly skeptical. "Take a peek, you don't believe me."

She stood there hesitantly.

"Go ahead, take a look."

She glanced around as if hoping for some other encouragement. Above them, at the peak, the wind made a low, sucking sound.

"Don't hurt to look."

She lowered herself into a crouch and tilted her head. She could see that it was, in fact, a passage of some sort and that there was light, something flickering.

"It's lit up," he said. "All kinds of candles."

She got to her feet and stepped aside. He thought she was going to back away, maybe bolt down the hill, but she drew her shoulders up and positioned her camera at her side. "You first."

"Sure," he said.

He waited for her inside and as she crawled through the entrance he held out a helping hand. Her eyes grew wide at the sight of the hidden shrines and he thought again that hell, yes, luck had turned his way. First the stash of leaves, then the return of his confidence, now the babe.

She started clicking away, photographing every nook and cranny, every flickering candle.

"Didn't I tell you? Knew this would be your kind of thing."

He couldn't vouch for the seeing-God-thing—maybe what Phil meant was that under the plant's influence you *felt* like God. Because gone was the feeling of being exiled, gone was the melancholy, the wounded belief in himself. In place of those things he felt the familiar bravado of his old life. He was sure he could do *any*thing, he was charmed, as blessed as anyone who had ever lived. In short, he felt like his old self. Only better. Left behind with all that downbeat stuff was the vow he'd made to change his ways. Why change, when the world was at his feet again? He'd gone through a bad period, that's all. A time of weakness. But that was behind him now. And he had a babe waiting.

She was moving quickly shrine to shrine, almost in a frenzy, the rapid stutter of the flash disorienting enough so it seemed the stone faces were mocking him, saints whose names he no longer remembered except for one: Crazy Lucy with her eyeless sockets, holding a plate on which her self-plucked eyeballs sat like two eggs about to be fried.

Being a saint meant being a whacko, he was thinking, they were all batso, they all had something weird about them. Who was it that spent a month at a time fasting in the desert? And that other one who let himself be shot up with arrows, just stood there like a girl and let them jab him to death. Must have been one of those weird doormat types, beat me fuck me call me Ruth. He didn't understand it, not one bit. What kind of God did they invent for themselves who would make them do that? What was wrong with them, why didn't they get a life?

Then he was jerked to his senses by her cry farther ahead in the passage. He'd gotten lost in himself, not quite a trance but he'd been suspended in a no man's land there for a minute, and she'd gotten farther ahead than he'd realized. When he caught up to her she was standing inside the little room with the packaged leaves, saying something about how amazing this was, how her boyfriend had gone traipsing into the mountains looking for this and all the time it was right here, bagged and neatly collected.

"What? What are you talking about?" he said, realizing how stupid he'd been for bringing her here, exposing his secret so that now it wasn't his anymore. She'd tell her boyfriend and god knows who else.

"Stop!" he shouted. "Stop!" But she had turned back to the shelves above the table, leaning toward them for a close-up. "You know what this stuff is?" she said, snapping shot after shot. "You know how many people are looking for this? Do you?"

It appeared to be the real thing. She identified it from the pictures Trace had shown her from botany books, from photos taken of ancient cave drawings. The silvery-green, oblong leaves, irregularly divided into a few narrow lobes, with its characteristic and unusual single wavy edge. That was the giveaway: the single wavy edge. A freak of nature that one edge of the leaf was fluid and unbroken and the other notched in small, wave-like bumps. The plant of the gods.

She couldn't wait to show Trace. Maybe she'd even— she felt a change in the tension of the room's air.

An intrusion.

She lowered her camera and stood absolutely still. In her excitement she'd nearly forgotten to raise the obvious questions. What was it doing here? Who had picked it, dried it and packaged it? And what did it have to do with the man standing behind her?

She felt a moment's panic and turned slowly to face him. Grim-faced, he watched her from the edge of the passageway. "Party's over."

Her eyes flashed to the opposite end of the passage. There had to be a way out in that direction. He'd said this cut right through the hill. She could run. She could. But she held her ground.

"Gonna have to ask you to give me that film." He came toward her with his hand out. Her instinct was to hold on tight, fight him to the death if need be. The photos were hers, an extension of her, her babies; but when he stood near her, so close she could feel the heat of his body, feel her own heat too, the trembling across the surface of her skin, she offered the roll to him without resistance. He took it from her, held it a moment as if weighing it, determining its value, before stuffing it into his pocket.

Then his lips were on hers, his hands taking pos-session of her body: one around her neck, the other shoved hard between her legs, grabbing her sex as if it were portable, something he could rip out and cast aside. He tore at her panties, jerking them down in one short quick motion and then his fingers found their way inside her, slippery in her juices, softer now and less rushed, calling her with an insistence that seemed both remote and familiar. She braced herself against the table, opening her legs and pushing herself against him, clawing at his shoulders in a way that was both fighting him and pulling him closer and she thought *you've been resisting this so long, so long, and now you can't, now you no longer have the strength or will.* Because she *knew.* She knew she'd been moving toward this force, this man, all her life and she'd known without thinking it when she first saw him, and again today when he stepped from the trees behind her, that it was inevitable, their coming together like this, this collision of forces, despite the fact or maybe because of it, that she disliked him, *despised* him, his swagger, his coldness, his pseudo-hip New York bravado, his contempt for women masquerading as desire. Her own desire was intensified by this in a way that both frightened her and drove her on.

When she took his sex and brought it up inside her she thought, *This is where I die, this is where I die* and she heard a small voice from a long-abandoned and forsaken part of her crying out *Your death is your home, lost girl, death is where you always wanted to be.*

—17—

Late in the day, soon after shadows had begun to stretch across the canyon floors, they heard the chopper for the first time.

It was the second major surprise of the afternoon.

The first occurred an hour earlier: they had come upon another encampment, this one high in the mountains on an open swath of ground between two canyons. It was a larger and gaudier version of the one at the base. The collection of wildly-colored dome-shaped tents had been assembled in a circular formation under a double-ring of Christmas lights strung pole-to-pole and powered by a portable generator that rattled and shook behind the tents. Beside it a bank of speakers a good thirty feet high rose like a dark tower on the flat dry land. In the center of the circle a crowd swarmed around an over-sized effigy of a wooden figure, stick-like and primitive, that was being mounted on a pedestal of crates.

"Their god, Joshua," Jessi Belle had said, standing beside Trace on a ridge above the camp.

Trace had been more focused on the human figures in

the crowd, what looked to be a mix of Goths, New Agers, hippies, punks, bikers and a few less immediately classifiable types. A generally ragged, if not rough and tumble and downright hostile-looking group. "Who *are* they?"

"Farley disciples. A splinter group. They've been threatening to break from the main organization." She said it as if she'd been expecting this, as if it didn't surprise her in the least. "They got tired of sitting around waiting for Joshua. They want to be *part* of the search."

"So they're here looking for him?"

"For him. For the plant. Anything they can get their hands on. Even Zeke. They blame him for sneaking off on his own. They think he's holding out on them. That he knows more about Joshua's whereabouts and the location of the plant than he's letting on. " She gave him a knowing look. She wanted to be sure he understood. "They're not our friends. They'll do anything to get hold of the plant."

"Meaning—?"

"They got some fanatics there. They think the plant's gonna save them."

At that moment violent sound erupted from the bank of speakers, a deadening blend of guitars, drums and synthesizers that reverberated across the open land, climbed the walls of the ridge where they stood. Within the circle, the stick-like effigy had been stabilized on the pedestal and the crowd stood back to marvel at it with a collective awe.

"Let's hope we find him before they do," Jessi Belle said.

"What will they do to him?"

"If they think he's hiding his father or the plant, God knows. They'll make him talk, that's for sure."

No sooner had she spoken when somebody in the crowd below—using field glasses, Trace concluded, because the distance was so great— spotted them. An arm was raised in their direction, followed by a shout. More arms, more shouts. Several people were running, then it was all of them like a clot of runners in a marathon, moving across the flat ground toward the path.

"O God," he said. He stood transfixed by the sudden turn of events until Jessi yanked his arm and began pulling him up the path.

"Come on, come on!" she cried out as the first of the crowd began climbing the hill to the ridge. "We've got to get into the canyons. We'll be harder to find there." She let go of him and started to run, her ponytail swinging wildly back and forth across the top of her knapsack. Beside her, he was running to keep pace. He pulled the strap of his back pack hard against his shoulder to keep the nylon bag from bouncing, from holding him back.

The ridge ran long and straight for a quarter mile. When they reached the entrance to the next canyon, they were out of breath and disoriented by the heat, the exertion. She glanced back to watch the first dozen or so Farleys surge onto the ridge, get their footing and break into a run. Her face had turned a deep red, glistening now under a sheen of perspiration. "Fuck my life," she said.

She squinted through her shades to assess the distance between them. Then she was shimmying her shoulders to free herself from her knap sack. When it was on the ground, she dug through it for her canteen.

"What are you doing?"

"Got my compass, got my water. We got to move fast now, or we're dead meat."

Trace had his bag off, too, pulling out his canteen. "What do they want from us?"

"Me. They want *me*. They're hoping I know either, one, where Joshua is or, two, where the plant grows."

"*Do* you?"

"Let's not go *there* again. We got to move." She was jogging ahead into the canyon, waving her arm for him to follow.

"What'll they do if they catch us?"

"Hold me hostage. Torture me, would be my guess. Till I give them what they want."

"You can't be serious."

"You want to wait around to find out?"

He was running a few steps behind her as they wove between juniper trees and clumps of mesquite.

"Let's pick up the pace," she urged. "Otherwise that stuff you're carrying about your father, all your questions—gonna be a moot point."

The canyon was long and narrow and they ran through most of it, far enough ahead of the angry mob behind them to remain out of sight, though reminded of the presence of their pursuers by occasional shouts that were amplified and carried by the rock walls. When they came to the far end, they were dry and breathless. They took a moment for a water break, before she pushed on again.

They followed a ledge that served as a path to higher ground. Steadily, they climbed to a flat precipice from which they could see the Farleys toiling through the canyon below. A hundred of them at least, Trace estimated. They had spread out in a ragged formation, trampling bushes, kicking up dust, moving at the pace of a forced march.

Jessi had already gone ahead down a wide, sandy alley that served as a vestibule of sorts to a series of canyons that opened to the west. "Here's the tricky part," she said when he caught up to her.

"What tricky part?"

"It's one of these on the left here." She turned and re-traced her steps, stopping in front of a chasm that opened between two tall rock towers. "I'm pretty sure it's this one."

"Pretty sure?" He pulled out his satellite map, the only other thing he'd salvaged from his bag.

"Or it could be that one," she said, pointing to another opening a short distance away that also had a tower of rock on either side of its entrance. She waggled her finger between the two. "Eenie meenie miney mo." She looked at Trace, the consternation in his eyes, and laughed. "Only kidding. It's this one." She moved toward her first choice, too fast for Trace to do anything but stuff the map back into his pocket.

They were running again, a fast jog across the hard-packed dirt of the canyon floor. She was a step ahead of him. After several minutes she pulled up short and groaned.

He was breathing hard, his legs aching from the strain of their cross-canyon run. "What's the matter?"

She pointed ahead. Nothing but rock walls on all sides. "Wrong one," she said. "Oops."

A raucous cheer rose from the far end of the canyon: they'd been spotted. Trace watched in horror as the phalanx of Farley disciples came running toward them. "The wall," Jessi said. "Our only chance."

The canyon walls rose straight-up and sheer, forty feet high at least, he estimated. Maybe more. "No way. I can't do that."

"Follow me." She was running to the right-hand corner of the canyon where the rock face seemed, marginally at least, less sheer. Taking one more look at the charging mass spread out now in a ragged line across the basin, he sprinted after her.

From the base of the wall she scanned the crevices, picking out her route. "I've done the rock climbing thing before. Do exactly what I do."

When she was eight or ten feet onto the wall, he began his climb. He pressed himself flat against the rock, placed his fingers where hers had been, his feet on the same narrow lips of stone, the toe of his shoes into the same crevices. Up close like this he saw that the ascent wasn't as sheer as he'd thought. But still it was harrowing, climbing at this angle, with little margin for error and his heart beating so hard.

Three-quarters of the way up he really started to panic. His fingertips felt raw. The ledges for his feet seemed narrower, slicker. Worse than that, though, was the sensation of hanging precariously in the air. A long way to the ground below. No net.

"We're almost there," Jessi said above him. "Get to this ledge here and we're home free."

He made the mistake of looking down at his feet to check the security of his position. What he saw was the ground gaping at him from far below and in the next instant that ground was swarming with bodies—big, beefy men and tough biker-type women, faces turned up at him with flat, angry stares.

A wave of dizziness left him quivering and weak. His body swayed out from the wall. With great effort he twisted his fingers tightly around a chunk of rock to steady himself. A prayer began to form on his lips and he thought how funny that was: he hadn't prayed in years. He slid one foot along a thin protrusion of rock. Then the other. One step and then a second. On the third step he reached the wider ledge that Jessi had promised. He threw himself onto the rim of the wall. She was bent over, pulling him by the belt, his canteen beneath his chest scraping on rocky ground.

Quickly, breathlessly, he was on his feet, following her through a thicket of pines, toward the sound of running water. When they reached the stream—a trickle really, barely enough water to cover the stones over which it meandered, but more than enough to cover their tracks— they waded in, running and splashing their way for nearly half a mile before they turned northwesterly onto dry land that took them back in the direction of the canyon they should have taken.

"You know where you're going now?"

" 'Course I know."

"You want to check the map?"

"What for?"

And that was when they heard the chopper for the first time: not yet visible but definitely close by, the clack-clacking of its rotors reverberating off the canyon walls.

They flattened themselves against a wall as the sound grew stronger overhead. The shadow appeared first, thrown across the far wall and then the chopper itself, its plastic bubble shooting back the setting sun's light as it banked and dropped out of sight beyond the canyon rim.

"They've got choppers, too?" Trace wanted to know, thinking it was a two-pronged assault they were facing, by land *and* air.

"I don't think it's the Farleys up there." Jessi had begun walking again, a forced-march pace in hopes of out-racing the falling sun.

"A TV crew, you think?"

Expressionless, she kept her pace and offered no comment. Trace looked to the sky again, the sound of the chopper fading into the silence. It was unlikely, he thought, that it would be a TV news chopper. Except for reporting his disappearance, the mainstream media had largely ignored Farley, had long ago bestowed him with quack status. It was only as a cult figure that he had received any notice.

"My boyfriend," she said finally. "He's done this before."

"Here? In the mountains?"

"Un-unh. Other times, though. Other trips I took." She glanced at him sheepishly. "He's prone to sudden fits of jealousy."

"You said you did *your* thing, he did *his.*"

"We do, mostly. Times, though, he gets in a mood. Times, he comes get me."

Trace shook his head in disbelief. First the Farley maniacs, now this. He imagined her boyfriend, in a jealous rage, doing harm to Zeke Farley, maybe silencing him forever. The last link to Joshua and the plant of the Gods severed. Gloom descended upon him.

"What? What's your problem now?"

This—the way this thing was turning into a circus—is the problem, he was thinking. Her crazy, mixed up life—

that was a problem, too. What he said, blank-faced as he could manage, was: "Nothing. Nothing at all."

"You think a thing's got to be all one way or all another, but that ain't the world."

He raised his hands in retreat. "Let's forget it. Let's just try to find Farley before anyone else does."

"What else would we be doing?" she said.

Racing the falling sun, Jessi Belle kept up a hard, steady pace. Every muscle in his body ached but Trace concentrated what energy he had left on not dropping behind. They had neither seen nor heard the Farley crowd in quite some time and he felt encouraged by that. "I think we've lost them," he said.

"Don't be fooled. They won't give up. They'll search for us all night, if they have to." She was looking for signs, a landmark, and asking him for help on this the final leg of their journey. "We have to find the tree."

"What kind of tree?"

"A crucifixion thorn."

She walked through the canyon without being more specific. When the walls fell away the land began to rise. On top of the hill a lone tree stood and he followed behind her as she climbed to it. "The Tree of Life," she said. "That's what Joshua called it." She stopped to admire it. "Look how its many branches reach for the heavens while its roots dig deep into the earth's darkness. Its trunk the cosmic pillar uniting matter and spirit."

"Is that what *he* said about it?"

"His very words. Feels like a prayer, doesn't it?" She looked at him to be sure he was fully appreciating the tree. "It gives off a vibe, like a wind blowing through you. Can you feel it?"

His skeptical self wanted to dismiss this vibe business

as nothing more than a mystic's ravings, but the truth was he *did* feel something, not a wind so much as a tingling in his toes and fingertips. He knew about the *Axis Mundi*, its place in metaphysical symbology, and he tried to open himself to the energy of the tree. No use. His psychic antennae were transmitting nothing but static. He was interested only in finding Farley. So he decided to attribute the sensation in his extremities to the cooling air of evening and said, "Which direction now?"

They followed the ridge-line until they reached a series of ledges that offered a stunning view of the desert below. Somehow in their journey they had turned in a way that surprised him. They were facing due west, toward the setting sun. What looked to be less than two or three miles distant, rising above the smaller hills, was the cross of Holy Land lit a garish orange-gold in the failing light.

"We're close now," Jessi said. "We climb here and keep in line with the cross."

"How far?"

"To the next set of canyons."

When he asked why she thought Zeke would be in the same place as last year, she said, "Plain and simple. It's close to where we think Joshua found the plant.

Trace gave her a questioning look.

"Joshua wasn't always what you'd call direct. 'Specially about the plant. He kind of gave it away, though, if you knew him good as I did. And he had a system for determining the best place to consume the plant—according to some ancient Mexican Indian text he'd found." She eyed him closely to see if he were following her. "See, in order for the plant to produce maximum effect, you have to follow certain guidelines. First, you have to have the right intention, you have to be pure and open of heart. Then you have to consume it in the right setting. Something about being no more than a hundred meters from where the plant grows and where the sun casts its last light of the day." She chided him with her smile. *I know what I'm doing,* it said. "So where else would Zeke be?"

It sounded like hokum to Trace. Either the plant had mystical properties or it didn't. He wasn't really interested in some Indian superstition. He'd had enough of tall tales and legends with the Catholic Church. All that mattered, though, was whether Zeke Farley believed it. If he'd be where she said he'd be.

—18—

It was dark when they saw the fire, a small yellow glow against the canyon wall.

They moved toward it cautiously. Farley was nowhere in sight but his equipment was strewn across the ground. Jessi recognized his bed-roll, his two-tone leather boots. "From last year," she said. "From that last sad time."

From a distance, off to the west, came the dull buzz of the chopper. Trace scanned the star-riddled sky. He thought the search would have been cut off at nightfall, but they'd heard the engine intermittently over the past hour. "Your boyfriend's crazy, staying up there in the dark."

"He gets something in his head, nothing stops him."

So far, at least, they'd eluded the Farley crowd. Trace was grateful for that. No sight or sound of them since their rock-climbing escapade. But still, he reminded himself, it was one more unpredictable element in the night's chaos.

Moving around the far side of the fire, Jessi Belle examined Farley's mess kit items and dipped her finger into the coffee cup. "Still warm."

Leaning closer to the fire she poked a stick into the burning ash, deciding something. Trace was about to ask which direction Farley might have taken when a voice said from the darkness behind them, "Don't move."

A thin, emaciated figure stepped into the pale of light. Barefoot, pants rolled above his ankles, his face sun-burnt around tired eyes, he stood there unsteadily, holding a rifle trained in their direction. It took a moment before he recognized Jessi. "It's *you*."

" 'Course it's me," she said with a disarming smile.

"Him?" He jerked his head toward Trace, kept the rifle on her.

"My bodyguard."

Farley snorted. "I'll bet."

"You got a dirty mind, Zeke."

"Why you stalking me?"

"You know why."

Wearily, he hoisted his shoulders to keep the barrel aimed at them. For a moment he rocked uneasily in place, before stumbling toward the wall where he used one hand braced against the rock to lower himself into a sitting position. His finger still on the trigger, he propped the rifle on his knees and stared at them warily.

"You don't look good, Zeke."

"Yeah, well—"

"You sick?"

"Yeah, I'm sick. Sick as hell."

"What of?"

He gave her a derisive smile. "God's flesh."

She stared at him wide-eyed. "You found him?"

"Him? Who? I found *it*. Damn thing's growing all down this end of the canyon."

"Oh," she said, disappointed. "I thought—"

"It's not what you thought."

"I was hoping—"

"It's not what you hoped." He gave her a brief, unflinching look to be sure she understood.

Her spirits dashed, she simply stood there watching

him, her mouth set tight, hands balled into fists at her side. Trace saw tears glimmer in her eyes. He wanted to say: let's go find the stuff, let's try it. But he didn't want to intrude on her sorrow so he crouched by the fire and waited.

Far off an owl hooted twice. Wind whispered in the spaces between the rocks. Night's serious chill was settling in the canyon.

She kept her eyes on Farley whose head had fallen forward. "How much?"

He was contemplating the ground with a dull, listless stare. "What are you talking about?"

"How much of it did you do?"

"Twelve leaves. What my old man said was the proper dose. I boiled them and drank the liquid."

"So what happened?"

"I got sick is what happened." He tried spitting into the dirt but his mouth was dry and nothing came forth but air. "I puked my guts out. For an hour, at least. Maybe more. Then I defecated. There's nothing left inside me."

"You were *purified*."

His lips curled in a half-smirk. "Yeah, I was purified."

"We are purified according to our need," Jessi said, remembering Joshua's words. He had learned that from the curanderos, the descendants of the Aztec shamans. She spoke matter of factly, without judgment. "*Your* need was great."

Farley glared at her. "Don't preach at me. I had enough of that from my old man." In protest he had pulled himself away from the rock, raising the rifle; but he had no strength to maintain the gesture and he sank back again in resignation.

Trace had read about the "purification" rituals associated with certain entheogenic plants—ridding the body of toxins—but he'd assumed the term was used metaphorically, a ceremonial cleansing of negative spirits and forces. Maybe there was more to that *Axis Mundi* image, he thought, than he'd given it credit for. Maybe

Heaven and Hell *were* inextricably entwined. First you puke and shit, *then* you see God.

Jessi Belle was on the same wave-length. "And then you had the Divine visions, right?" she was asking.

Farley threw his head back and laughed. It was the most life he'd shown. "Visions, yeah. I saw the old man."

"*You did*?" She fairly leapt at him. He swung the rifle to keep her at bay. She backed off then, crouching, searching his eyes which were both frightened and defiant. "*Where*?"

"In my head. Where else?"

"What did he *say*? What did he *do*?"

"What he always did. Ignore me. Pretend I wasn't there. Stare right through me to prove how little I meant to him." He rolled his eyes then at the incredibility of it all. "And talk. Talk talk talk talk talk. Spouting his theories. Babbling on about his journeys in search of the angels of salvation. That was his latest pet name for the leaves: *the angels of Salvation*. He had more of a connection to that plant than he had to his own son." He tried to spit again but his mouth was too dry. He reached for the water-bottle propped against his mess kit and drank in small, careful sips.

"Did he have any message? For *me*?"

"Why should he?"

"I don't know. I thought maybe—"

"He was too busy talking about himself. Jabbering away non-stop and so loud I had to cover my ears. I thought I'd go deaf from the sound of him." Shoulders slumped forlornly, he sat holding the rifle across his knees, leaning toward the fire. "Pathetic, isn't it? Even dead, he haunts me, he dominates my life. Even dead, he has the last laugh. I'm expecting to see God and what do I get? *Him*."

With brooding eyes he stared into the fire. Jessi watched him intently but said nothing. She was calculating something. Trace could tell by the energy she gave off. From her eyes, especially. A probing force that filled the air around her.

"Maybe your intention wasn't right?" she said. "Maybe

you were too filled with guilt."

Farley shot her a nasty look. "For *what*?"

"You tell *me*." She regarded him coolly.

"Don't know what you're talking about."

"Don't you?"

"Maybe your energy channels weren't open," Trace offered. "Maybe you weren't ready to receive—"

Farley swung the barrel in Trace's direction. "What the hell do *you* know?"

"Nothing. I just meant—" What he meant was he was only trying to break the heavy silence hanging over them. He was trying to make the guy feel less hopeless. But Farley was right. What business was it of his? He was a stranger who showed up with the guy's father's mistress; he was, from Zeke's point of view, a hostile witness. So there was no sense trying to ingratiate himself. He huddled closer to the fire for warmth and scanned the black sky for any sign of the chopper.

"Dead," Jessi said. "You said he was *dead.* I thought all we knew was that he was missing."

"That's what I meant," Farley mumbled. His sat with his shoulders pulled in against his neck like a roosting bird.

"But you said *dead.*"

His eyes flared at her then narrowed to fine points. "It was a figure of speech. I meant *gone, missing.* And that's what we think anyway, right? How could he be alive? He's been gone a year, without a trace."

"You were the last one to see him—"

"Yeah, so?"

"You said he just walked off, into the night—"

"What are you, a cop now? Get off my back."

"It's not me who's on your back, Zeke."

Farley held the rifle close to him, rocking toward the fire and away. "I don't want to talk anymore."

She leaned toward him. "You've got to talk. Don't you see that? For your own sake, if not mine."

He was on his feet now, leveling the rifle at them. "I don't want to talk. It's time for you to scram. I want to be alone."

Jessi Belle stood her ground. Beside her, Trace shifted uneasily and took a step backward. There was a crazed, unnerved look in the man's eyes.

"I said, beat it." Farley stumbled at the edge of the fire and stepped toward them, jabbing the rifle in their direction. "I mean, *now!*"

"Come on, Jess." Trace took her arm but she shook herself free.

"It's all right," she said calmly to Zeke as well as to Trace. "We can work this out. Can't we, Zeke?"

"Nothing to work out, far as I'm concerned."

"Sure there is. You know there is."

He was advancing on them, rifle raised at eye-level, his finger curling around the trigger. His walk was uneven, but the determination in his eyes was unflinching. "Leave me the hell alone. You hear? You hear me? I'm through with all that."

They backed away from him slowly. Trace had his arms raised, but Jessi looked unruffled, her eyes on Farley. The more she looked at him, the more agitated he became. A tic quivered under his eye. His finger played nervously with the trigger housing. "Through with what, Zeke?" she asked.

"My old man, that night, the plant. All of it can go to hell."

"It's not that easy. You know that. You can't just turn your back on it."

"I can do anything the hell I want."

"If that was true, you wouldn't be here now. You wouldn't be suffering like you are."

She stopped backing away then and stood her ground. "Put the gun down, Zeke."

He made a sound that was half snort, half snarl. "Now why would I do that?"

"Because you need me. You need *us*."

"Like hell I do."

"Zeke, listen to me—"

But he was listening to something else: the far-off drone of the chopper cruising above the dark hulks of the mountains. His lips curled in disgust. "They've got planes now, too."

"And that's not all," Trace interjected, figuring to capitalize on the man's miscalculation. "Planes up above and an angry mob on the ground. A hundred people, at least. We barely out-ran them."

"The hounds of hell." Zeke spit the words like a curse.

"They can't be more than a couple of miles away," Jessi said. "The darkness is on our side but still—it's only a matter of time. They'll follow our tracks. You know that, don't you?"

Under the dim light of the stars, the defiance seemed to drain from Farley's face. "They hate me," was all he said.

"What do you think they're going to do to you when they get here?"Jessi asked.

"I don't know." But it was clear from the terrified look in his eyes that he'd already considered the possibilities.

"No Joshua. No plant. They're going to want answers or—"

"They'll tear me limb from limb." He lowered the rifle and hung his head. "I'm doomed."

"Unless we give them the plant."

"No way!" He jerked the rifle up as if he would defend his territory, his *inheritance*, no matter the cost.

"How many of them you gonna kill before they rip you apart?" She saw that he was contemplating what she said so she waited a moment before adding: "Why not give it to them? You'll be their hero."

For the first time, he offered no protest. He simply stood there, thinking it over.

"It'll be a peace offering," she said. "We'll help you

gather it."

On the opposite side of the canyon, the plant grew in a long, narrow swath along the wall.   Jessi let out an involuntary gasp. For a moment she stood frozen, before fingering one of the leaves. A slow, timeless caress.

"Out here there's three or four dozen of the plants," Zeke said without enthusiasm. He stood there shining his flashlight on the leaves, his shoulders heavy with resignation.

Trace's heart was beating hard. He, too, reached to touch a plant, to assure himself it was real. Not far off he could hear the sound of water dripping on rock and he thought he could detect a silvery glimmer in a crevice of the wall. Which would explain how the plant could survive here. From what he had read, its Mexican cousin, and virtually all the plants in its class, grew best in well-watered but well-drained soil. It could tolerate neither drought nor frost. Which was where the rock wall came in. Providing sufficient shade but also absorbing the heat of the sun, acting as a radiator at night.

The tallest of the plants, those closest to the wall, had grown to three or four feet. The leaves were large and oval-shaped. In the flashlight's beam they shone a pale silvery green.

Jessi was thinking of the hungry crowds to come. "Is this all there is? They're going to need more."

"There's more," Zeke said.

"Where?"

He swung the flashlight down the length of the canyon. "A box canyon. Beyond this one. It's completely hidden."

"I want to see it."

Trace, reading her face, knew what she was thinking. That must be the secret canyon Joshua had written about. That was the sacred ground he had walked upon.

"Too dangerous," Zeke was saying. "It's guarded."

"By what?"

"Wolves."

"*Wolves*?" Trace and Jessi said the word at the same time.

"On the rock ledges. Along the top of the walls."

"I want to see it, Zeke. I have to see it." She started along the wall, Trace right behind her. He was as anxious as she was to walk where Joshua Farley had walked.

"You'll never find it."

"Show me then. *Please*."

Holding the rifle in one hand, the flashlight in the other, Zeke watched her without expression. "It's dangerous," he said again.

"What are you worried about? You've got *that* thing." She laughed then. "Wouldn't go shooting it off, though, less it's a matter of life and death. Too many ears out there."

Trace thought the man was going to refuse to show them. The secret canyon. One last thing he could call his own, a belated if unintended gift from his father. But he may simply have done the math and realized Jessi was right, these few dozen plants wouldn't feed the hounds of hell. He started walking past them, moving toward the far end of the canyon. A pocket of trees grew there and right beyond them was a thin opening in the rock face. It looked like no more than that: an indentation, a hollow. But it went far deeper than it appeared. They followed him through a narrow, zigzagging passage that opened into a second canyon the size of a grid-iron.

Somewhere in the past few minutes, unnoticed, a quarter moon had risen. In its cool ivory light, the plants fanned out before them, a faintly shimmering sea of leaves that filled the confines of what those who had come before called the Canyon of the Gods. A sob issued from Jessi Belle, and Trace felt his heart racing again. He couldn't remember the last time he felt so filled with anticipation.

Zeke said this was as far as he was going, but Jessi

had already moved into the canyon, *floating* not walking it seemed to Trace, so delicately and gracefully did she glide among the luminous green abundance of the plants.

"Look," Zeke whispered, pointing to a series of ledges on the canyon's left side where shadows seemed to move.

For a moment or two, Trace couldn't be sure if it was a trick of the eye. The canyon wall held pockets of darkness, still and deep, black spaces where no moonlight penetrated. Caves, maybe. Except that the caves, or something within them, was in motion. Shadows detached themselves from the larger darkness, leapt from precipice to precipice. Along the top of the wall where the light was better, he thought he could make out thin, rangy shapes skulking low against the rock. "Coyotes, maybe."

"Coyotes, wolves. What difference does it make? They're not happy we're here."

It seemed that way to Trace, too, because the wall had come alive with shifting motion. He tried to count the individual shapes, but because the motion was constant now, more agitated it seemed than before, he gave up. Thirty, he thought, at least, maybe more—on that one wall alone. And as he looked around he saw that the dark shapes weren't only on the left side of the canyon, but on *all* sides. He thought he could make out the glint of their eyes—hundreds of pairs of eyes, he thought, but that couldn't be, could it?— reflecting the moon's light.

He was reminded of what Father Martin had said of the Indian superstitions—that there was a curse on those who violated the sanctity of the holy ground where the plant grew—and for a moment he thought the curse might be real, that he could feel it then and there, a palpable thing in the air, in whatever vigilante army of animals was massing on the rock around them—manifestations, perhaps, of the shape-shifted spirits of the Anasazi. It's only the eeriness of this place, he told himself, hidden away at the top of the world: the bone-like pallor of the unnatural light, the strange and inexhaustible stillness, the presence of the plant itself and the magical hope it inspired.

He blinked and for a moment the glinting eyes were gone, the shadows stopped moving. He thought it odd that if they were dogs of some sort, there had been no barking, no yelping, nothing remotely like a growl.

Jessi came wading through the plants toward them, her eyes glowing with a rapturous light but her voice steady, assured. "We've got things to do. While there's still time."

With Zeke standing guard, rifle at the ready, Jessi Belle and Trace took turns cutting down the plants. They used Zeke's hunting knife, cutting the stems close to the ground. While one cut, the other stacked the plants in bunches to be transported to the outer canyon.

Jessi Belle seemed unperturbed by the presence of the shadows, concentrating instead on the work at hand, as if she possessed some secret knowledge that she was immune to attack. Trace, on the other hand, kept a wary eye on the canyon walls. The animal-like shadows—he would bet they were coyotes and not wolves—had moved lower on the ledges but so far, with occasional shouts and the almost constant gesticulation of his rifle, Zeke had kept them at bay.

Not for the first time that day, but for the first time so consciously and directly, Trace thought of his father. This was the kind of ordeal he would have gladly endured for his faith— climbing mountains, overcoming obstacles, exposing himself to danger if necessary—and it made Trace feel closer to him in ways he hadn't felt since childhood. Of course, whether faith was waiting for him at the end of this, only time would tell. And if it wasn't? Well, then the joke was on him, on both of them, on all those who suffer for their God. The possibility of that, the very real possibility of that, left him with a sinking feeling.

When they had cut nearly a third of the plants, Jessi said she thought that was enough. An even greater stillness, it seemed, had settled upon the canyon. Trace glanced again at the walls. There were no moving shadows, no eyes. Only the black hollows of what might have been caves, motionless and impenetrable.

They brought the bundles of plants to the outer canyon and laid them in neat rows next to those growing along the wall.

"We must prepare ourselves," she said and directed them to sit with her at the fire.

Zeke took his seat against the wall, the rifle propped against his leg.

"You shouldn't need that now," she said, but he made no move to put the rifle out of reach. He had retreated inside himself once more. His sullen eyes stared at her with reproach. "Why should I humiliate myself again?"

"You don't know that. No two trips are alike. And you weren't ready the first time. You didn't prepare yourself. You had too much darkness within you. That's why, before we begin, you have to tell me what you're holding inside you."

He looked about to protest but he sat in silence, playing with the hem of his jeans. When he raised his head, there was resignation in his face, his eyes aquiver with some new recognition, as if he'd finally acknowledged to himself the truth of what she said.

"That last night," she said. "What were you arguing about when you two walked off?"

"Who says we were arguing?"

"Come on, Zeke." She said it so gently, so softly, it sounded more like a plea than a challenge. "I heard you shouting. You were cursing at him like he was your worst enemy."

When he looked at her, whatever resistance had reared

itself left his eyes. Later Trace would think it was the residual effects of the plant that made him confess, that weakened his defenses enough to allow him to pour his heart out, or maybe the softness of her voice when she prodded him, or maybe simply the pressure of the guilt from holding his secret so long.

"What were you fighting about?" she said in the same soft, coaxing voice.

Farley closed his eyes, squeezing them tight as if there was something he didn't want to see. "Nothing. Everything."

She held her breath, waiting. "You can tell me. *Please*."

"The usual," he said finally, opening his eyes. "What we'd been arguing about for months." He spoke more to the fire than to Jessi. "I knew he'd found the plant. I knew he'd tried it, even though he denied it. I begged him to let me take it with him, the two of us, but he wouldn't hear of it. Too soon, he said. He didn't want to make the same mistake *they* made. He meant Alpert and Leary, the 60s crowd. He said they went public with LSD too soon."

His face was lit with firelight, his eyes unflinching in the brightness as he released more of the story. "He had this theory that as soon as Acid spread through the masses, as soon as it exploded into a hallucinogenic circus, it became a threat the government had to stop, at all cost.

The Pols had no idea how to get their minds around it. So they passed all those ridiculous drug laws that killed even legitimate research. No university, no academic scientist would dare continue work on mind-expanding substances. He kept shouting at me that we lost forty years, forty precious years, because Leary had rushed things, had let it all get out of hand. That wasn't going to happen again. Not if he, Joshua Farley, could help it. There was too much at stake. There was the 90% of our brain that we weren't using that was at stake. So he had it all figured out. He'd been planning for years what to do if he ever located the plant. He would work in isolation and secrecy. He wasn't going to let mass hysteria ruin his life's work."

Trace thought he saw tears in the man's eyes but it may have only been the shadows playing tricks again.

"I said it wasn't mass hysteria he was talking to, it was *me*, his son. But I didn't count for anything, I never had, so why should it have been any different that night? He said he wanted to test it himself first, he wanted to be sure it was safe. How long, I wanted to know, how long? And he laughed at me, said as long as it takes, my boy, as long as that."

He was close to sobbing now. Trace looked at Jessi but she didn't return his glance, rapt as she was in Farley's account.

"I called him a liar. I told him he didn't care about anybody else. All he wanted was the ego-trip of being the first to publish research on the plant, the one who got all the glory. And he accused me of being another Leary, willing to sell my soul to the masses for my fifteen minutes of fame. He called me irresponsible and immature; he called me a fool. He said I had no idea what serious research meant, that I'd learned nothing from him. Nothing at all."

He hung his head in shame, as if he were hearing it again, his father's voice upbraiding him. "All I wanted was to share something with him, to be part of what he loved so much. He was right, I *was* a fool. A fool to even imagine that could happen. He'd been shutting me out all his life, why should it be any different now? Going off the way he did every summer, leaving me and mom behind like we didn't exist, showing up again in the fall like he'd been away only for the weekend. The guy was oblivious, totally cut off."

He drifted off, lost inside himself. In the details of that night? The residue of the plant's hallucinatory images? Trace could only wonder.

"So, that night, what happened?" Jessi asked. "What

happened after you argued?"

He nodded to something behind Trace and Trace turned quickly, expecting someone had crept up on them, but there was nothing except the darkness of the canyon with its faint grey outlines of trees and shrubs.

"We were on that narrow path that leads into this place. The one you came in on, the only way here. He told me I was in his way, that he had things to do, and he tried to push me aside. Like a branch he was pushing aside or a pesky fly, an annoyance. Just shove it away like it was nothing, like he'd been doing to me all my life. But I wouldn't budge, I wouldn't step away, and he—he lost his footing, he teetered there a second, flailing his arms. I reached for him, I did, I tried to grab hold of his coat but he was already off the edge, falling—"

A gasp escaped from Jessi Belle and for a moment Trace thought she might collapse where she was sitting, her body seemed that liquid, that unsure of itself. With great effort, it seemed, she pulled herself together and kept her eyes on Farley. "You didn't even—? You—left him there?"

Farley tipped his head, barely a nod.

Her face had frozen in disbelief. "What if—?"

"It's a half-mile drop, at least. All those rocks—"

"But—"

"There's no way he could have survived. No way. *Nobody* could have survived that."

"You left him lying there, all broken." It was a statement, a realization.

"I thought about going down. I *did* think about it—" He looked lost, bewildered, and Trace didn't know whether to condemn him for his callousness or feel sorry for him. "It's too steep," he said in his own defense. "No one could make it down there alive. Could they?" He looked at her as if asking for absolution. "What would have been the point?"

"He was your father," she said.

"I was afraid. I was afraid to see him like that."

"The police. Why didn't you tell *them*?"

"I didn't think they would believe my story. A lot of people, like you, knew we didn't get along." A flame of defiance flared again in his eyes, and a self-righteous anger which he directed at her. "I didn't want to rot in jail. I wanted to finish what he'd started. I wanted to show him, even though he was gone, that I could bring this plant to the world, and the world would be transformed by it."

He was sobbing into his hands, his grief amplified by the walls of rock and the night's deep silence.

Some time passed before Jessi got slowly to her feet. There was something trance-like about her movements, slow and measured as they were. "I want to go down there. I want to see him."

"Don't be crazy," Zeke said.

"I want to."

"There won't be anything left. The vultures will have seen to that."

"The bones. I want to see the bones." She stepped around the fire and walked toward the canyon entrance.

"Jessi, wait!" Trace was on his feet, hobbling from the day's exertion. "It's not safe out there in the dark."

He caught up with her on the narrow path that bridged the escarpment between two canyons. Wind channeled between the faces of rock. She stood midway on the path, some twenty feet from him, gazing down into the ravine's blackness, shivering in the sharp air. Hope destroys us as it saves us, he was thinking. Gave her sustenance for a year, but made her descent now to earth more merciless.

His body, aching with fatigue, felt unsteady. He spread his feet to stabilize himself and stayed where he was so as not to disturb her. She would draw her own conclusions. She would see the impossibility of entering the ravine.

In the wake of Farley's story, he felt unsettled and he found himself studying the contours of the path before him. Its width was three feet at its widest point, maybe two feet at its narrowest. Certainly it would have been possible for a man, an *older* man, to slip off the edge, particularly if he had been made unsteady by his own anger, by his effort to push away an obstacle the size of Zeke Farley. But it was just as likely that in a fit of jealousy the old man was pushed. Or that even if he simply slipped his son made no attempt to reach for him.

All kinds of permutations of Farley's tale were possible. It came down to what you wanted to believe. And in this case Trace wasn't sure *what* he wanted to believe: Zeke Farley as murderer, or sad victim of twisted fate? Nor did it really matter what he thought. What mattered was what Zeke Farley thought, whether he believed his own story and where his belief—or lack of belief—would take him from here.

Truth, like the face of a stalker, slipped in and out of sight.

And truth, he thought, was what his being here was all about. *Ultimate* truth. *Constant* truth. *That which could be no other*, as one of his Theology professors had phrased it. *That which is complete in itself and beyond which there is no more.* The precise point where he, Jessi Belle, the Farleys and their disciples were hoping the plant would take them.

Once in my life, Trace was thinking, if I could get there once in my life. It had become an unvoiced prayer to the God he doubted. *Lord, lift me for one moment above the clouds of uncertainty and confusion so that I may see your face. I ask for no more.*

Then he became conscious again of the night around him. The vast lonely reaches of the mountains seemed to mock him. How foolish he must sound to a God, if there was one, or to the endless void of the universe if there were not. Throughout the centuries how many must have pleaded for the identical privilege: *just one glimpse, that's all I ask. Just one glimpse, so I know.*

Why should the mysteries be revealed to *him*?

And yet the preposterous nature of his request did nothing to contain his yearning.

Jessi had shifted her stance. She raised her eyes from the ravine. She called his name and he went to her, moving carefully along the path until he was close enough to hold out his hand to bring her back.

"The plant," she said. "We can find him there."

—*19*—

When they'd left the catacomb, Vee walked beside him down the hill. The sun had moved farther west, there was no bright or shocking glare, but even so he'd donned his shades the moment he stepped outside. Crawling back, she thought, under whatever rock would hide him. Still, she stayed close and went with him to his cottage.

Inside the room, as austere and penitential as the one she shared with Trace, he told her to take off her clothes.

"I'm going to rock you from here to kingdom come," he said. He took off his shades and set them on the dresser along with the two bags of dried leaves he'd mail to Phil.

She did as she was told, removing her halter top and slipping out of her shorts. By the bed she stood waiting for him.

"Those, too." He meant her panties, torn and stretched and still wet from her juices.He watched while she stepped out of them. "On your belly. This one's for your boyfriend."

On the unmade bed she stretched herself out, hands reaching beneath the pillows, face pressed against the wrinkled sheets so that she could smell the faint residue of him on the cloth: a trace of body oil and sweat, a salty smell.

With the room heavy with the day's heat he came into her, hard and unforgiving. She took her punishment without complaint, balling her fists and muffling her cries in the pillow, knowing she deserved this pain though for the life of her she could not remember her crime.

When he finished with her that way, he wanted her on her back. She flipped over and gave him whatever he asked, turning this way and that, swiveling her hips, pumping them harder or more gently at his command, taking him in her hand, her mouth, and always his presence above her, large and looming, a weight she couldn't bear but knew, again without knowing why, she *must* bear.

When he stopped demanding things of her, when he took his hands from her and lay back on the bed, she still wanted him. Even more now because he'd abandoned her, set her adrift on her own and she wasn't ready for that—how could she be? she thought—*will I ever be?*

She ran her tongue over his nipples, touched his neck, his shoulders, the soft skin on the inside of his thighs, thinking all the while how much she disliked him, even his body-type, his thick trunk and his weight-lifter's muscles, and even more so the way he lay there, sated and indifferent, communing with the ceiling rather than her, not even touching her, not even a kiss before leaving her.

She wouldn't release him. Not yet. Not yet.

She ground her fingers into his flesh and took him in her mouth, drawing him out until he was swollen again. Lifting herself into position she bore down on him, clenching her muscle until he was wrapped so tight he couldn't possibly leave her. Not for a while, at least. Not until she was swept into that tide of obliteration where she wouldn't have to wonder who she was or where she was going. And when the tide caught hold of her, hurling her again like flotsam from wave to crashing wave, she thought: this is what you wanted.

Are you happy now? Are you?

Later, her back to the stranger who snored more loudly than the wind which had risen and now worried the window glass, she was thinking about her mother, what she would think if she had witnessed her daughter's behavior this day. Would she disown her? Would she curse herself for this groveling savage she had created?

Then she was thinking of Trace, the man she loved, or thought she loved, and she began to weep violently.

From the common room, Father Martin had watched them come down the path from Holy Land and enter the far cabin.

Lovers.

They had become lovers that afternoon. He was sure of it. The way she leaned into him as they walked. The way she held his arm. The way she would pull away every so often to study his face, as if waiting for him to tell her something she needed to know.

He rummaged in his desk for a pack of cigarettes left over from his smoking days. Outside in the colonnade, he inhaled deeply, pacing the tiled floor far earlier than his usual nightly routine, staring through the graying light of the garden in hopes that it had been a mistake, her going into the man's cottage, hoping that she would quickly realize that and emerge, return to her own cottage—or, better yet, come running across the garden to be with him, to ask his advice, to ask for confession.

What made this even more hurtful, more humiliating, was that he'd been waiting for her all afternoon.

After he had dropped her off here earlier, after what he thought of as their moments of intimacy in the car, he was confident there was a bond between them. He was certain he had convinced her he could offer comfort in her troubles, he was sure he had, sure she understood that when she left him, the *lingering* way she left him. And he had actually prepared himself in case she came to him for counsel. He had showered and shaved and dressed himself in fresh clothes. He'd forgone his afternoon nap, afraid he might miss her. He'd made certain to remain in the common room at all times, in case.

His disappointment had grown as the afternoon wore on, he felt as jilted as a lover, and then *this*. He should have known better, he told himself, a man of his age. When would he cease being so susceptible to illusion?

He made a decision then, or thought he did. He snuffed out the cigarette and strode across the lawn. A confrontation was what he had in mind. He would inform Mr. Joseph Francis Xavier Dillon that he had overstayed his welcome, time to move on; but when he reached the cottage door, the room dark beyond the windows, the shadows alive with secrets and whispers, his feeling of humiliation overcame him. He turned away, defeated.

What would he have said, anyway?

I want you to leave immediately.

You go, but the girl can stay.

I have guests arriving. I need the room.

He would make a fool of himself, wouldn't he? Reveal himself for what he was—a jealous and frustrated and lonely man, growing old with too much time on his hands.

And if he had ordered the man to leave, what then? He was armed, to be sure. Would he have turned violent? Or would he simply have laughed in his face? He didn't know which of those possibilities was worse.

And if he had pressed his face to the window, what would he have seen?

O, you know what you would have seen. You would have seen the way of the world. Why should she be any different?

To the voice inside him, he defended her: but she's

different. She is.

Fool! Fool! She's as common as the others. Why can't you face it? Why?

Disoriented, he stood uncertainly on the path. Then, ignoring his own admonitions to his guests, he did another thing he hadn't done since the Refuge ceased functioning as a rehab center. He climbed the hill behind the cottages into Holy Land.

This had been his getaway, albeit a perverse one, when he needed respite from the troubled souls in his charge, when the tide of their anxieties and depressions swamped the increasingly fragile shore of his sensibilities. He would exchange the demons below for those on the hill. The abandoned exhibits with their butchered icons had seemed a simulacrum of his lost faith, though the faith he was losing was not so much in the Church as in himself.

Now he climbed as far as the gate where he stopped for breath beneath the cut-stone arch. From here he could see to the top of the hill, the crucifix a thin shadow in the dimming light. Over time, he had become all too familiar with Ezra Holmes' ill-fated dream in all its incarnations: the sullen and breathless quiet under a noonday sun in summer, the odd and incongruous cheerfulness of its springtime bloom of wildflowers, the pale as death countenance of the grey facades under a thin dusting of snow.

He had learned, too, to measure the day by the park's variations of light and shadow: dawn's pink-gold liquid spilling from the crucifix to the tops of the tallest trees, the facades' flat white glare at midday, and what was happening right now around him—the murky shape-shifting shadows at dusk.

This, he thought, was the most unsettling time of day.

This was when the plaster bodies of the statues seemed most like visitors from beyond the grave. He imagined that the spirits of those who passed through the Refuge had migrated here, had taken up permanent residence, and that this was the time they were most restless.

Branches lifted in the breeze, shrubs made whispering sounds. He squinted through the charcoal-grey air as if he might see a statue turn its head or raise an arm.

You're a rational being, he told himself. You've been here too long to believe this is anything but a junk-pile of plaster and cheap wood.

And yet. . . .

He looked down the path to the cottages, his eyes drawn to the first of them, still dark, still silent, as if nothing were happening there. But something was. Something was. Another soul was being lost to him.

One more failure among many. One more proof that he had lost his usefulness.

He began climbing again. He would have to walk a long way tonight, he would have to walk for hours, to calm his nerves. His failures had mounted too strong a case against him.

He was thinking of *that* time, that one wild night several years past, when one of his damaged priests, Father McElroy, a fifty year old man with an insurmountable attraction to altar boys, fled from the Refuge and went into hiding here in Holy Land. With torches and flashlights, the staff scoured the hill until nearly dawn at which time he sent them back to the Refuge for rest. On his own he'd continued the search, finding the fugitive priest several hours later, distraught and shivering in one of the catacombs.

"I want to be left alone," Father McElroy had told him, choking back his tears. "I want to die here, alone. I'm not worth saving."

"Of course you're worth saving. You're one of God's—"

"I'm a disgrace. To myself, my family, my church, my God."

"God's love and mercy is all embracing—"

"But not *yours*."

He had been taken aback by the accusation. That was the moment he first acknowledged to himself a growing, deep-seated repulsion for those he served. The wayward priest cowering against the catacomb wall had seen it before he himself had. So he stammered out the only words that came to him, "God's love is all—"

"I despise myself," Father McElroy said. "So I surely must be despised by you. I see it in your eyes."

In response, he said nothing. Instead he offered his hand. The runaway priest was too weak to walk on his own, so he locked his arm around the man's waist and half-coaxed, half-carried him down the hill.

He learned much that morning about his own inadequacy. For the priest he was helping down the hill exposed what had been festering within him: that he'd turned his back on those he was supposed to save, that he'd said to them in the secret chambers of his heart, *you disgust me.*

He admitted to himself that he had come to dread his sessions with them, their whining and cajoling voices, their ceaseless craving for drugs and alcohol, for having sex with children. Unlike Saint Martin whose love for living things was so boundless, so the stories went, that in the evenings he would go outside the friary gates to feed scraps of bread to the vermin scuttling in the ditches, he saw that his capacity for love was pitifully limited.

He was ashamed at his inability—even more so at his unwillingness—to offer them more than perfunctory comfort in their struggles. This was the knowledge that would shape his self-doubt from that point on.

The knowledge of a fool, the voice said inside him as he climbed the hill. It might have come from one of the statues rising from the shadows.

Why? Why am I a fool?

Because of your naiveté. Because you believe that God's plan for the universe must be recognizable and absolute.

I want it to be. It disappoints me when it isn't. It fills me with inconsolable grief.

Like the girl disappointed you.

Yes.

Like McElroy and all the others disappointed you.

Yes.

You want the world to stand at moral attention.

Yes.

And if it did, then what?

I'd be capable of love.

You grow more foolish by the hour. But your greatest failing is this: You expect God's plan for **you** *to be recognizable and absolute.*

How else will I find my way?

The way is all around you.

I don't understand.

Of course you don't understand. That's why you mope around as you do. That's why you wallow in your precious despair.

You make it sound like I created it.

Of course you created it. Where else would it come from?

The world, Father Martin wanted to say, this world so unequal to the needs of a man. That's where it comes from. But he stopped himself. The voice would only mock him, accuse him of self-pity, of being faint of heart.

Doubt is the condition we're born into. A test of our love. It's a gift.

A gift brings joy.

Eventually, yes.

Then I've grown tired of waiting. Perhaps I should leave the priesthood.

More self-pity.

Maybe I should.

But the mere thought of that terrified him. What would he do? Where would he go? Faith was a family from which he'd been orphaned, yet he clung to it in his isolation, felt its presence like a phantom limb.

Your friend, Father Avila. He's found his way.

Because he's a good man.

We're all good men. If we choose to be.

I'm too weak—I'm not—I'm incapable of—

There you go again. Your addiction. Your self-inflicted despair.

He looked around in desperation, as if one of the statues might console him. How? How can I be a good man?

Open your eyes, the voice inside him said. *Reach out your hands. There's always a way.*

He waited for something more, but the voice was silent. He felt at loose ends. Nothing, it seemed, had been resolved.

In his distraction he'd strayed from the path and found himself wandering through one of the exhibits. Two angels were escorting the risen Christ to Heaven. The angels' wings had been hacked to a rubble of plaster chunks at the Lord's feet. Father Martin winced as he passed by. The atrocities here still shocked him. Even in this make-believe world, the moral order had been subverted.

When he returned to the path again he was breathing hard. This was the steepest part of the hill. The stone steps to the summit lay just ahead. The wind had picked up and he had to fight it as he climbed.

Standing beneath the crucifix in the last light of day, he felt bereft and lonely. Why had he come up here? What purpose did it serve?

Far below, the Refuge lay in heavy shadow, its collection of plain adobe buildings, its manicured garden, so neatly enclosed within its walls. From this distance it seemed too small, too fragile a place to offer any true protection from the open, ragged space of the desert or the bruised and gaudy spectacle of the hill. From this distance it seemed no refuge at all.

As he started back down, the wind shook the shadows

loose on both sides of the path. Surely, he thought with a laugh, the ghosts had come for him now. One of the shadows veered close to him and he jumped. Brother Brendan— materializing, it seemed, out of thin air— stood beside him, matching him stride for stride.

"Brendan, you startled me. Where did you come from?"

His companion shrugged in a way that made the question seem irrelevant.

"Don't you find it disturbing here? This time of night?"

The man stared back at him with soft blue eyes that offered no opinion.

"Of course, you don't. Nothing disturbs you, does it? Things like doubt and despair don't exist in your world, do they? You have your shrubs and flowers." The notion crossed his mind, as it had before, that his co-worker's connection to Holy Land was deeper than he knew.

Could he be the one responsible for these strange acts of vandalism?

Instantly, he rebuked himself for the thought. That was absurd, wasn't it? Surely, this mild-mannered man wasn't capable of such destruction. "Are you?" he said.

Brother Brendan stared back at him with Buddha-like composure and now, as always, confronting that blue-eyed mask Father Martin was left simply to imagine what the deaf-mute might be thinking.

—20—

Jessi laid out careful conditions she insisted they follow. In order to have a pure experience, she said, a truly mystical one, they must proceed with reverence and caution. It seemed to Trace that grief had bestowed upon her a stillness: in the way she moved, in her eyes which had lost their jittery drive. Her country girl roughness had been replaced by a kind of elegance.

Along the canyon wall, she moved from plant to plant, deliberate in her choices, picking the largest of the leaves. When she had gathered thirty-six leaves, she counted them a second time out loud, then followed the sound of the water until she reached the stream. She filled her canteen by holding it against the rock. She wanted to use the water that nurtured the soil. This land, this water had been blessed and it was most beneficial to respect it. She learned this from Joshua, she said. He had spoken to her time and again of the ancient procedures: the practices of the Shamanic world to ensure the highest level of interaction with the Divine.

At the fire she used one of Farley's pans to cook the leaves. She knelt close to the flames and stirred the mixture with a twig she had snapped from a nearby yucca tree. At times her eyes were closed, her lips moved, and Trace thought she might be praying, invoking a spirit from the lost world. At other times she stepped outside her trance-state to comment on her preparations. "I've done this so many times in my mind. I've followed his instructions down to the smallest detail, in preparation for the time we—Joshua and I—would, together, commune with the spirit of Jesus."

It seemed to Trace she was moving and speaking in slow motion, as if she were already intoxicated by the boiling leaves, as if he himself were high as well. Against the wall Zeke Farley had resumed his slump-shouldered position. He stared into the fire and seemed unaware of them which made Trace wonder if he was still under the influence, or if it was his confession that had sedated him. At one point he raised his eyes to Trace and said, out of nowhere, that he liked sitting here, his back to the wall, so that he could see them when they came for him.

"The hounds of hell?" Trace asked.

"*My* disciples now. If they'll have me."

The boiling leaves had formed a slurry, a yellow-green watery mush that Jessi said had to cool for ten minutes. "In the meantime, we must find a peace within ourselves."

"He never told me these things," Farley said, rousing himself from his torpor. "He never explained these rituals to me."

"Maybe you weren't listening. Maybe you weren't ready to hear them."

He glared at her, the muscles around his mouth tight again and it looked as if he might spit at her; but in her calm she appeared impervious to his rage.

"We must set aside our darkness. We must open ourselves to the light." She held his gaze until he submitted to her and lowered his eyes. "Ezekiel, do you understand?"

Again Trace was stunned by her newfound calm, the high-priestess tone to her voice, and the craziest of notions entered his head: that she was no ordinary being like himself or Zeke, that she was a visitor here from some higher plane, from that lost world he was trying to reach. He caught himself immediately, mocked himself for even thinking such a thing, the absurdity of it. This place, this place, it was spooking him, as was what they were about to do, what might hang in the balance.

He tried to talk himself down, find for a moment the ballast of the physical world in the solid rock of the walls, the dusty trees and shrubs that poked from the darkness, the clear bright starlight above and the silt-like dirt they were sitting on.

Far off he heard the sound of the hoot owl.

He looked over at Farley who seemed miraculously calmed again by Jessi's voice, the simplicity of her words. The tension had eased around his mouth. He'd drawn a blanket around his shoulders and settled back from the fire, his eyes contemplative and brooding as if he'd finally realized how much distance he still had to travel.

"We must clear away earthly distraction," Jessi Belle was saying. "We must stand at the threshold with the innocence of a new-born child."

Trace felt chills down his spine. He wondered again, against all logic and reason, if she was channeling, if she had become some other being. Her voice had changed, hadn't it? The way she spoke, the words she used. Jessi Belle Lynch, the teenage sexpot turned earth-mother.

At the fire's rim she sat with her back straight, hands clasped in her lap, eyes closed. "To receive the Lord, we must be filled with nothing but silent darkness."

Trace turned into himself then, to his own darkness. He could not say it was silent, muddled as it was with uncertainty and doubt. At her prompting, he tried to set aside the emptiness he felt, the troubling distance he'd been unable to cross to reach Vee, his growing concern that he might be incapable of love, either the giving of it or the receiving. And his father—the chaos of his feelings for the man. Unlike Jessi, whose grief had ennobled her, his grief had only left him angry and at loose ends. He didn't know the extent of the sea he was adrift in, only that he *was* adrift.

Who was he? Who was he trying to become?

He waited for the silent darkness to take him.

When the liquid had cooled they drank it, in turn, from Zeke's tin cup, though not before Jessi washed the cup in the waters of the stream. She drank first, then Zeke. Trace, for a moment stepping outside himself, suppressed a laugh at the weirdness of the situation: the three of them sitting around a campfire partaking of a vile-smelling, disgusting brew of crushed and dissolved leaves that they hoped would open the doors to eternity. He was reminded of Boy Scout camp, only then it had been marshmallows and the purpose of the communion was simply to have fun, to eat something sweet and gooey that tasted good.

When it was his turn he held the cup with both hands before putting it to his lips. The potion was thicker than he'd imagined—with a bitter, sour taste. He gagged at first and thought he'd never be able to drink an entire cupful. Sipping it, though, he managed to get it all down. He set the cup near the fire and looked across at Jessi who sat serenely watching him.

"We must destroy all barriers and allow ourselves to be thrown into inconceivable new worlds," she whispered before closing her eyes and drifting into silence.

Trace kept his own eyes open, both longing for and fearful of what awaited him. It wasn't that he'd never tried drugs before. In his teen years he'd experienced the usual high school fare—pot and hash, a peyote button or two—but he'd abandoned the drug scene quickly.

He'd wanted to find his highs naturally, without

chemical encouragement. But now the stakes were so much higher. Now, it seemed, it was his future at stake.

He felt his stomach rumble and for a while he suffered from cramps. From time to time he glanced across the fire at Jessi Belle who had assumed a Buddha-like pose. If she was experiencing gastro-intestinal distress, it wasn't evident either in her face or the composed stillness of her body.

With his eyes closed at last he listened to the fire's murmur, the dry hissing of ash. Otherwise the night was free of sound. No bird calls. No chopper's buzz. In his mind's eye he saw the sky, a vast plane of darkness pricked with points of light, different from his own darkness which seemed so much smaller, so much more contained. He tried to expand his darkness, pushing out its edges, stretching it left and right, top and bottom, until it touched the sky's darkness, until he could step from one to the other, taking long steps, hopping or jumping kind of steps, the way kids do in the playground, hop-scotching their way square to square, careful not to touch the lines or go beyond the boundaries.

Here there were no boundaries—only one long unbroken darkness and for a moment, one timeless moment, he felt he belonged to the sky, that he'd been consumed by it—but then there was a rift again between the darknesses, his own like a cloud he was standing on, drifting backward, a vantage point from which he was observing with a sad and helpless feeling the receding sky.

He didn't know how much time had passed.

There were stars again. Not pinpricks of light but gaudy flashing splashes of white that expanded and contracted. And then the splashes assumed color: pinks and reds, deep golds, deep scarlets. It seemed they were real enough to touch and he did, in fact, reach for them. He could feel his hands moving at his sides, collecting handfuls of air. He thought perhaps the source of the color splashes was the firelight refracted by his closed eyelids. When he opened his eyes the leaping flames seemed larger and wilder than he remembered, richer in texture, revealing hidden levels of pigment that produced colors he couldn't quite identify though they seemed somehow familiar.

Once he got up—or it seemed he did—to touch the canyon wall, to ground himself in the physical world, to assure himself he had not been abandoned. The surface of the rock felt warm with the sun's residual heat. There were crevices deep as valleys, crags as sharp and pointed as mountain peaks. His hand felt lost in the landscape of permutations as though it had separated itself from him, following a destiny that was not his own. He moved along the wall, many miles it seemed, until his hand finally returned to him like a prodigal child and he was seated again.

Beyond the flames he saw Jessi, far away and barely visible. She was crying, that much he could see, though her eyes were closed. She was crying and he said something— or thought he did—to comfort her; but it didn't look as if she heard. She said, or he thought she did, that her son had died.

When? he asked, though he couldn't hear the sound of his own voice.

A long time ago, she said. *It seems like only yesterday.*

Yesterday. It was a term he didn't understand.

I am the Mother of God, she said, without moving her lips. *He was my only son.*

Take me to him. Show me your son.

Her face, still as stone upon which tears had dried, stared back at him across the flames.

He closed his eyes again, waiting to see Jesus. He recalled the image he once prayed to: a statue of the Sacred Heart in the Jersey City church he belonged to, the over-sized marble figure before which he knelt in adoration— how many times?— side by side with his father; then he tried to find the other Jesus, the steadfast figure who walked beside him in the neighborhood, the Jesus to whom he confided secrets, the receptacle of his hopes and prayers.

But that Jesus was nowhere to be found. What presented itself instead was a face vaguely like his own, sad-eyed and lost.

A thinner and younger version of himself was standing in a hallway of some sort, looking for a way out. A fleeting shadow—*Jesus?*—was ahead of him, turning the corner. If he could only run faster he could catch him. If it was Jesus, he would know the way out. If it only was.

He watched himself running down long dark halls. One turned into another. He ran through basement rooms of cold yellow concrete that reminded him of the basement of the housing project in Jersey City. These subterranean rooms opened into other halls, other passageways and he thought finally he understood: it was a maze, a trap, a game. If he kept playing he would find out the answer, but a voice inside him was shouting *what answer? what answer?*

And someone else said—his father's voice, he thought— don't be a fool. *The* answer, the only answer there is.

So he kept running, growing more and more exhausted until he thought he might collapse. There was no end to this hall, to the complex of underground rooms and tunnels, and he began to feel he should stop this foolish running, quit it once and for all.

If you do, something terrible will happen, his father's voice warned from the darkness.

Then he saw scrawled on the walls in what looked like his father's handwriting, the words QUIT AND YOU DIE, QUIT AND YOU DIE. Over and over again these words were written as far as the walls went on.

A towering cross loomed above him, above the fading hallway, and he thought he had reached the pinnacle at Holy Land because all around him lay the broken icons of his long-lost faith. If he looked down he would see the Refuge of Good Hope and maybe Vee, taking photographs of the decimated hillside, making permanent the images that in his mind were only evanescent.

But when he opened his eyes what he saw, at the heart of the canyon's darkness, was Jessi Belle Lynch standing behind the fire with her arms outstretched.

She wasn't looking at him but he sensed she knew he was watching. Her eyes were unwavering, fixed somewhere on the rock wall behind him. Slowly she began to undress, pulling off her sweatshirt first and then unhooking her bikini top. When she had slipped free of her shorts and panties her body, perfectly formed and glowing in the fire's gold light, began to sway ever so slightly, following the beat of whatever music she was hearing.

Trace looked to Zeke Farley as if to verify what he was seeing but Farley, breathing uneasily with his eyes closed and his head resting against the wall, seemed to be asleep or passed out, or maybe simply preoccupied with the images being screened behind his eyelids. On the rock wall behind him fire shadows twitched like spirits unleashed.

Jessi was lost inside her dance, her arms raised and undulating in time with her hips. The fire light threw flickering lines on her. It seemed to Trace that she had two bodies moving in and out of one another, a skin of darkness and a skin of light. She seemed as fluid and connected to the elements of the universe as the tree of life: sky and earth, body and spirit, the sublime and the depraved.

There was something both terrifying and comforting in her beauty. He wanted to reach out to touch her—her soft girlish curves, her luminous skin—thinking, she'd be so much easier to love than Vee was. Immediately, he felt ashamed at the thought. Love was neither simple nor easy. It was the dark place you entered, hoping to find a light at the end.

Despite his arousal, the tender turnings of Jessi's body, what he felt for her this moment went beyond the senses. It was the same thing he'd experienced the first time he saw Vee naked: a state of mind, a *place* he had not been able to reach with her since. In a way he couldn't explain, it seemed he had been shown all of her secrets. Whatever followed would be, if not disappointing, then at least different and far more ordinary.

Like faith, he thought. It promised so much.

She was touching herself, exploring her body as if discovering it for the first time, when shouting voices disrupted the night's stillness.

At first, Trace thought the voices were inside him until he saw the bursts of fire sliding this way and that, and beneath the bursts and behind them shadows emerged, assuming three-dimensional form. In the wavering light of the torches and the pinprick circles of flashlight, faces bore the strain of triumph and relief.

At the canyon entrance, the hounds of hell spread out like a wave of immense proportions suddenly unleashed upon an unsuspecting shore.

—21—

Jessi stood by the fire with her hands cupping her breasts. She stared at Trace with an intensity that disturbed him, speaking to him with her eyes: a long and complicated and necessary message.

"*What?*" he said.

She continued to watch him, saying nothing with her lips.

Zeke Farley had been jerked back to consciousness. He sat bolt upright, staring wide-eyed at the surging crowd. There was no fear in his voice when he said, "I'm ready for them." He got to his feet unsteadily and teetered in place, blinking repeatedly to clear his vision. "God didn't show me his face. But he has shown me his children."

When he lurched past the fire, he steadied himself to greet the hundred or so disciples. He approached them with open arms and a cheer of sorts erupted when he pointed them to the sheaves of cut plants and the section of the wall where the plant grew. Cries, shouts filled the night and the crowd divided around him, became a stampeding mass rushing across hard ground. Farley turned to watch them run, his hand raised at half-mast in benediction as the mass of bodies fractured. Shadows broke off here and there among the plants, others knelt before the cut stalks, each man for himself.

Jessi had turned to watch them now as well. "At least they gave us time."

At first, Trace thought he understood what she meant.

"Enough time to be with *him*—"

"Jesus?"

"Joshua," she said. "One last time."

"Oh."

"And you, too. You were with me, too."

Now she was confusing him. Was that what her striptease was about, that touching herself? Some kind of sexual fantasia? He wouldn't have thought so. It seemed larger than that, more universal and impersonal.

He was about to ask her what she meant when a thunderous drone filled the sky, rising above the noise of the disciples' frenzy. Within moments the chopper rose from beyond the rock walls, a grey shadow beating deafeningly, its searchlight sweeping the canyon floor.

"Time to go," Jessi said. In the same unhurried and deliberate way she had been touching herself she reached down for her panties and began to dress.

"How did—?" But there was no need to raise the question; he could answer it himself. The torchlight parade had given them away. It would have been noticeable from miles off. From the air, from the cruising chopper, it would have been easy to track that procession of light.

"He *knows*," Jessi said. "Sometimes I think he has second sight."

"Who? Who knows?"

"Bobbie, my boyfriend. He knows when I'm having sex, or when I'm about to. No matter how far away he is." She said it without irony. It was simply a matter of fact. When she saw Trace's doubtful look, she said, "It's true. He just *knows*."

The chopper was lowering itself in an empty section of the canyon. Amid the swirl of wind, the stuttering clatter of its rotors, its searchlight swooped across the mad orgy of disciples wildly gorging themselves with leaves.

Trace squinted to find the faces inside the bubble. "He going to hurt you?"

"Bobbie *never* hurts me. He wants me too much." She picked up her back pack and slung the strap over her shoulder. "Come on. Walk me over."

She took her time, her step sure and confident—almost queenly, Trace thought—nothing like the forced-march pace she had set on their way here. Walking alongside he felt oddly attached to her, as though they were key players in a ceremony still unfinished.

Ahead of them, at the edge of the rotor-generated wind gusts, Farley stood some fifty feet from the chopper. Starry-eyed he gawked as if it were the descent of the Holy Ghost, or an alien spacecraft preparing for an abduction.

She held out her hand. "Bye, Zeke."

His head shot back as if she'd bitten him. "Yes. Yes. Goodbye." He touched her hand briefly, then let go.

She turned to Trace. "There's room for you."

He looked toward the chopper warily. The door hadn't yet opened. The figures inside were sitting in the dark.

"I'll tell Bobbie you saved my life. Which is true, in a way. He won't be mad at you."

It was too soon, though, for him to go back. The experience had ended too abruptly. Still active in his head were cobwebs of images and sensations that he needed to re-visit. And there was, of course, the still unfolding drama at the opposite end of the canyon: the fate of the raving vision-seekers. "I'm a journalist," he said. "I've got a story to cover."

She looked disappointed. "You sure?"

"I'll need a ride out of here in the morning, though. You

think your boyfriend would send a chopper back for me?"

" 'Course he will. If I ask him to." A familiar, suggestive smile eased across her lips. A trace of the Jessi he first knew. She leaned in to kiss him. The firm pressure of her lips promised more. "Remember me."

Then she was moving toward the chopper with her head lowered against the force of the wind. The door had opened and two occupants were visible: the pilot, a heavy-set man in his thirties; and an older and thinner, grey-haired man with wire-rimmed glasses. The older man's face revealed neither pain nor pleasure, simply a look of weary patience as he leaned from the bubble to help Jessi Belle in.

When the sound of the chopper had faded, Trace was still standing mid-canyon beside Farley. Their attention had turned to the ongoing feast of the disciples. Some were still in the process of ingesting leaves, others were hoarding the plants that hadn't yet been picked clean, stuffing them whole or in parts into their back packs.

"Look at them." Farley's eyes had lost their starry-eyed glow. What replaced it was a look of dawning horror. "They're sub-human. They'll eat themselves to death." He moved unsteadily in their direction, presumably to offer his counsel.

"One question," Trace called after him.

Farley stopped and turned, weaving slightly as if suddenly wracked with a wave of dizziness. "What's that?"

"Why did you wait a year to come back? I mean, you knew your father had found the plant. You knew it had to be somewhere close by."

Farley looked at him as if he didn't understand the question. "I don't know. Fear, I guess."

"Of what?"

But Farley had turned away, moving with a shifting gait

toward the disciples.

Later that night Trace huddled close to the fire for warmth. His muscles ached and his body was heavy with exhaustion, but his mind was alert, restless still in its search for answers.

Nearby, disciples had scattered across the open ground. Some sat in a stupor in the dirt. Others wandered along the rock wall in various stages of intoxication. So far they hadn't discovered the secret canyon and he was grateful for that, that something might be left behind for the next wave of seekers, whoever they might be.

Informally he had interviewed, or tried to, as many of the disciples as would talk. He wanted to know if they had seen God, and in what form or manifestation. He wanted to know if their visions had been anything like his own.

For nearly three hours he'd listened to their ramblings—images, hallucinations, what some of them thought were visions of the Divine—all of it too personal and chaotic to make much sense. From what he could see, there were no common threads or motifs, other than that in nearly every case the experience was deeply felt. None of them had seen Jesus as a shadowy figure at the end of a hall. If he *had* appeared to them, it had been in a private and equally uncommon form. As for Zeke Farley's second experience with the plant, all he would say was that at least his old man hadn't dominated his visions this time. Other images, other voices came to him as well. One of them might have even been Jesus on the line, he said, though it was a bad connection.

From time to time Trace would still hear someone retching—there had been a lot of that during the night. This crowd, it seemed, required an extreme degree of purification. In a matter of hours this pristine sanctuary at the top of the world had been transformed into a septic field. Maybe Jessi was right: true visions come only to the pure of heart. Few would qualify.

And of his own visions, what could he make of them? Were they messages from God? From his father? Or simply instructions to himself about the life he should lead? Certainly, there was not the affirmation he had hoped for. Yet he had learned something, some tiny thing perhaps, that would have little or no relevance to any other creature on the planet. He had learned that in his dream life he was a wanderer of hallways and secret passages, and Jesus was a shadow's flicker at the edge of—of what?

Instead of reaching the end of his search, he had found only its beginning. That, at least, gave him purpose.

So he could be sure of this: certainty was as elusive as heat shimmers on a desert road.

And maybe Jessi Belle was right: certainty wasn't some outside thing. It came from within. Maybe it was, after all, however unconscious, a choice one made. So he would have to accept his father's inscrutable faith and its consequences, just as his father—or whatever residue of his spirit remained in the universe—would have to accept his son's doubt.

He was crying, silently at first and then uncontrollably, his grief rising from the deepest part of himself, because he missed his father so much.

Through his tears he watched Zeke Farley on the far side of the canyon, stoop-shouldered and gaunt-faced, move between the ravaged plants, a shepherd ministering to his flock.

-- PART THREE --

—22—

Dillon awoke with the girl beside him and the barrel of a gun in his face. It was a bad dream, right? But when he saw the knife-like slants of light cutting in from the windows, when he saw the face that belonged to the arm that held the gun and several feet behind the face, standing in the middle of the room a fat-bellied, grinning Vinnie Fargo, he knew it was no dream.

The man who held the gun on him was Louie DeFazio —Fazz, as he was known in the East Bronx neighborhood Dillon had bolted from—a tall skin and bones creepo with deep-shadowed eyes and stinking breath. "Looks like Casanova here's been having a time of it."

"On the boss' money, too," Vinnie Fargo said behind him.

"I didn't take that dope."

"That a fact?" He took a step toward the bed, his eyes fixed on Vee who had pulled the sheet over her breasts and backed herself against the headboard. "General consensus is, you the man. Ain't that right, Fazz?"

Fazz forced the tip of the barrel into Dillon's skull. "Yup."

"Ain't that right, Elmo?" Vinnie said to the cement-faced guard at the door, a strapping hulk with a military bearing, the only one of the three formally dressed in a dark suit.

"Right by me," Elmo said.

"*I* think you took it, *Nicky* thinks you took it, the Bozzoni brothers outside think you took it. What's that, five, six to one? I'd say you lost the vote, wouldn't you?"

"I didn't take that dope, Vinnie. You know it."

"Almost don't matter whether you took it or not, when you got public opinion against you like you do. You down six to one, the way I see it. You're just plain fucked, guy, a hundred ways to Sunday." He had a broad, fleshy face and when he grinned, as he was doing now, his cheeks puffed up around his eyes and gave him a clown-like look. He wore a yellow sport shirt decorated with tiny green alligators that made Dillon wonder if they'd been looking for him in Florida—which was where he'd been headed until Phil talked him into coming out here.

"You want me to do them right here," Fazz was saying, "in their conjugal bed?" He had trouble pronouncing *conjugal* and it came out sounding like *con-juggle*.

"Take it easy, take it easy." Vinnie's eyes had drifted back to Vee holding the sheet. "We got to assess the damage here. It ain't just this goofball stole big-time from my brother. We got other considerations here. Like how much we had to suffer chasing him around the goddamn country while he's shacking up here getting his rocks off with this one. We got to account for that, too." His eyes were drooling now, spilling out it seemed over the rims of his fleshy cheeks. "She's a looker, all right. Which in my mind raises the ceiling on what he owes us." He stood at the foot of the bed, grinning. "I want to see just how much of a looker, so's I can fully calculate the exact amount of the debt." He flicked his hand toward her. "Come on, honey. The sheet. Let it go."

She gripped it tighter and cowered against the headboard.

"Why don't you leave her out of it?" As Dillon moved to pull himself into a sitting position, the barrel of the gun swung across his face and he was knocked back into the pillow. Vee screamed.

"Whatsa matter, sweetie? In over your head?" Vinnie rocked back on his heels, sneering at her. "What kinda slut are you, anyway? You don't do a background check on the guys you screw? You don't google them before you spread your legs?" He shook his head in mock disappointment. "Your mama didn't teach you how to be a good girl? That the problem, huh?" He motioned to Elmo. "Help her show us what she's got, El, will you? She got real modest all of a sudden. Turned into a prude right before our eyes."

She screamed again when the man came toward her. He walked stiffly and yanked the sheet from her hand, pulled it all the way back so that both she and Dillon were fully revealed. But nobody's eyes were on Dillon.

Vinnie gave a low whistle. "Ain't that somethin' now. Ain't that somethin'."

In the narrow space between the bed and the window, Vee had backed against the wall, her arms crossed over her chest.

"Your tits," Fargo said. "Let me see." And when she made no motion to lower her arms, he said, "Elmo."

The big man came toward her again. She said, "No, no," and lowered her arms slowly, turning her face to the wall while they gawked at her.

Vinnie whistled again. "Ain't that somethin'." He stared at her chest without speaking, without breathing it seemed. "Step away from that wall now, honey. Stand up straight."

She watched him, calculating something, before she took a step forward and straightened her shoulders, her hands opening and closing at her sides.

"That's better," the fat man said. "No sense hiding what

you got. No sense hoarding it for this low-life here. You give it up for him, you can give it up for anybody, right?" His eyes had hardened, his face showed no pleasure. "Now turn around, real slow. Lemme take a look at that back door."

Her body was shaking. She turned unsteadily. It seemed she might faint.

"Real slow, now. That a girl. One more time."

She had her back to him and he said, "Guy wouldn't know where to start on you, would he? Front, back, top, bottom, you got it all, don't you?" She was shaking so hard he said, "All right, get dressed." He shot a look at Dillon. "You too, hotshot, before I remove your appendages right here."

When Dillon stood beside the bed, Fazz said, " Lookitthat. He's got a dick like a fire plug, short and stumpy."

Vinnie gave him a dirty look. "Shut the hell up, DeFazio, you think about dicks too much."

The gunman's mouth dropped open. "What? *When?*"

"You're always talking about them."

"I do not. Tell him, Elmo."

"Just shut the hell up," Vinnie said.

Fazz wiggled his finger in the trigger housing. "You sure you don't want me to waste them right here?"

"Good thinking. Real good thinking. That way we can have monks crawling all over this place. That way we can have a goddamn monk massacre, too." He stared with disgust at his gunman. "You got to learn to think before you open that yap of yours, you know that?" He flicked his hand at the door. "Put'em in the car. We'll drive up a mountain somewhere."

"Wait." Dillon had finished buckling his khakis and was pulling on his shirt. "I got a way to make good on what I owe."

"*900 G's?* Right."

"I swear, Vinnie."

"Where's a two-bit punk like you get 900 G's?"

"What I've got's worth way more than that. Way more, I swear it."

"Hope you're not talkin' about that bullshit sage bush."

"How much you know about it?"

"Your buddy, Phil." He held a pack of Luckies, tapped one free and hung it from his lip. "Talked our bloody ears off about that damn bush. How you was gonna find it. Make us all rich. Yadda yadda yadda."

"I found it."

"The thing ain't been seen here in four hundred years and you found it. *You*, Mr. Lucky, who couldn't pick a winner in a one-horse race." He took the cigarette from his mouth and waved it as he paraded across the room. With his fat gut and skinny legs he moved like a pigeon, more a wobble than a walk. "For gods' sakes, Joey. Gimme a break, will ya?"

"I swear, Vinnie."

"I swear, Vinnie," Fargo said in a squeal-y, girlish voice.

"I can prove it."

"I can prove it." Same falsetto squeal.

"Right there." Dillon pointed to the dresser. "Right there's a sample. Plenty more up on the hill."

Vinnie half-turned to catch sight of the two bags. It seemed at first he would dismiss them, tell Dillon to go diddle himself but he snapped his fingers. "Elmo."

He's at least interested, Dillon thought. The guy's too damn greedy not to be.

The dark-suited hulk brought him a bag of dried leaves. Vinnie studied it in the man's hand before taking the bag, unzipping it. He stuck his nose between the plastic flaps. "Smells like piss."

"It ain't what it *smells* like," Dillon said. He stood by the bed, dressed except for his shoes, leaning toward Fargo.

"It's the way it gets you off."

"Is it now, smart guy? Anyone ever tell you what a smart guy you were?" He looked at Dillon with amusement. His eyes flashed to Vee who was dressed and huddled in the corner, arms still crossed to cover her breasts. "This what you gave to Miss Hotbox here? This what got her to open wide?"

"It's supposed to let you see God. It made me feel"—he had nothing to lose, he figured, if he exaggerated a little—"like *I* was God. Like I could do anything."

"That a fact?" The fat man seemed genuinely amused now. "Made you feel like God, huh? A lame-ass, shit-for-brains, numbnuts like you from the Bronx? This must be some dynamite shit then, right?" He held out a leaf, examined it. "How you take this stuff?"

"I don't really know. We'd have to ask Phil. But I—I chewed it."

Vinnie bit into the leaf, then spit it out. "*Tastes* like piss."

"You got to swallow it," Dillon said. "It won't take unless you get it down."

"That a fact, Mr. Big-time expert?"

"You got to at least give it a chance," Dillon pleaded. "The potential here is incredible. I mean, if this stuff does a tenth of what they say it does, people'll go apeshit over it. And the thing is—"

"I know, I know. It's not addictive, it don't show up in blood or urine tests. Your buddy went through the list. A miracle drug, according to him. But who the hell is he? Could be a psycho for all I know, coulda just been trying to save your ass, and his own. How the hell do I know?"

"You got to think of the potential here," Dillon repeated. "Athletes, businessmen, lawyers—who's not gonna want to feel like they can take on the world. To say nothing of the club crowd. There's a billion dollar industry here, Vinnie. All ours."

"All ours, huh?"

"It can be."

"All *ours*. One big happy family, right?"

"So cut me out if you want. It's yours. You and Nicky. For what I owe."

Vinnie jabbed the unlit Lucky at the bag. "How do I know this is the real thing? How do I know you didn't bag some damn cactus bush in anticipation of our meeting up like this? How do I know this stuff does what you say it does?"

"Up on the hill behind us." Dillon jerked his thumb at the back wall. "There's a stash, all neatly bagged like that one. And there's a garden full of the plant. One of the monks—the gardener here—he's cultivating the stuff. He wouldn't be going to all that trouble if this stuff was worthless. He's got his own private goldmine out here. He's been entertaining himself and maybe his friends for god knows how long. And that guy Farley—"

"Yeah, yeah, I seen him once on Cable." He was pacing again, along the edge of the bed. "Real space cadet—"

"He spent his life searching for this plant. All through Mexico and Central America, talking to all kinds of witch doctors and medicine men who knew what this stuff could do—" Out of breath he stopped to assess Vinnie's mood.

"Yeah, yeah. I told you I seen the guy—"

"And on top of everything else it's a—" Dillon hesitated before going on. ""It's an aphrodisiac. You can go for hours on this stuff."

Vinnie whistled in mock astonishment. "You don't say." His eyes ogled Vee again. "That why Sugar Tits got those circles under her eyes? You wouldn't let her get her beauty sleep? You did the boogie all night long?"

"I swear, Vinnie. You can forget about Viagra—"

"Whoa, you sayin' I can't get it up—?"

"No, no, I—"

"You tellin' me I got a limp dick? That what you're

tellin' me?"

"I didn't mean *you*. I meant anyone, a person—"

"But that ain't what you said now, is it? You said *you*, and a sensitive guy like me takes that personal, real personal. A sensitive guy like me feels he's got to punish someone who insults his manhood like that. Defend his honor, know what I mean? I mean, what else does a man have if he don't have his honor?"

"Come on, Vinnie, you know I didn't mean—"

"You screw up every which way, don't you, Romeo? What you say, what you don't say, what you do, what you don't do. You just can't get it right, can you, boy?"

"All I'm asking is give it a—"

"All I'm asking is, all I'm asking," Vinnie said in a girlish squeal. "Top of everything else you're a whiner, Joey, you know that?" His mood changed abruptly then, from disgust to contemplation. He slipped the Lucky back into his mouth, lit it, and held the bag out in front of him. "I don't know." The Lucky wiggled between his lips as he spoke. "I got to think about this."

That was when Dillon knew. The guy was putting on a show, acting like it was *his* decision to make. Something in the way he paraded around the room gave him away: King of the Pigeons, chest out, drawing on the Lucky like he was sucking on gold. Taking his time, keeping everybody waiting. Vinnie Fargo's little power trip. Because there was little chance he hadn't already discussed this with Nicky. The what-if scenario. Little chance Nicky wouldn't have told him to give it a go. If Dillon had his boss—ex-boss now—figured right, this was more than likely the kind of thing he would love to gamble on.

"All right," Vinnie said finally. He turned to Elmo who had taken up his station at the door. Tell Franco and Cheechee to bring that gardener over here. And anyone else holed up in this damned sand trap."

Father Martin had made it only as far as his chair, a distance no more than ten feet from his bed. He was feeling sluggish and particularly useless this morning. His dreams had been jumbled and chaotic. They followed him now into the murky light of dawn.

He was in the Holy Land, the real one not the one on the hill above the Refuge, during the time of the Crucifixion. Bearing the weight of the cross, Christ was being led through the streets, up the long hill to Golgotha. Father Martin saw himself skulking along behind, trying to stay hidden within the crowd of onlookers. He was dressed in a cloak and he kept the hood pulled tightly over his head. He didn't want to be recognized or identified in any way; he didn't want to be called upon to help his condemned Savior.

But why? Someone in the crowd asked him. *You're a priest. You devoted your life to serve Him.*

He tried to explain that he didn't want to be jeered, he didn't want to be spat upon and cursed. But he knew that was a lie; even in his dream he knew. It was because he was afraid: that he would be called upon and he would fail and all the world, and his God, would be witness.

The dream ended without resolution, and that was the way he felt now: unresolved. Idle in his chair. Struggling to begin his morning service. For inspiration he looked to his window with its view of the garden. The winged angel in its perpetual pose of flight shimmered in the first rays of the sun.

Long since had he forsaken formal prayer. His morning service had evolved into a kind of meditation, a meandering preview of the day ahead: how might he, in his limited and humble capacity, serve the Lord?

This day one possibility suggested itself. The woman, Vee. She might yet need him after—after last night. She might see things more clearly in the morning light. She might come to him, in repentance.

Immediately, he upbraided himself. Hadn't he learned his lesson yesterday? How many disappointments would it take before he accepted the fact that she had no use for him? Because even after he had seen what he had seen, even after his tormented excursion into Holy Land, he had still held out hope she might come to him. He had kept the lights burning in the common room until nearly two in the morning. He had sat there reading, or trying to at least, attentive to every sound, thinking one of them might be her step, her knock upon the door.

And here he was again, the morning after, *still* playing the fool. Thinking she would be repentant, that she would come to confess her night's sin. Thinking he could help her make her peace with God.

Today, at least, he would break free of his inertia. Today, at least, he would be a man of action. He would tell Joseph Dillon he had to leave. Violation of the rules. Conduct unbecoming of a Refuge guest. He didn't care if the man laughed in his face. He would have the police come and remove him by force, if necessary.

And without him here, without his seductive presence, maybe. . . .

Maybe what? the familiar voice taunted him.

Maybe the girl would come to her senses, come to *him.*

Your hope is pitiful. You're pitiful.

He was groping for a response, for something to keep his hope alive, when the door burst open and a man with the largest handgun Father Martin had ever seen shoved it in his direction and told him to get the fuck up.

—23—

Dillon sat on the edge of the bed, head in his hands, cursing himself. Bad enough with the chick, showing her the stash, but then getting caught with his pants down. Pumped as he'd been, he hadn't even bothered to set up his make-shift defense. At least the dresser being knocked over would have a given him a moment's warning; but he'd been too busy focused on Vee's body. The Derringer under his pillow? Useless to him now.

In the blink of an eye, it seemed, his luck had turned again. His plan of sending a couple of bags of leaves to Phil this morning, stuffing the rest into his Toyota as his bargaining chip and taking off, keeping on the run until Phil could process and test the damn stuff—all that had fallen down around him. He blamed it on the leaves. Whatever drug they contained had confused his senses, tricking him into thinking he was invincible, stuffing his head with crazy riffs about saints and God and getting laid. *This* was how he'd ended up.

Charm is like a snake. Charm is like a snake. His father's words rattled around inside his head like a tin can trailing in the wake of a speeding car.

God, did his head hurt. Fazz hadn't been kidding when he swung at him.

No break for old times' sake. Not from Fazz the finagler, the guy who never stopped cadging: butts, a beer, twenty bucks for a cab. He never seemed to have money, or *enough* money. Dillon remembered the time not three months back when the guy hit him up for a C-spot. Had a tip for the fifth at Aqueduct, couldn't pass it up, *a little short at the moment*—his usual line. So Dillon had come across. Turned out the horse was a long shot, 60-1, paid off 6 G's. Not only didn't Fazz offer to split it with him, Dillon never even saw his C-spot again. That was Fazz. Fazz the grateful. The prick couldn't have hit him any harder, could he?

Dillon touched the wound. Not a lot of blood but enough to make a sticky mess. Shit, was it sore. Sore as hell and getting sorer, swelling to cover the whole right side of his head. He thought maybe it was the worst he ever felt. And that made him laugh. Because bad as his head ached, that was the least of his problems. Vinnie was out to get him, with or without the plant. And with Fazz standing over him pointing a gun to his head, Elmo at the door, and the Bozzoni brothers as backup, his chances for escape were worse than zero. The most he'd managed was to buy himself some time.

"What are you laughing at?" Fazz was asking him.

Dillon grinned. "You, you cheap prick."

Fazz the finagler would have struck him again but the door burst open and the priest, white-faced and shaking, was shoved into the room. Right behind him, also unsteady from the push he'd been given, was the phony retard gardener.

We got all the cages represented now, Dillon was thinking, all we need are the dipshit zoo keepers. And right on cue the Bozzoni brothers appeared: Cheechee first, wearing a red St. Louis Cards baseball cap, his trademark, and Franco a step behind. He'd run into them once or twice

in the Bronx. Plenty of muscle, dumb as meat loaf. Standing side by side they were even funnier looking than Vinnie. A real freak show. Nearly identical vacant-eyed mugs, narrow
heads too small for their barrel-chested bodies.

"This is all we got," Cheechee announced.

Vinnie got up from the bed where he'd been ogling Vee. He puffed on a Lucky, his third in a row, and coughed while he appraised with a mixture of reverence and distrust the newest hostages. "Glad to have yas with us, Fathers." He coughed again and cleared his throat before swiveling his glance to Dillon. "Okay, Mr. Big-shot deal-maker. Let's see what you got up there."

Dillon was told to lead the way.

On the hill he ignored the heat, and the pain in his head, and kept a strong pace until Vinnie yelled to slow it the hell down. He was thinking if he could only. . . .Only *what*? Tire them out enough so that he could make a run for it? Forget it. Not with five guns at his back. They weren't going to get *that* tired. Yeah, but maybe. . . .Maybe *what*? Maybe he had to think longer term. If he could wear them down, even a little, he might increase his chances for making a break when the time came. He might be able to take advantage of their slower reflexes, diminished energy. But reality came back to him like another blow to the head. There's no more long term for you, buddy. You're strictly a short-timer now.

But still—

He glanced behind him to check out the situation. Fazz was right on his tail, maybe three paces back, walking with his gun at his side. The man's gun hand jerked upward. "Eyes straight ahead, dickface. Nobody asked you to turn around."

"Yeah, yeah." Dillon turned back to the path but he'd had enough time to see what he was up against. The priest and the retard walked behind Fazz and behind them Elmo in his suit and tie, striding like he was in a military parade.

Behind Elmo was the girl. She hadn't looked at Dillon once since the morning began; she'd stayed as far away from him as she could get. And now she was walking in front of Vinnie who, between occasional coughing outbursts, had his eyes pinned to her ass. The Bozzoni brothers brought up the rear.

From the looks of it, Vinnie and the Bozzoni's were having the toughest time. Vinnie's face was red and he kept dabbing at it with a handkerchief. The Bozzoni's were moving at an even slower pace, swinging their massive arms to gain momentum. At least some of them were hurting, he thought. He was counting on that, and the sun climbing higher in the sky. He was counting on a brutally hot day.

That was when he made his vow a second time. He meant it this time, he told himself. Swear to God. If he got out of this alive, he *would* change his ways, be a better person. He would start over.

Gradually, in hopes it wouldn't be noticed, he began to pick up the pace again. Wear them down, wear them out. He was going to need all the help he could get.

At the gate Vinnie yelled to hold it up. Dillon turned to look behind as Fazz raised the gun to his face. Quickly he stepped back and lifted his palms. "Easy, man, easy. Where you think I'm gonna go?"

Fazz waggled the gun at him. "You got that right, smart boy."

Down the path Vinnie was telling Cheechee to stay by the gate and keep an eye out. "You got a view of the whole kit and caboodle down there." He turned to Brother Brendan. "This the only way *in* here?"

Brother Brendan nodded his head.

"He doesn't speak," Father Martin interjected. "He's mute."

"Mute, huh?" Vinnie Fargo, thinking it over, studied the silent man.

"The answer to your question, though, is yes. This is

the only entrance to the park."

"You wouldn't lie to me now, Father, would you?"

"It's the truth," Father Martin said. "It's all mountains on the other side."

"You expectin' anyone else today? Anybody stopping by?"

"Our next guests aren't due for three days."

Vinnie regarded the priest thoughtfully. "You know, Father. Was a time when you could take a man of the cloth at his word. Not no more." He shook his head in disappointment. "Not no more."

The priest stiffened and lifted his head in defiance. "I can only tell you what I know to be the truth. Whether you choose to believe me is another matter."

"No offense, Father. Nothing personal. The times we live in. You know?" He swatted his face with the hanky. "I'm just sayin' we'd be better off without any new arrivals. They'd only complicate matters, if you see what I mean."

"I think I see," the priest said evenly.

"Good. That's good." He looked around him, taking a close look at the broken down exhibits. "This place looks like shit. What happened?"

"It's rather a long story. I can't imagine you'd be interested in hearing the details."

Vinnie stared at the Annunciation exhibit where a beheaded Virgin Mary knelt beneath a larger statue of the Angel Gabriel. He wiped the sweat from his brow and seemed genuinely distressed. "It's a shame."

"A shame?" the priest asked.

"About this place. The condition it's in." He looked at the priest as if he should understand. "I'm a Cat-lic too, Father."

"Really?"

"St. Antony's parish. Gun Hill Road. If you know where that is."

"I'm afraid I don't."

"Went to school there. Gonna be a priest till sixth grade. About the time girls in class started, you know, developing. Touch and go there for a while, tits or Jesus. Tits won out." He was amused by the memory but when he looked at the priest's solemn face his smile vanished and he cleared his throat. "All right. Let's get moving."

The sun had climbed higher in the sky and between the rising heat and his aching head Dillon had all he could do to keep focused on his objective: keep up the pace, keep things moving. Vinnie yelled again to slow it down—a good sign to Dillon, a sign that his plan, such as it was, was working. He slowed the pace for a few steps then began walking briskly again. Fazz claw-clamped his shoulder and yanked him back. "You heard the boss. Slow it the hell down."

He shrugged away from Fazz' grip. "Whatsa matter? You guys don't work out anymore? You guys turned pussy on me?"

"I'll show you a hard-on twice the size of yours any day of the week, faggot."

"There you go again with those dick jokes. Vinnie was right." He leaned forward, expecting retaliation in the form of a gun barrel across the back of his head. What he heard was Fazz' strained breathing and plodding footsteps. He glanced around to see the man had fallen a few steps behind. He was showing his age, which must have been way past fifty. His face, in contrast to Vinnie's, had grown paler so that his skin looked unhealthier than usual, if that were possible. His eyes had begun to glaze over.

"Just slow it down, will you?" It was as much a plea as an order.

"All right, all right. I walk any slower we'll be going backwards." He slowed down briefly then picked up the pace again.

"Where the hell we going?" Vinnie called out.

Dillon stopped again to look back. Vinnie had fallen even farther behind so that there might have been a hundred feet or more from the head of the line to Franco Bozzoni at the rear. "Top of the hill." Dillon pointed through the trees. "We're almost halfway." He took a moment's pleasure in the grimace on the fat man's face.

He began climbing again, past the path that led to where his money was hidden. He'd thought about offering it to Vinnie as a down payment. 250 grand. Nothing to laugh at. But even that was no guarantee the man wouldn't do him in anyway. What was stopping him? There was no one for miles around. It would be days at the earliest before the bodies would be discovered. Offering him the money would be like offering a bribe to the grim reaper, wouldn't it? And there was another reason he hesitated. That was *his* money. He'd earned it. He'd be damned if he'd give it to a prick like Vinnie. Besides, and maybe it was only the residue of the drug talking, he was going to need it. He was going to find a way out of here. Some way.

When he reached the first of the Christ-bearing-the-Cross statues, he thought about making a run for it. Behind him, the line was strung out a good hundred and fifty feet. If he took off up the hill, he could weave in and around the statues till he reached the catacomb.

Not so fast. Think this through.

Stressed as Fazz and Vinnie and Franco looked, there was still Elmo to contend with. The man was strong as iron. Shoulders straight, head up, he showed no signs of fatigue. Even *if* he made it to the catacomb, he'd have to come out the other side. It would be nothing for Elmo to be at the giant cross by then with a perfect shot at anything moving down the hill.

Wait it out, Joey D. Wait it out. But the reality of the situation nagged at him. *The clock is ticking, boy. Ticking real fast.*

He looked at the sagging figure of the stone Christ on the path ahead. *I'm as doomed as you are, man. I'm right there with you.*

The path grew steeper and even he was straining now. Pools of sweat had formed in his armpits and across his back. His head had grown much heavier, drums beating inside with the fury of a tribal dance.

"Where the hell you taking us?" Vinnie called from far behind.

"Where you want to go, Vinnie. The land of buried treasure. The source of hopes and dreams."

"You better not be jerking me off."

"Who me?"

"Yeah you, stud cakes."

"Why would I do that? Sweet guy like you."

"You're funny as a turd, you know that?" Fazz said, closer to him now. The old fart had gotten a second wind. Really kicking ass, Dillon thought. Breathing down my neck again. Maybe I *should* have bolted back there.

As he passed the last of the statues he let his hand slide across the brittle stone. Each of the four stone figures had been vandalized, this last the worst. One side of Christ's face had been battered to a concave hollow. The cross had been lopped off at the top so that it resembled a T.

He stopped to catch his breath. From here, the path was straight and clear to the top. A buzzard cruised the skies above the cross. He tried to see it not as an evil omen but as something positive: a soaring escape from the sweaty toil of this earth. He tried to ease his pain by letting his mind drift with the bird on what he imagined to be cool mountain breezes.

No relief came.

His head pounded, intensified by the heat of the sun which had risen higher. Blinking to clear the sweat from his eyes, he took a look back at the line. Vinnie and Bozzoni were closing the gap, Vee walking slowly but steadily ahead of them. For a moment her eyes crossed his, but she looked away.

What did she mean to him now?

A mistake, he told himself. Bad judgment, regret. And the fading memory of how good her skin felt in his hands. He repeated his vow to change his life, if—

"Who's the pussy now?" Fazz wanted to know.

Dillon grinned. "Hey, I only stopped to give you suckers a break. I'm ready to rock n' roll."

"You look like shit," Fazz said.

"That's what happens when I look at you."

Fazz lunged at him but Dillon stepped back quickly. "Last one to the top is a dick-sucking, foul-breathed old fart," he said and forced himself to push hard the rest of the way. Even the renewed Fazz couldn't keep up. His fuming rage didn't help him, either.

In front of the catacomb entrance Dillon stood waiting for them. Elmo was the first to make it. The man stood beside him, head thick as a cinder block, his bearing rigid as the rock formations around him. In his dark suit he appeared unruffled, none the worse for the climb. He might have been standing in his usual position outside a limo, waiting to open the doors.

Vinnie made his way through the boulders tentatively, bracing himself with one hand against the rock surfaces. With every step he teetered and, top-heavy as he was, it seemed he might topple backwards at any moment. He stopped to gaze up at the one-armed Christ hanging from the cross, pondering for some moments as if he didn't know what to make of it.

When he began climbing again he made a high, whistling sound with each breath. The whistle evolved into a cough which slowed him down even more. Finally Fazz and Elmo reached down to pull him the last few steps and Bozzoni pushed from behind until he was standing on flat ground, wheezing and waving his hanky like a fan.

"Need a smoke." He fumbled in his pants pocket for his Luckies. He was still weaving slightly and his hand trembled when he struck a match. He took a deep breath of smoke like it was fresh air and began coughing. He punched his chest until the coughing stopped. "All right, so where the hell are we?"

"In here." Dillon indicated the opening in the rock wall.

Vinnie scowled darkly. "A cave?"

"A catacomb. The stuff's in there."

"You're kidding me, right? You're yanking my chain."

"Swear to God."

Vinnie had a what-the-hell? look on his face. He turned to the priest. "Father, what's he talking about?"

"This is the Holy Land, remember." Father Martin smirked at the preposterous nature of the claim.

"You got bodies in there?"

"These catacombs are more figurative than literal."

Vinnie drew on his cigarette, thinking it over. "They ain't real, you mean?"

"They're simulations," Father Martin said.

"Simulations, yeah. I know all about simulations." He looked at Bozzoni standing shoulder to shoulder with him, and then at DeFazio and Elmo. They were all laughing with him. He took another drag on the Lucky and stepped in front of Dillon. "You don't come outta there with something I'm interested in, you're a dead man."

Dillon nodded. "You won't be disappointed."

"Fazz, Elmo." Vinnie waved toward the opening. "Accompany lover-boy here." Both men moved at the same time, nearly colliding. "One at a time, one at a time," Vinnie said like he was reprimanding children. "Elmo, you first then our guest of honor, then Fazz. He gives you any trouble, blow him to kingdom come."

—24—

Dillon waited for Elmo to lower himself through the opening. Stiff as the man was it seemed he might break in the bending, but he made it through without so much as a grunt. When Dillon came into the passage Elmo was standing erect, hands clasped in front of him. He seemed not the least bit curious about his surroundings, his eyes on Dillon.

Once Fazz was inside, Dillon led them past the alcove statues and flickering candles.

"I feel like I'm in grammar school," Fazz said. "What's that church on Bronxdale Ave's got shit like this? Grottoes and stuff?"

"I don't know," Elmo muttered in his monotone.

"Hey, Joey. What's that church?"

"St. Lucy's."

"Yeah, that's it. St. Lucy's."

"It's on Williamsbridge, not Bronxdale. Just for the record."

"Williamsbridge? You sure?"

The passage widened ahead and Dillon stood in the room-like space, staring at the empty table. The shelves above it had been cleaned out, too.

Fazz crowded into the space beside Elmo. "So where is this shit?"

"It was here. I swear it was here." Dillon went to the table, ran his hand over the surface, then touched the first of the shelves above it, groping for something, a stray leaf, a shred of plastic bag, to verify what he had seen. "Yesterday. Bags of the stuff. Right here."

"Ain't nothin' there now," Elmo said

"Like that one in my room. Bags and bags. I *swear* it."

Fazz smacked his lips. "You're history, Joey boy. You're gone."

Outside Dillon went after Brother Brendan, throttling his neck, forcing him back against a boulder. "Where is it? Where is it, you bastard. You faking bastard."

The man's face colored but his brilliant blue eyes stared back with a dreamy serenity.

"Hey, what's goin' on?" Vinnie was shouting from his seat of stone.

"Nothin' in there," Fazz said. "Not a freakin' thing."

Dillon was swinging at the gardener who held his hands up to protect his face. Father Martin had rushed at Dillon, pulling at his arms to restrain him. "Leave him alone, leave him alone." Then Elmo came behind Dillon and, grabbing him under the arms, yanked him backward.

"*He* took it," Dillon said, struggling to free himself from Elmo's iron grip. "It was in there yesterday, I swear it. Bags and bags of the stuff. That bastard took it."

"Shame on you, Joey," Vinnie said. "Beating up on the weak and infirm. The man's afflicted, can't you see?"

"Afflicted, my ass. I heard him whistling. *Strangers in the Night*. I swear to God. The guy was whistling Sinatra."

"My, my." Vinnie stepped close to Brother Brendan and studied his face. "Looks afflicted to me." He turned to the priest. "What do you say, Father? This man afflicted, or not."

"In all the years he's been here, I've never heard Brother utter a sound. Mr. Dillon must be mistaken."

"I can prove it, Vinnie, I swear. The guy's got a garden other side of the hill. He grows the stuff there. Saw it with my own eyes."

"A garden, huh?"

"Rows and rows of the plant. I seen him yesterday watering it. He picks the ripe leaves and brings them in the cave here to dry."

"Except nothing's in there, correct?"

"But there was. I swear."

"But there was, I swear," Vinnie whined. The mockery receded from his eyes. He gave Dillon a hard look. "How long I got to put up wid you, Joey?"

"Let me show you the garden, that's all. You'll see."

"And how far is this alleged garden?"

"Other side of the hill. Not far."

"Not far, huh?"

"No, I swear."

Vinnie gazed at the catacomb entrance. "You know I ain't crawling through that hole."

"There's a path." Dillon pointed beyond the rim of boulders. "Goes around the hill."

Vinnie rocked on his skinny legs, still not convinced. His eyes drifted to the crest of the hill where at least half a dozen buzzards hovered in the sky. "You know, the more hoops you make me jump through—and I'm countin' each and every one of 'em—the more you're gonna hurt before you leave this world. You know that, right?"

"I swear, Vinnie, I won't let you down. Gimme a chance."

"Last dance, last chance," Vinnie said. "Make it fast."

They walked single-file around the base of the summit. Overhead the buzzards sketched lazy circles against the sky. "They know supper's on the stove," Vinnie mused.

Dillon tried to ignore the remark. Concentrate, he told

himself. Figure out the plan. Which was, plain and simple, this: when he showed them the garden, in that initial excitement and curiosity, he would bolt for the trees. Try to make it into the ravines beyond, lose them in the mountains. The only one he thought had a chance of catching him was Elmo and he figured he could eventually out-run the guy. He was a chauffeur/bodyguard, right? He stood around a lot, sat on his ass behind the wheel of a limo. How much of a runner could he be?

Not a great plan, but the best he could come up with. Its main flaw? Those few seconds it would take for him to get to tree cover. Fazz or Elmo or Bozzoni—any one of them might get off a shot quick enough to fell him. In fact, there was a good chance of it. But what choice did he have? Time was counting down. And once Vinnie had the plant, he had no need for the finder of the plant.

They were approaching the cluster of trees this side of the garden. Once inside its spotty shade Dillon strained, through the prism of leaf and branch, for a look ahead. He entertained the fleeting thought that like the bags of dried leaves the garden, too, might be gone; but when he stepped out from the trees he saw it there, the relief he felt quickly turning to shock and rage. The plants had been replaced with shorter bush-like clumps of vegetation, and patches of yellow flowers. Not one of the plants he'd seen yesterday was in sight.

He turned then—he would have choked the life out of the gardener if he could have reached him—but Elmo stood in the way, chest puffed out, arms extended like a road barrier.No way he could run now. With the attention on him, he wouldn't make it halfway across the garden.

He thought, for a moment, he might cry. "He dug it up," he said to no one in particular. "The son-of-bitch put in different plants."

Vinnie stepped into the garden, his black shoes crushing the smaller plants. He bent down to pick a yellow flower.

He held it by the stem and twirled it. "That's always been the trouble with you, Joey boy. You promise more than you deliver."

"I swear, Vinnie—"

"I don't wanna hear it." He tucked the flower into a buttonhole and lowered his eyes to admire it. "Goes with my shirt."

"You wanna take care of him right here?" Fazz wanted to know.

Vinnie stared across the garden at the long view beyond: rising hills and dry gulches, sand and rock and sky. "Nah. Them mountains there. They depress the hell outta me."

They ended up at the Tomb of Mary, the first shady place they came to back inside the park. It was a tree-encircled clearing in the center of which lay a sarcophagus-style coffin with its lid partly raised. A hanky pressed to his head, Vinnie peered inside. No replica of a body but on the bottom, along with the words *Mater Dolorosa*, there was a painting of the Virgin in faded colors of blue and gold.

When he had seen enough he withdrew his head and stood unsteadily beside the tomb. "My mother prayed to the Virgin every night," he said to the others who were standing in the shade of the trees, awaiting his instructions. "For *me*. That I wouldn't take the wrong path like my brother. That I'd be a son she could be proud of. A *good* boy."

Fazz laughed. He thought Vinnie was mocking the foolishness of his mother's intentions, but his boss shot him a look that shut down what was left of his mirth.

"She was a good woman," he said. "Immaculata. The purest of the pure. Worked fourteen hours a day in a sweat-shop downtown so's I'd have new clothes for school. So she could afford to send me to St. Antony's. When I made my first communion she broke down and cried. Said she had a dream about me. In this dream an angel told her I'd been chosen to be a priest of God."

He ruminated on this. "I broke her heart."

His voice was choked and his henchmen shifted uneasily and stole glances at each other, wondering what was up. The boss didn't look good. Something distressed and unsettled in the way his eyes were lifted to the top of the hill, the damn buzzards floating high above the cross.

"You want we should do them right here," Fazz said to get him back on track. "That what you're sayin'?"

Vinnie blessed himself, put his fingers to his lips and kissed them. "Madre Mia. May she rest in peace."

His boys dropped their heads and there followed an unofficial moment of silence. Wind made a sudden sifting sound in the leaves. The quiet that followed was unsettling.

Fazz cleared his throat. "Say the word, boss."

Vinnie pointed to a ditch beyond the circle of trees. A metal plaque identified it as the Valley of Jehoshaphat. "We'll do our business there." He pulled out his cell phone, stabbed at it with his over-sized thumb, and held it to his ear. "Hello, hello, Cheechee?" He held it away from him and squinted at the display. "What the hell kind of no man's land don't have phone service?"

He looked over at Bozzoni who was using his arm to wipe the sweat from his face. "Franco, go down and take over for your brother. Tell him go get the shovels and drive the car up to that gate so we's don't have to hump it all the way back."

"Sure, boss." He turned toward the path and started down the hill at a slow trot.

"Who first?" Fazz asked.

Vinnie leaned against the tomb, an arm propped against the raised lid. "Hold your horses, Louie. We got to do this right. We got to make sure the punishment fits what they all done to us. And we gotta show some respect. On accounta this place and our Cat-lic heritage." His eyes roamed across the ravaged hillside. "Damn shame what happened here. No reason for it. No reason at all." He seemed to drift off into reverie again.

"You feelin' all right, boss?"

"Feelin' a little nostalgia, that's all. My mama, you know? Woulda been eighty-two tomorra."

"So what you're sayin' is—"

"What I'm sayin' is, what with havin' Father here, everyone gets last rites. If they want it, a course."

"I ain't never seen you like this, boss."

"Lotta things you never seen, Louie. Lotta things I never seen about you, neither. That's the way it is. Buncha strangers knockin' into one another like pigs in a chute. Shouldn't be that way." He looked at Father Martin who sat beside Vee on a stone bench. "Ain't that right, Father?"

The priest's head jerked as if he'd been struck. He drew his shoulders up and straightened his back. "Yes. Yes."

"It's this place," Vinnie said in his own defense.

"Perhaps you're feeling remorse," the priest suggested. "For what you're about to do. For the sins of your past."

"Woulda been fine, we never come in this here park." He glared across the clearing at Dillon. "Stirring up all this stuff inside me. It ain't natural here, I swear it."

"Perhaps it's your conscience speaking, telling you not to do what you're planning," Father Martin said.

"Ain't no choice." Vinnie shook his head in agreement with himself. "Conscience or not."

"There's always a choice." Father Martin fumbled for the right words. He fell back upon the only argument in his grasp. "Man has free will. He can choose—"

"Got to finish what you start, Father. My line a work, that's the rule."

"Why? *Why?*" was all the priest could think to say."You've got innocent people here. We've done nothing—"

"Shame about that, Father. Shame you folks had to be

associated with this low-life here. But the way I see it, that's no fault a mine. You got to take responsibility for that. Just like I got to take responsibility for the job I come here to do."

"Your mother." Father Martin heard the desperation in his voice, his last-ditch effort."What would your dear mother think of what you're about to do?"

"You got a point there, Father. You got a point." He tipped his head back and stared at the vast blue sky, blinking against the brightness. When he lowered his eyes, they were moist with rumination. "Hope she ain't lookin'. I sure do. But where she is, nothin' can hurt her. Ain't true for me, though. Ain't true for me, at all. So it ain't real fair for her to judge now, is it?"

As if shaking off a chill he stepped away from the tomb and lit a cigarette. "It's this place, I swear. It's breakin' my heart." For a moment, looking at the wreckage spread out on the hill below, his face held a genuine sadness, before turning back to the priest, to the matter at hand. "Lemme ask you, Father. You got everything you need?"

The priest hung his head in defeat, speaking softly but firmly. "I'll need some oil, and some privacy."

Vinnie nodded as if he understood. "Beyond the trees there, Father. By the ditch." He dragged deeply on the Lucky and turned away from the tomb to let the smoke funnel out across the clearing. "Fazz, give them the space they need. Don't be breathin' down their necks."

Happy that at last things were moving forward, Fazz motioned the priest toward the ditch. "Who first, boss? You got a preference?"

The boss jerked his thumb toward Brother Brendan. "The afflicted one."

—25—

It was nearly noon when Trace drove the Chevy through the Refuge gate. It felt strange to be back, as if his time in the mountains had become more real than this, the familiar world. There, at least, his purpose had seemed closer at hand. Here it seemed remote, at best. He attributed that feeling to the fact that he hadn't fully re-entered the realm of earthly logic, that he was still under the influence of the plant, and the all-consuming intensity of his mountain trek.

He had an article to write, he reminded himself.

Yes, that was a definite, though he still hadn't decided what he would say. What kind of visionaries had he consorted with? Nut cases or true shamans? Maybe, as in the case of Jessi Belle, she was both way out there *and* spiritually enlightened—which only served to complicate the situation. As for Joshua Farley himself, he could say only that from all appearances the man seemed to have truly believed in the divine source of his visions, though that seemed far less true for his son.

Throughout the night, awake/ asleep/ imagining/

dreaming by the fire, he'd had a lot of time to think things through. And when the chopper came for him as promised, shortly past day break, his mind and body still seethed with a restless energy. From the air the Farley people, roaming like scavengers through the devastated canyon, seemed as insignificant as the rock and sand. Lonesome figures shrinking with time and distance. And he himself, being helicoptered over the mountains' peaks and valleys, suspended in the vastness of the sky, had felt equally as lonesome and insignificant. He thought, maybe our actions always come down to *this*: how lonely we are. So we cling to whatever idea is most dear to us, until that idea crowds out all others, becomes more valuable to us than life itself, or at least *inseparable* from life itself. Which seemed to explain people like Joshua Farley and his father and— he was beginning to see— even himself.

That, he thought, was what he might write about. If he could find the words.

And on that chopper ride he'd thought, too, of Vee, how much he missed her, how he had allowed his work, his purpose to stand between them. He would have to find a way to tear down that barrier and share more of his inner life with her. He would have to learn to make her happiness as much a priority as his own.

As he parked next to the priest's van, he looked toward the garden in hopes of seeing her, perhaps taking photographs, capturing the essence of this forlorn, desolate place. Nothing moved in the stillness.

A black Lincoln was parked under the trees where the Eldorado had been. New guests, he assumed, though as he walked toward the cottages he saw no signs of activity.

Inside his cottage the bed was made, things neatly put away. The room had a strangely unlived-in look.

No sign of Vee's bag so he assumed she was out *somewhere* taking pictures. On the porch he cupped his hand above his eyes to search the grounds once more. Nothing moved in the bright, unfailing light.

A car engine turned over. The Lincoln lurched across the sandy parking area and came straight toward the cottages, jouncing and creaking on the uneven path. It stopped short of him, engine idling. A face watched him through the dark windshield. Four, five seconds. Enough time to make him uncomfortable. He shifted his feet but kept his eyes on the tinted glass.

The car lurched forward then, stopped directly in front of him, and a big man in a red cap got out. "Who are you?"

"I'm staying here. Who are *you*?"

"You with that broad?"

"Vee? Yes. Where is she?"

"Up the hill." The man came around and opened the passenger door. "I'll take you to her."

There was something in the man's voice and the way he stood at the door— the insistent hulk of his body and the flatness in his eyes—that let Trace know he wasn't being given a choice.

Father Martin knelt on the ground above the ditch and blessed himself. This was, he thought, the most difficult thing God had ever called upon him to do: prepare these unfortunate souls, and himself, for eternal life. This was what his dreams had been warning him of. He murmured the words, "O God, give me the strength. . . ," but did not finish. Instead, he tried a second prayer, "Lord, I am not worthy," but gave up on that one, too.

He glanced at the line of trees behind him. Watching him was the man called Fazz, still as one of the tree trunks, holding his gun at his side. The priest turned so that neither the man nor the trees were visible. Brother Brendan knelt beside him, head bowed.

When his colleague opened his eyes they were as blue and innocent as always. If there was the capacity for deception in the man's nature, it was not evident in his eyes. Father Martin looked at him a long while; the blue eyes did not falter. Simple, smiling eyes, depthless as the layers of the stratosphere. Was it possible, he wondered, to have lived and worked beside this man for all these years, in such an isolated environment, and not to have sensed a deeper, inner life?

Anything was possible, yes. He'd lived long enough to know that. But if it were true, if Brendan had pulled off this miracle of deception, how should he—the man's mentor and confessor and companion—be feeling now? Angry at the betrayal? Bitter at being deprived of hours of conversation that might have endured late into the lonely night? How much more of their days in the sun might they have shared? And did it matter, now, with death so close?

"Have you made your confession yet?" the priest asked.

Brother Brendan nodded.

Father Martin found himself nodding, too, holding the man's gaze. "We're entitled to our secrets, Brendan. They're ours to keep. My only regret is that . . . ." He hesitated at the awkwardness of putting his jumbled thoughts into words. ". . . is that we might have. . . ." He didn't finish. What was the point now? Looking at the man's child-like, untroubled face, the words *heavenly pothead* came to mind and he smiled. "You did spend an inordinate amount of time up here. I often wondered what enthralled you so."

He attempted a joke. "Anyway, if it is true, you might have asked me to join you once or twice. Who knows, it might have helped me sleep as soundly as you." Brother Brendan's benign look did not change. The priest sighed and raised his hand to make the blessing: "*Te absolvo, in nomine Patris et Filii et Spiritus Sancti. Amen.*"

He reached for the tube of sunscreen oil, compliments of

Fazz who'd had cancers removed from his face. He carried the oil with him when he had to work outdoors.

Father Martin squeezed some oil from the tube and rubbed it between his fingers before administering the last rites. He anointed his colleague's forehead, hands and feet. "Eternal rest grant unto him, O Lord. And let perpetual light shine upon him."

When he finished, Brother Brendan got slowly to his feet. Before leaving he rested his hand on Father Martin's shoulder. The flection of light in his eyes, and his grin, hinted at—what? The joke he'd played on all of them?

The girl came to him next, trembling and hesitant. "What do I do, Father? I'm not really a believer anymore, as you know."

"Sit with me a moment." He held out his hand to her. "Is there anything you wish to ask forgiveness for?"

When she settled herself on the ground, she was half-turned from him, facing the ditch and the rock wall beyond. "It's not God I need forgiveness from."

"Who then?"

She was thinking, if only Trace hadn't left me, if only. . . .But she knew that was like blaming the river for a drowning man's fate. "Do you think—is there such a thing, Father, as necessary sins?"

"*Necessary* sins?"

She was thinking about what Bonnie Tauber had said about taking *step after lonely step*. Her next step would be loving Trace the best she could, with all her heart and soul and mind, if he would let her. Of that she was certain. "Things you do because you have to, because you can't move on with your life unless you do?"

"I don't know. I've never thought about it in quite that way." A moment's panic rose in him. He felt at a loss. She was asking him for something, he was pretty sure he knew what, but he was afraid he might fail her. "I do know there are things within us and around us that affect everything we do. And while I do believe in free will I know there are forces that push our will strongly one way or another." He searched her eyes for some sign she was taking comfort in his words. "I had a theology professor once, at seminary, who said it wasn't so much what we did or didn't do that determined whether we went to heaven. He said God took into account the extenuating circumstances, the internal pressures that we faced."

He thought he saw the tension recede in her eyes. Or was he only imagining it?

"Thank you, Father."

"Thank *you*, Victoria."

She looked at him as if she didn't understand. "For what, Father?"

"Yesterday. For spending part of the day with me." He reached over and touched her forehead. "Go in peace, my child."

Walking back into the clearing she saw Trace coming up the hill with the red-capped man who reminded her of the bouncers at the off-campus clubs. She ran to him and wrapped her arms around him, murmuring "Trace, Trace" like a prayer, vowing to herself she would make it up to him, whatever way she could.

"Who's this?" Vinnie Fargo wanted to know.

"Says he came with *her*," Cheechee said. "Says he's her boyfriend."

"Touching," Vinnie said of the way she clung to Trace. "Breaks my heart." He gave Trace the once-over. What he saw amused him. "Know what you are, buddy boy? Classic case of wrong time, wrong place." He stifled a cough and reached for another cigarette. "Ten minutes later and you'd a had your whole life ahead a you. Now you're gonna lie in the ditch with the bitch."

He lit the Lucky and blew smoke in Trace's direction. "*Ten* minutes. Think about it. If you'd a stopped for a smoke, or a beer, or to fill up with gas. If you'd a gotten outta bed ten minutes later this morning. Anything, man. Anything. *Ten lousy minutes.*" He motioned toward the trees. "Get up there and see the Father while I'm still in a generous mood."

"They're going to kill us," Vee whispered in his ear.

Trace nodded. It had taken him only a matter of moments to understand the gravity, if not the facts, of the situation. She leaned in to kiss him before he crossed the clearing, passing the tomb and approaching their fellow guest at the Refuge, the one who acted like any number of toughs from his old neighborhood. The man sat on the grass, staring across the clearing at Vee. When Trace turned, he saw her lower her eyes. Something in Dillon's disdainful smirk made Trace think that, while he was gone, things had happened between them. Given their present circumstances, he wondered if he would ever have the chance to ask her about it.

Then he stepped beyond the tree-line to find Father Martin at the edge of a ditch, solemn-faced, extending his hand to him.

"I'm sorry you couldn't have been spared," the priest said.

Trace was still too stunned to speak.

"I've been asked to—I know your position on the role of the clergy—but if there's any way I can help you in making your peace with—" What could he say to help this man, a good man, he believed, a man like himself who had simply fallen prey to his doubts? "You must be in shock."

"Yes, Father." He hadn't expected to turn a corner one day and, like his father, find death staring him in the face. Once again he found himself searching for meaning, looking for design. "What if—?" But he wasn't even sure what his question was.

"What if *what*?"

"What if it's God's plan to intentionally withhold himself from us? To never let us see his face? In life *or* death."

It was a question that Father Martin, too, had considered. When the night was full of hours. "Perhaps in the end it comes to this: we see what we want to see. No more, no less."

Beyond the ditch an enormous black vulture had settled on the rock wall. Father Martin had seen too many of them for too long to attach any special significance to its appearance at that moment. He was thinking of the young man before him, what he might offer in the way of comfort. What he said finally—he wasn't sure it was true, though he hoped it was—was this: "Those who search are also blessed."

"By whom, Father? With what?"

"If we're fortunate, we may yet find out one day." He raised his hand above Trace's head and made the sign of the cross. "We're not so different, you and I, after all."

When Trace returned to the clearing, Vee came to his side and took his hand. Vinnie sneered at them before turning his attention to Dillon. "All right, Joey, your turn. And make it snappy. You're gonna burn in hell no matter how many times you say you're sorry."

Dillon had no intention of confessing anything. His plan was to bolt soon as he got beyond the trees. "Can I ask you something first? In private."

"Well, I sure as hell ain't comin' to you. You wanna ask me somethin', get your ass over here."

Dillon came toward the end of the tomb where Vinnie was leaning. He shoved his hands in his pockets and tried to see beyond the brown opaque surface of the fat man's eyes. "Why'dya have it in for me? I mean, what'd I ever do to you?"

"So, what, you're some deep thinker now, looking for reasons?"

"I just wanna know. That's all."

Vinnie's eyes bulged over the thick slopes of his cheeks. "I don't like you. That's why." He lit a Lucky, flipped the burning match at Dillon's chest. Dillon stepped back, brushed the spent match from his shirt.

Vinnie drew on the Lucky and coughed. When he could clear his throat, he said: "You had too many broads fallin' over you. It pissed me off."

"That's *it*?"

"What more you want?" He grinned at Dillon's shock and coughed again, longer this time. He leaned back and pounded his chest until he began to recover. "Come to think of it, there is somethin' else.

"Yeah, what?"

"The way *every*thing just fell into your lap. You didn't have to do nothin'. Like you was exempt or somethin'. You didn't have to sweat like the rest of us." He drew on the Lucky, sending the smoke in a hard stream at Dillon. "And you know what really pissed me off? That you took it all for granted. You didn't have a clue how lucky you were."

Dillon stared at him, unblinking. Everything on the man's face had turned hard as brick.

"We're gonna dice you up. Spread your pieces on that hilltop up there. Sky burial, if you catch my drift. Just so you know. Now get the fuck outta my sight."

"Sure, Vinnie. Whatever you say." He hiked up his shoulders, turned slowly toward the trees. Not a chance he was going to slouch away from the fat prick. Walk tall and proud, he told himself. Then Vinnie's voice rang out behind him and his heart sank.

"Fazz, stay on lover lips here like a fly on shit. He so much as twitches his ear, blow his nuts off."

"My pleasure, boss." Fazz stood at the edge of the trees, grinning as Dillon approached.

On the opposite side of the tree-line, there were three vultures now, sitting side by side on the rock wall. The unholy trinity, Father Martin joked to himself, come to bid us farewell. Their turkey-like heads remained motionless, their eyes—it seemed to him—unnervingly impersonal. When Dillon, with Fazz right behind him, stepped out from the trees, two things happened at once: the buzzards lifted from the wall and Vinnie Fargo took a coughing fit so severe both Elmo and Cheechee Bozzoni rushed to his side.

The birds raised a clatter as they swooped low over the ditch with their enormous black wings beating fiercely and casting dark shadows. Fazz, his head and arm jerking upward in fear, fired off a round as he stumbled backward. Dillon body-slammed him from the side, driving the rattled man head-long into the ditch.

"Run!" Father Martin screamed, though he needn't have. Everyone in and outside the clearing—save the felled Louie DeFazio and the gasping, apoplectic Vinnie Fargo—was already in motion.

—26—

Dillon and the priest moved in opposite directions, Dillon side-stepping the ditch and leaping downhill into a tangle of underbrush, Father Martin skirting the circle of trees and making his way toward the main path.

Dillon picked himself up and fought his way through dense bushes until he reached a cobble-stoned walkway which soon gave way to dirt. This section of the park hadn't been developed except for the path which rose and fell as it wound in a generally downhill direction past stands of trees, matted undergrowth and occasional outcroppings of rock.

Behind him he heard footfalls and heavy breathing, someone gaining on him. When he turned, the gardener was coming at him full-steam ahead, so fast in fact that he had to jump free of the path or risk being run down. Near the hill's bottom the man tripped, pitching forward head-first and landing hard on the sharp rocks that dotted the path. His body bounced and rolled its way to the bottom.

When Dillon reached him, he lay writhing in the dirt and clutching his leg, his normally placid face in anguish. His pants' leg had been ripped open. Through the tear, blood and bruised flesh was visible.

Tough break, Dillon thought, but not my problem. Besides, the guy had it coming to him, didn't he? Why didn't he open his mouth back there? Was the stuff that damn good that he had to hoard it for himself even if the price was death? He wanted to scream at the man but didn't, afraid of giving away their position. "Too bad, asshole," he muttered and stepped over the body.

But he had gone only a few steps before he stopped and turned around. At the moment there was no one visible on the path above them. He hesitated a few seconds more before going back and lifting the man under the arms.

You see, I can change. I can.

The guy was heavier than he looked and it took a lot of bending and twisting to get him off the ground. They swayed uneasily on the narrow path. Dillon had never carried anyone like this before and the close presence of the man—the smell of his sweat, the limp weight of him—repelled him at first.

"Which way?"

Brother Brendan— his eyes wide in pain, and holding his ribs as if he'd been hurt there as well— nodded to the right.

With the monk propped against him, Dillon guided them through a cluster of smoke trees and desert willow. Several hundred feet beyond that they came to the base of a craggy rock wall that rose in a series of ledges to the summit. The man could barely stand on his own. He leaned forward, breathing hard, one hand pressed against his ribs.

From what Dillon could see they hadn't been followed; but he wasn't going to wait around to find out. "Which way now?"

The gardener pointed along the wall.

"Come on then," Dillon said, taking the man's arm, thinking *You see, you see, I have changed. I have.*

Brother Brendan limped alongside him and Dillon

helped steady him, all the while waiting for him to take the lead. But he moved too slowly for Dillon who became impatient so he walked on ahead, leaving the monk to struggle on his own. Dillon followed the base of the wall into an area of large rocks, a maze of ice-age boulders fallen from the hill's higher elevations.

He turned once to be sure the man was behind him and he was, laboring slowly with one hand using the wall for support. He looked like he needed help but Dillon's fury at the faker consumed him again. He wanted to yell out *Hurry up, you fool. Bad enough you got us into this. Least you can do is get us out.*

The man's pace remained unchanged, slow and uneven but determined. Dillon went back to making his own way through the maze—at his own pace, the pace of a forced march, not the limping, snail-crawl the damn gardener was doing.

When he turned back again, several minutes later, the man was gone. Dillon re-traced his steps part way.

No dice. The guy was nowhere in sight.

Maybe he'd found a way out. Another catacomb, maybe. Hadn't the priest said the hill was riddled with them?

Or maybe he'd fallen, unable to get up. Maybe he needed help. *He might be too hurt to walk. He might need me.*

Dillon thought about going back. He had vowed to change his ways, hadn't he? He should follow through on his promise, shouldn't he? But he went on ahead, moving rapidly through the maze of boulders.

A shadow fell from above and he thought that explained it, the gardener had climbed onto one of the ledges. When he looked up, though, it was Elmo standing on the ledge in his carefully pressed suit, his unblinking limo driver's face expressionless as he aimed the gun point-blank at him.

I shoulda stayed with the Brendan dude, was the last thought Joey Dillon had.

The shot reverberated across the hill.

The man in the suit turned then and strode back along the ledge. One down, one to go.

He scanned the labyrinth of rocks below. Nothing moving. Nothing hidden among the jagged shapes.

At the end of the ledge he stopped. A slab of wall jutted outward, blocking his way, blocking his view to the east. For a better look he leaned away from the ledge, using for support the curled trunk of a tree that had managed to take root in the wall's crevice. It felt sturdy to the touch and he applied more pressure, testing it. Satisfied that it was securely imbedded he leaned out farther, just enough to widen his view.

The trunk shifted then, he felt it give, and he kicked at the ledge to regain his footing. There was a cracking sound as the wood split. His free hand flailed at the wall, the trunk broke free, he felt his breath rush out of him in one quick gust and he was swimming backwards in the air above the jagged-toothed rocks below.

Trace stiffened at the sound of the gunshot but kept running, pulling Vee him by the hand. Father Martin, close behind them, kept calling out directions: "Left here . . . left again . . . straight ahead now. . . that's right. . . keep going, yes."

They were traveling on a secondary path, west of the main path. They passed the Tower of Babel, the Mount of Olives, and the Temple of Jerusalem. The priest considered having them hide in the Temple, one of the buildings on the property with a real interior, not simply a façade, but decided the catacomb behind the manger was a wiser choice. It was pitch-black and narrow but relatively straight and, though one had to crawl through part of it on hands and knees, it opened out farther down the hill, a short distance above the cottages. Not that he'd traveled it himself. But he'd passed more than one sleepless night musing over an old blueprint of the park, begrudgingly admiring the intricacy and ambition of Ezra Holmes' design.

As they moved toward it a second shot rang out, this one louder and closer by. "Hurry," Father Martin urged, we're almost there."

The manger's support posts had been battered so that the thatched roof nearly touched the ground on the back side, making it look more like a lean-to than a barn. On the exhibit's perimeter they stepped over the plundered bodies of farm animals.

Father Martin led them behind the sagging roof where a hole opened in the hillside. He pushed them toward it. "Go, go, hurry."

Behind him he heard coughing. Through the holes in the collapsed roof he saw Vinnie Fargo, not more than fifteen or twenty feet away, moving toward the manger, gun in hand.

Instinctively, as if he'd made this decision long ago, the priest stepped away from the catacomb entrance toward the far end of the manger. The motion caught the fat man's attention and he shouted to his henchmen, "I've got them. They're here."

Father Martin was running hard along the path, away from the manger. Not the bearer of Christ as his dreams had proclaimed, but his decoy. Behind him the fat man was running too; he could hear the labored breathing, the hacking cough.

The first of the shots missed him and, when the path twisted to the right, he glanced back to see that for the time being at least, he was alone. Ahead of him loomed the Tower of Babel. He headed for it, yanking open the door and climbing the spiral staircase. The steps quit halfway to the top where, breathing hard, he pressed himself flat against the hard concrete wall.

Coughing violently, Vinnie had to stop on the path. He choked and snorted and spit, finally clearing his throat. "They're here," he yelled out to the trees around him, "they're here."

Fazz and the Bozzoni brothers came running up the path behind him. Fazz, gun raised, head swiveling left and right, moved along a row of withered hedges. "Where, boss, where?"

"Here, right here. I just saw the Padre. The other two got to be real close." He straightened up now and wiped his brow. "Franco, Cheechee. Check out that temple thing there. Fazz—?"

"Yeah, boss."

"Take that path there. I'll take this one. We'll trap the monk somewhere in the middle."

"The pincer effect," Fazz said.

Vinnie gave him a sidelong look. "Yeah, whatever. Long as we nail the mother."

On the path's far side the brothers, arms cocked, guns pointed skyward, stalked the temple's perimeter.

"The hell you doing?" Vinnie screamed at them.

"Checkin' to see if they's any other entrances," Cheechee said, going red in the face.

"Just get the hell in there. These people ain't armed."

Vinnie Fargo moved along the path to the cock-eyed tower directly ahead. He had a feeling. He could smell a rat. When he swung open the door the smell got stronger.

It took some effort to squeeze himself through the doorway. Once inside he had to lean with his neck crooked to see around the spiral twists of the staircase. There he was, the good Padre. Flattened against the wall to make himself less visible.

He climbed the steps until the priest was directly above him. "Make you a deal, Father. Tell me where the guy and girl are, I shoot you once in the head, you go out easy. You don't tell me, I start with your kneecaps and work my way up. Whole process could take a while, you know?"

A calm had settled upon Father Martin and he looked down at his assailant without fear. "I don't make bargains with the devil."

"Sorry to hear that, Father. Real sorry."

The priest raised his eyes to the circle of sky visible above the unfinished roof. "Deliver me, O Lord, from the evil man. Preserve me from the violent man—"

Vinnie pointed the gun at the priest's knees, flicking it back and forth. "Eeenie, meenie, miney, moe." He grinned, taking his time to decide. At the last minute he changed his mind and fired directly into the priest's heart.

Fazz heard the shot and came running down the path in search of his boss. He'd been spooked by the eerie stillness, the ghost town atmosphere of the place. He called out, "Vinnie? Vinnie? Where'd you go?"

He had wandered into an area of trees and bushes away from the main section of the park. Nothing seemed familiar. He stopped to get his bearings and turned in a slow circle hoping to catch sight of the boss or the Bozzoni's or a landmark of some sort. He hadn't been through here before, he was sure of that. He was lost and now he couldn't even decide which direction the shot had come from.

"Franco. Cheechee," he called out.

Panic ate at his nerves. He had a sharp, sudden longing to be back in the Bronx where everything was arranged according to streets and street corners and you always knew exactly where you were.

He decided to leave the path and strike out across a patch of overgrown weeds and bushes, swinging at the obtrusive stalks with his gun hand. When the land began to rise he could see above the tree-line the grey tower and, with relief and a renewed sense of well-being, he began to jog toward it.

Vinnie watched the priest fall against the staircase railing, one arm draped over the metal rim, dangling in the air. The weight of the body pulled it downward along the rail until the feet caught between the steps and snagged it.

"Rest in peace, Father."

He pushed against the door and when he stepped outside something came at him. He tried to raise his gun hand but the thing struck his chest and his gun discharged, a burning sensation searing both his hand and the region above his ribs.

On his knees he looked up at the man who had hit him, the deaf and dumb Brother of Mercy who stood holding a long-handled shovel. The man turned and limped away, out of his vision, and Vinnie pressed the palm of his good hand to his chest to stop the bleeding.

Fazz came running toward the sound of the latest shot. Past a stand of trees, the tower was directly ahead. He could see the grey thread of path beyond a small rise. At his sides his arms swung wildly to give him momentum. He was nearly there, nearly at the crest when a man sprang from the tall grass wielding a shovel.

He was able to get off a round before the metal spade struck his head, spinning him backward into tall grass and darkness. Brother Brendan pitched forward, bleeding leg exposed and arms spread wide, to land on top of him.

A passerby, coming upon them, might think they were lovers united in a suicide pact.

—27—

Inside the Temple of Jerusalem, the one big room was murky with shadow. Here and there pools of light spilled from holes in the roof. Birds flittered in the upper reaches and their constant chitter in the dark unnerved Franco who stayed close to his brother. As they moved toward the back of the building, the wood floors creaked under their weight, a noise that further roiled the nesting birds.

Franco had his head tucked in close to his neck. "There's bats in here, Cheech."

"Where you see bats?"

"Place like this got to have bats. Hundreds I bet, hangin' from the ceiling."

"I don't like bats," Cheechee said.

"Me, too."

They might have been Siamese twins then, standing close as they were shoulder to shoulder, five-hundred-plus pounds of meat moving as one great mass.

"Anybody in here?" Franco asked the darkness.

"We got to go all the way back, case they're hiding

there," Cheechee said.

"A course, a course we do. I was just askin'—"

They passed through a cascade of light, the flood of brilliance so blinding they had to blink against it. When Cheechee stepped forward there was something wrong with the floor—it was uneven or lowered—and then it gave beneath him. He grabbed for Franco, the two of them plunging downward like an elevator in freefall, their legs flailing in the darkness.

Twenty, thirty feet. Neither of them could have said for sure. Then they hit bottom. Cheechee's knees buckled under him and he was in pain, kneeling in the dirt. Franco had landed with a heavy thump beside him. Cheech could hear him, *feel* him in the dark but it was too black to see.

"You hurt?"

"Yeah. You?"

"Yeah."

"Where the hell—?"

"Some kind of mine shaft maybe," Cheechee said. "Can't move my legs."

There was a long moment of silence.

"Help!" Franco cried out in a hoarse, rasping voice.

Then both of them were yelling in chorus. "Somebody somebody *helllllllpppppp!*"

Vinnie had gotten to his feet and was climbing the hill. He was having trouble breathing and he thought if he only could get some air he would be fine, he would make it through. It would be easier to breathe at the top, he was convinced of that, above the trees and rocks and the dilapidated ruins. It would be pure and clean up there. Breezes blowing, soothing his wounds, cooling the fire within. The wind would bring him new life.

He had given up trying to stop the bleeding. His entire

right side was dark with blood; he was leaving a trail in the dirt behind him, but he didn't want to dwell on that. Think positive. His mother's advice, from when he was a boy. Think *good* and good comes to you. If he could only make it to the top, he'd be okay. Think positive. Think *good*.

With his left arm he wiped the sweat from his eyes. It was like his body had sprung a leak, sweat and blood draining out of him. He blinked to clear his vision. There were dark spots in the sky directly above. He blinked again.

Buzzards. The damn buzzards.

He raised his good arm and made a fist. "I'll outlive all a ya's. I swear it on my mother's grave."

And then it wasn't sweat but tears in his eyes. He was thinking of his poor dead mother. Nothing now but bones in a ditch.He struggled past the cross-bearing Christs and looked up at the hill ahead. Not far. Not far. He could make it, he could. He was almost there.

A coughing fit stopped him. His chest heaved and it felt like sand and gravel had been dumped down his throat. It took all of his effort to drag himself between the large boulders. But the wind was stronger here and he could feel it breathing life into him.

The open ground of the summit lay directly ahead, unmarked except for the stripe of shadow cast by the cross. He thought he would sit at the base of the wooden structure, rest his back against it, but he was too weak to keep going. Legs out, he sat in the dirt and tried to fill his lungs with the pure breath of the wind. Think *good*. Think *good*.

Fat black shadows moved like stains across the surface of the hill. "Damn birds," he muttered. With his good hand he squeezed off a round to scare them.

When the sound of the gunshot faded, he rocked himself gently in place. Fever burned out of control inside him. Worse than anything he'd felt as a child. Barely could he manage the words, "Mama, forgive me."

He raised his eyes to the weathered cross so that the

wind might comfort his face.

One of them had settled on the cross-beam.

Trace, within the protected womb of the hill, heard neither the shots nor the cries for help. In darkness unyielding he was inching his way along the passage, on hands and knees. He was thinking that his vision on the mountain had come true in a way: except that it was a cave and not a hallway he was traveling through, and it was too dark to know what, if anything, flickered in the space ahead. Soon, if Father Martin was right, there would be a smear of light that would grow larger and they would run to the Chevy and the relative safety of the world beyond.

He shuddered at how alone he felt.

"Vee?"

"Yes?" she said behind him

"Vee—?"

"What is it, baby?"

"Nothing, I—I only wanted to hear your voice."

"I'm here," she said. "I'm right here behind you."

Philip Cioffari is the author of two books of fiction: the mystery/thriller, CATHOLIC BOYS, and the short story collection, A HISTORY OF THINGS LOST OR BROKEN, which won the Tartt Fiction Prize, and the D. H. Lawrence award for fiction. His short stories have been published widely in commercial and literary magazines and anthologies, including *North American Review, Playboy, Michigan Quarterly Review, Northwest Review, Florida Fiction,* and *Southern Humanities Review.* He has written and directed for Off and Off-Off Broadway. His Indie feature film, which he wrote and directed, LOVE IN THE AGE OF DION, has won numerous awards, including Best Feature Film at the Long Island Int'l Film Expo, and Best Director at the NY Independent Film & Video Festival. He is a Professor of English, and director of the Performing and Literary Arts Honors Program, at William Paterson University. He can be reached at: www.philipcioffari. com